If Only for One Night...

If Only for One Night...

ShaRhonda L. Sharp

SLS Publishing, LLC

Contents

Dedication **viii**

one   **1**

two   **11**

three   **33**

four   **51**

five   **64**

six   **77**

seven   **91**

eight   **104**

nine   **121**

ten   **137**

eleven   **149**

twelve   **166**

thirteen   **181**

fourteen   **204**

Contents

fifteen   225

{ EPILOGUE }

About The Author   246

This story is dedicated to those who need to be reminded that Love is a many splendid thing that comes into your life and changes you for the better. It never comes to hurt you.

{ one }

March '22

"*What* is that noise?" Treena asked, agitation present in her voice.

"I'm running bath water," Denai replied dryly as she flicked her fingers under the spout to check the temperature.

"Again?!" Treena screeched into the receiver.

"I'm sorry. Should I *not* bathe daily?" Denai asked sarcastically with a frown.

"Not with a bottle of tequila and a Toni Braxton playlist to keep you company," Treena replied with her own dose of sarcasm.

"Good thing it's Mary J. Blige and wine this time," Denai mocked, sticking out her tongue as if Treena could see her. "Anyway, I ran outta tequila two days ago."

"Good lord!" Treena huffed.

Denai Powell had been in a grouchy mood from the second she answered the call from her best friend, Treena Thompson. She had half a mind to ignore the incessant vibrating of her cellphone against the sink's counter, but knew if she didn't answer now, Treena would just keep calling until she did. There was really no escaping or avoiding that woman. Denai wanted nothing more than to be a hermit, wallowing in her sorrows of sadness, without any interruption, and Treena just refused to let her be great in her misery.

{1}

Denai was on day four of her "mourning period." She had broken up with her boyfriend of three-years, Ryan Lattimore, and it was a very ugly, tumultuous break-up, indeed. From the moment they began dating, Denai just knew in her heart of hearts that Ryan was the man of her dreams and they were destined to be together forever. Well, "forever" had a very short timeline, apparently.

After a year of dating, Denai had moved in with Ryan and quit her job, all at his behest and promises to take care of her every need for the rest of their lives. Yet, here she was thirty-years old, single, jobless and back at her Mama's house living out of a suitcase until she had a chance to get the rest of her stuff from Ryan's. This "mourning period" was certainly well-earned and much needed, as far as Denai was concerned.

"Denai! Hello!" Treena shouted through the phone.

"Yeah? What?" Denai responded absentmindedly as she lit the chamomile and lavender candles along the edge of the tub.

"Did you hear what I said?" Treena asked.

"Nope," Denai said plainly.

"Of course not," Treena said, smacking her lips. "I said I'm going out tonight and want you to come with me."

"Oh, no ma'am. Thanks, though."

"D, you need to get out of the house. You think that negro sitting up somewhere wallowing and worrying about you? Hell no!"

"I don't care what he's doing, Treena."

"Bullshit."

"I *don't* care what Ryan is doing. I *don't* care that you're going out. I *don't* care how long it's been or that my coping mechanisms aren't like yours. I don't care about *anyone* or *anything* except getting my ass in this tub and trying once again to drink until I forget. *That* is what I'm doing with *my* Friday night."

The silence that followed Denai's rant was heavy. All that could be heard was the subtle popping of foam bubbles in the tub as she sprinkled in Himalayan sea salt pellets and her own angry breathing. Annoyed, Denai put the phone on speaker and tossed it next to her wine glass on the white utility cart by the tub. She twisted open the bottle of Yellowtail Merlot and filled the stemmed wine glass to its rim.

Denai was just about to start undressing when Treena finally spoke.

"You're not alone in your heartbreak or your suffering, D," she started earnestly. "I'm your best friend. When you hurt, I hurt. You know that. And I worry about you because I know how you get if you sit with your pain for too long. I'm not rushing you to do anything you're not ready to do. But when you are ready, you already know I'm with you."

Denai exhaled a heavy sigh as she gingerly lowered her body into the hot, sudsy water. The still dissolving bath salts scraped and fizzed against the tub floor under her legs and buttocks as she situated herself in the bath. Denai reached over and grabbed her wine glass off the utility cart, bringing it to her lips. The sound of Treena calling her name through the phone's speaker made Denai halt her sipping.

"I hear you, Treena," she simply replied.
"Good," Treena said. "Well, imma let you get back to Bath-Time Karaoke. Love you, Toots."
"Love you, Toots," Denai said flatly before closing her eyes and taking a hefty sip of wine.

The three beeps from her phone let Denai know Treena had hung up and she was finally able to get back to her routine. She put on metallic gold under-eye gel pads and laid her head on the cushion hanging on the back of the tub. Denai closed her eyes, trying to relax her breathing as she tapped her short nails against her wine glass.

"Hey, Siri," Denai called out to the virtual assistant feature on her cellphone. "Play Kelly Price radio on Pandora."

As the melodious sounds of Kelly Price soulfully singing about laying with someone else's husband came through the Bluetooth speaker on the window ledge above the tub, Denai quietly hummed along as she took another generous gulp of wine. The feel of the water lightly lapping waves against her body helped soothe the tension and anxiety that had crept into her muscles.

Talking to Treena in that short amount of time had agitated Denai so much. She was already on edge emotionally, so the slightest thing would easily set her off. Soon, the angelic tones of Chrisette Michele's "Get Through the Night" began wafting through the Bluetooth speaker, invading Denai's tortuously plaguing thoughts.

She was submerged neck-deep under the water that was already beginning to cool off, but presently she was numb to everything physical and tangible. Except for the cracking of her heart with every breath she took; the heaviness of her weighed-down soul; the strangling of her spirit with every memory of the last time she saw Ryan – it all felt too real.

Every time Denai shut her eyes, she vividly saw flashes of the fiery rage that was in his. The way his mouth twisted in anger with every venomous word he spat out would forever be etched in her mind. Denai had never experienced Ryan's anger that way. Certainly, she had seen how worked up he could get, especially with him being a high-powered Corporate Attorney handling million dollar negotiations everyday.

He had a very passionate personality fueled by his constant need to be right and have the last word. Of course, Ryan appreciated anyone or anything that provided him with a challenge, but he wouldn't relent until he emerged the victor, no matter what. And with Denai Powell, that is exactly what he got – a challenge.

An equally passionate, high-spirited young woman with a brilliant mind, quick wit and just as venomous mouth when provoked. All of which sparked Ryan's attraction to Denai in the first place. He was enticed by all of it, until he was on the receiving end of it. Then it became his mission to "bring her down a peg," as he so often said.

At first it was hurtful words masked as snarky sarcasm and jabs at Denai in the midst of arguments that would leave her at a loss for words, just as Ryan had intended. Then later he'd come along toting some peace offering and half-hearted apology ensuring he didn't mean what he had said and it'd never happen again...until it did. Denai participated in this song and dance production for much too long, as it was; but after what happened four days ago, she knew it had gone too far.

Denai took another long, closed-eye swig of red wine, trying to wash away the tightness forming in her throat. Then the tension of tears welling up in her tightly shut eyes prompted Denai to shake her head feverishly, trying to ward off the heavy emotions and tragic memories of her last night with Ryan.

The power of Chrisette's lyrics packed a gut punch like Denai had never felt before. The songstress declared that she will rise up and stand tall tomorrow. She just needed one night to let it all fall apart first. As the music faded out, Denai opened her eyes to truly take in the nature of her situation.

It was three o'clock on a Friday afternoon. She had spent the earlier part of her day in bed in her pajamas and bonnet, with the curtains drawn closed and the room bathed in darkness. She had gathered up enough energy to grab the wine out of the refrigerator in the kitchen downstairs. Then came up to the bathroom to run a bath, light candles and drink herself numb.

Honestly, that's all she'd been doing every day since she broke up with Ryan and started crashing at her mom's. Chrisette Michele, a musical superstar, only asked for *one* night, but here was Denai succumbing to emotional torment all day long for four days and three nights straight, and to what end?

At that realization, Denai bravely decided her pity party was over. What good would it do to become a depressed drunk behind a break up when she now had to figure out what the rest of her life was supposed to look like? She slammed down her wine glass on top of the utility cart and quickly grabbed her phone to switch to her Dance Party playlist on Pandora.

Denai always felt it was important to have a soundtrack to support your mood. Now that she was determined to shift hers from sadness and woe-is-me to an epic evolution, the tunes had to match. The bombastic bass of Janelle Monae's "Electric Lady" came blaring through the speaker and Denai ripped the stopper out of the tub almost ceremoniously as she belted out the lyrics with all her heart.

She turned on the showerhead to rinse off the suds from her bath, as well as the darkness and negativity she had been shouldering all week; watching it all go down the drain and far away from her. The pulsating spray of the shower's water was just the shock to her system that Denai needed to get her Bad Ass Babe edge back, because tonight she absolutely planned on doing whatever she wanted.

*****

Treena Thompson eyed her reflection in the mirrored closet door and was pleased with what she saw. She liked to refer to herself as a "Delicious Amazon," due to her curvaceous five-foot, ten-inch frame. She was equal parts busty and punky, with full 38 D-cup breasts she didn't mind showing off and a curly mohawk haircut with hot pink tips.

Treena's smooth butter pecan complexion, courtesy of her biracial African American and Puerto Rican heritage, was flawless with the exception of a large, colorful Phoenix wings tattoo that covered her entire upper back. Her flat stomach and perfectly rounded hips made Treena look like a statuesque figure eight. All features she fully intended to dress up and accentuate shamelessly.

Her ensemble consisted of a red and black satin strappy corset top that propped up her cleavage just right and hugged her narrow waist, showing off the perfect amount of stomach and lower back. Skin-tight leather leggings tucked into the tops of red suede, silver-studded peep-toe booties brought the whole sexy get-up together. Treena was putting in large heart-shaped bamboo earrings when she heard the doorbell chime.

She looked over at the clock on her nightstand and saw it was almost 8:30PM. Her friend, Freddie J, who she hosted events with sometimes, was coming to pick her up, but it was certainly too early for him to be at her door. Treena narrowed her eyes questioningly as the doorbell rang out for a second time. She strutted out of the room and rounded the short corner to head down the stairs.

Treena opened the door to find Denai standing in the gap between the wooden main and black metal screened doors. She gasped at the surprising sight of her best friend and before she could get a word out to express her confusion, Denai simply blurted out, "I need something to wear and you gotta do my makeup." Then she stepped across the threshold, briskly brushing by and heading towards the stairs leading to Treena's bedroom.

All Treena could muster was confused murmurs and throaty sounds, trying to find the words, but nothing came out. So, she quietly closed the front door and followed Denai's path upstairs. She found her surprise guest raking hangers across the bar in the closet, searching for something to wear.

"Uh, excuse me, Miss Ma'am?" Treena finally spoke up in a high pitched voice, her arms folded across her chest.

"Yeeesss?" Denai sang over her shoulder as she continued to rifle through Treena's wardrobe.

"I am confusion! What exactly is happening right now?" Treena asked, lifting a perfectly arched eyebrow.

"I'm taking you up on your invitation. You're right. Enough is enough and it's time to move forward, but I have nothing to wear for such an occasion," Denai smirked as she looked over at Treena still standing in the doorway.

"Well, shit! That's all you had to say! I've got just the thing. Move!" Treena giggled as she shooed Denai out of the way.

An hour later, Treena was putting the final touches on Denai's makeup and sending her to the mirror to get a look. A bold red, ombre lip with gold and bronze blended eyeshadow and dramatic eyelashes highlighted her full lips and almond-shaped eyes. Denai refreshed her short pixie haircut with soft curls and feathered them lightly across her forehead just above her eyebrows. Her heart-shaped "face card" was a hit, for sure!

Treena's choice of outfit for Denai didn't disappoint either. A black, faux leather asymmetrical one-sleeve top clung to Denai's petite torso, showing off her hazelnut-complexioned neckline and butterfly tattoo on her left shoulder. Coffee-brown denim, low-rise jeggings with slits across the thighs showcased her slim-thick frame just how Treena intended.

Despite their body shapes being so different, Treena would hold onto clothes she could no longer fit because somehow they always ended up fitting Denai just fine. Denai's entire look was brought to-gether by a pair of burgundy, closed-toe pumps, large thick gold hoops and a gold rounded cuff bracelet worn on her uncovered arm.

The two friends stood next to each other, assessing themselves in the mirrored closet door and fluffing their curls so they'd lay just right. Being pleased with what they saw, they each blew a kiss to their re-flections, turned on their heels, and walked out of the bedroom. When they got downstairs, Treena grabbed two leather jackets out of the closets – a black Moto style jacket for Denai and a cropped PU jacket for herself.

Even though it was late-March and creeping up on Spring, it was still pretty chilly in Chicago, especially at night. So the jackets were definitely needed; plus they just accented their outfits so well. Denai offered to drive tonight, so Treena called Freddie J to say she'd just meet him there and to save some seats in his VIP section.

"Where are we going anyway?" Denai asked as she grabbed the leopard print clutch she borrowed.

"TAO Chicago. Freddie's throwing a party there tonight," Treena replied while locking the front door behind them.

"Oooh! Never been there before," Denai said excitedly.

"It's a dope ass spot and the food is good, if you're hungry. If not, the drinks are even better!"

two

The heavy bass and cheers of the partygoers reverberated off the windows and walls of *TAO Chicago* and sent a wave of excitement crashing over Denai and Treena as they stepped inside. A DJ was bathed in neon strobe lights on a raised platform at the front of the club and unitard-clad dancers jirated on miniature stages to the left and right of the DJ booth.

The party was already standing-room-only by 10:30PM when Denai and Treena arrived, but luckily they spotted Freddie J standing at the corner of the bar. They were hopeful he still had a VIP section they could slide into when their feet needed a rest.

"Hey, baby!" Treena shouted behind Freddie J's shoulder.
"Hey, boo!" Freddie greeted with a tight hug and huge smile, showing off a top row of pearly whites and a gold grill-covered bottom row.

Freddie J was a tower of man with honey-blonde ombre dreadlocks, two small slits cut into his left eyebrow and a gold septum ring dangling from his nose. He had gold crusted pinky rings on each hand with a matching cuban link bracelet and watch combo on his left wrist. He wore a black t-shirt with a gold bedazzled lion head on the front, white ripped skinny jeans and hi-top gold and black Nike Dunks with his name spray painted on the side.

Treena met Freddie J about five or six years ago when he promoted a fashion show she walked in. They clicked right away and before long she became the face on many of his party flyers, and then went on to become his part-time business partner throwing events around the city. She decided to come out tonight just to show support and take advantage of as many free drinks as she could handle.

"Lady D! Ain't seen you in ages!" Freddie said as he greeted Denai with a hug and quick cheek kiss.

"I know, right?!" Denai laughed, pulling out of their embrace.

"Whatchu getting me to drink?" Treena chimed in as she laid her head on Freddie J's shoulder and batted her eyelashes.

Freddie J cut his eyes at Treena and smacked his lips before gruffly saying "Whatchu want, girl?" Treena broke into a cheshire grin and clapped her hands in glee as she ordered her favorite drink – a strawberry-lemon drop martini. Freddie J huffed after taking her order, then turned to Denai to see what she wanted and all she said was "Surprise me!" He laughed heartily and said "Aight, bet!"

Denai was standing behind Treena and Freddie J, who was now leaning on the bar to place their orders, when the beat for "Cry Baby" by DaBaby and Megan the Stallion dropped, and it instantly put her in the party mood. She stood back-to-back with Treena and started dancing against her, which was promptly reciprocated.

For the first time in days, Denai was moving her body to do more than just schlep from the bed to the bathroom and back. She was laughing and feeling excitement where pain and anguish once took up space. She was so glad to have accepted Treena's invitation. Tonight was going to be epic. She could feel it.

The DJ transitioned from one club banger after another and Denai had yet to stop dancing. Now she was body rolling with her eyes closed, sipping on her second Dark and Stormy of the night. Suddenly, she had this intense feeling she was being watched, but it didn't feel creepy or unsettling. Denai slowed her dancing and opened her eyes to survey the room around her.

The phantom eyes felt like a warm hand slowly dragging an ice cube across the nape of her neck. That strong sensation felt so real, Denai gave in to her curiosity and covertly did a full 180-degree turn on her heels until she spotted Him. She locked eyes with the mysterious stranger standing at the opposite end of the bar leaning against the wall. His eyes were deep and dark, flickering in the quick moving strobe lights each time they passed over his face.

Denai turned to look behind her, thinking He must be eyeing someone else, but when she looked back at Him those darkened eyes were still fixed on her. He never broke eye contact or made any sudden moves, just gazed across the crowded club as if no one existed except Him and Her. As the bartender slid his drink in front of Him, He broke their connection just long enough to retrieve the glass, then slowly lifted his head to meet Denai's eyes again.

Even in the club lighting, Denai could tell He winked at her before disappearing into the crowd. She searched through the sea of faces surrounding her, trying to spot Him, but to no avail. Then deciding she didn't want to appear too pressed about it, she shrugged it off and went back to sipping her drink. Just as Denai started to tell Treena about what happened, she felt strong fingers lay against the small of her back, making her arch in surprise.

Denai spun abruptly to her right and there He was. The woody, aromatic fragrance of Bleu de Chanel greeted Denai's senses before He ever spoke a word. Now standing this close, his chestnut eyes looked just as intense as they did from across the room, but there was something so inviting about them that piqued her curiosity.

"Oh, shit! Dell?!" Freddie J shouted over the music.

Just as the mystery man parted his deliciously moist lips to speak to Denai, He snapped his head around at the sound of Freddie J's voice. They greeted each other with a smile before slapping hands and embracing. The smiles and laughs never ceased as Freddie J and his friend briefly played catch up.

The entire time He engaged with Freddie J, He never removed his hand from Denai's waist. It rested there comfortably as if to say "I'm not going anywhere" and "I ain't forgot about you." It felt so normal and familiar, even though they were complete strangers.

"Uh, Freddie," Treena interrupted the guys' exchange. "Don't act like you're ashamed of us. Introduce us to your friend."

"Yes, ma'am," Freddie J replied with a laugh. "Ladies, this is my homeboy, Dell. He breezed into town for his cousin's birthday. Dell, these lovely ladies are some of the dopest people I know. Ms. Treena Thompson and Ms. Denai Powell."

Freddie J dramatically framed his hands around each of the ladies as he introduced them, making everyone chuckle a little. The moment he revealed Denai's name, Dell's eyes lit up because one of the biggest mysteries of his night had just been solved. Now that he knew her name, he wanted to know everything else. Dell leaned forward and shook Treena's hand, flashing a charming smile. She did a fake curtsy and smiled back. Then Dell leaned over and sensually whispered in Denai's ear, "Hey, you."

His warm breath caressed Denai's entire ear and set the nerves in the back of her neck on fire. She could feel instant wetness pooling in her panties as the butterflies fluttered frantically throughout her whole body. Denai drew in a deep breath, trying to get her bearings, and as she exhaled, her head turned slowly to face Dell. They were so close, so intimate. Afraid she might forget all of her good sense, Denai simply whispered, "Hey," before turning away to nervously gulp the last of her drink.

Treena watched the heated exchange between Denai and Dell, intrigued by what she just saw and what it could possibly mean. Whatever it is or could be, was a vast improvement from the last guy Denai dated, and Treena was in full support.

"Hey, Dell, where's E-Man anyway?" Freddie J inquired with a frown. "Why he ain't tell me he was coming? I would've hooked him up!"

"I think somebody else planned this for him." Dell explained. "He forgot this was one of your spots. He definitely would've hit you up. But, shit, y'all wanna come crash the VIP?"

"Hell, yeah!" Treena exclaimed. "Lead the way!"

The group burst into laughter as they followed Dell over to his cousin's section. He grabbed hold of Denai's hand, guiding her through the crowd; and she grabbed Treena's, trying to play off the fact that she was holding hands with a random man she didn't know. As they arrived at the steps of the VIP section, they could see the bottle girls dancing with sparklers and two bottles of D'ussé. The section was full of men and women dancing and celebrating the arrival of more liquor.

Freddie J walked up as the bottle girls were leaving and spotted Dell's cousin, Emmanuel "E-Man" Tipton, sitting on the leather couch rocking to Meek Mills blaring throughout the club. E-Man was a very handsome, light-skinned man with long thick black hair that was styled in two straight-back braids that swung back and forth as he danced. He had full, dark eyebrows and eyelashes, with a heart-shaped beard adorning his face and surrounding reddish-pink lips.

He was wearing an army fatigue denim jacket over a beige tank top and army green rockstar jeans that hugged his thighs nicely as he sat. Everything about him piqued Treena's interest the moment she laid eyes on him. *Tonight is gonna be interesting,* she thought to herself.

"Yo!" Freddie J called out over the music as he came to stand in front of E-Man.

"Yoooo! Freddie, my guy!" E-Man said gleefully, getting up from his seat to embrace his friend.

"Man, why the hell you ain't tell me you were trying to pop out for your birthday?" Freddie J asked with narrowed eyes.

"Bruh, I ain't plan none of this! All I was told was what time to be ready tonight." E-Man said innocently with a shrug. "I didn't even know this was one of your spots."

"Bro, *every* spot in Chicago is my spot!" Freddie J said with a wink and a grin.

"You right! Respect!" E-Man replied with a grin of his own.

"Well, since we're boys and it's your bday, imma look out for you. Your bottle service is on me tonight. Oh, and I brought you some company, if you got room for two more." he said with a smirk.

"Depends," E-Man replied skeptically.

Freddie J stepped to the side to reveal Denai and Treena standing on the steps behind him. Treena was the first one E-Man saw. His eyes widened and he immediately started to salivate like a starving lion in the Serengeti. He quickly slapped hands with Freddie J, silently saying, "You are the man!", but he never took his eyes off Treena, and she never took her eyes off him.

"Hell yeah, I got room!" E-Man exclaimed. "I'll kick niggas out if need be!"

"That's what I thought," Freddie J chuckled.

Freddie J beckoned to the ladies to come over and meet the birthday boy. As Denai started to ascend the three short steps of the raised VIP section, she was suddenly hit with the realization that Dell was still holding her hand. His palm was soft and warm, and his fingers were firm and strong.

It's crazy how something so innocent and simple could make her feel so secure, especially from a total stranger. His four fingers were wrapped around her hand tightly as he stroked her knuckles with the pad of his thumb…like it was something they did all the time. Familiar.

E-Man walked over to Denai and Treena, standing on the middle stair, almost wedging himself between them. He introduced himself, shaking each of their hands gently. He thanked them for coming out and expressed how glad he was they ended up in his section.

"Y'all know my cousin, Dell?" E-Man asked, gesturing towards the man standing next to Denai, still commandeering her hand.

"We just met tonight, actually," Denai answered somewhat nervously until she felt a reassuring squeeze of her hand.

"Oh okay, cool. Well, any friend of Freddie J's, that looks like you two, is definitely a friend of mine! My section is your section. Let's turn up! It's my goddamn birthday!"

The group erupted into a rowdy cheer and the liquor quickly started flowing. Freddie J and Dell both provided rounds of shots for the birthday boy and his new guests to drink, and the bottle girls strutted over with a third bottle of D'ussé for the party. The rest of the night dissolved into a boozy blur with an epic soundtrack.

Once it was time for the club to close down at 3AM, Denai, Treena and E-Man wanted to go to the famous White Palace Grill on Canal and Roosevelt for a late night breakfast binge. Dell tried to back out, but they wouldn't let him.

"Come on, man! It's my birthday!" E-Man pleaded.

"Nigga, your birthday was *Thursday*! I just tolerated your shenanigans for an extra day," Dell chuckled.

"Boooo!" Treena chimed in on the berating.

"Really?! Woooowww!" Dell exaggerated as he grabbed his chest, feigning hurt feelings.

Dell was adjusting his cashmere-wool blend Burberry print scarf under his wool trench coat when Denai flirtatiously stood in front him to "help" fix his lapels. He could feel her soft touch even through the fabric of his coat and clothes. It formed an anxious knot in his stomach and made him swallow hard, though he tried to play it off.

"You're really not coming?" Denai asked softly and sweetly as her hands rested against the flattened lapels of his coat, which also happened to be laying against his chest.

"Do you want me to come?" Dell asked in return, his husky baritone seeming to drop even lower the softer he spoke to her.

Denai slowly brought her eyes up from Dell's chest until they met his. His chestnut brown orbs mixing with her honey-sage colored ones like a perfect recipe for combustion. Denai gave one long blink that added a heavy note of pleading to her eyes as she silently nodded in response to Dell's question. Her delicate, yet direct, subtlety was enough for him to give her whatever she wanted.

Dell softly whispered, "Okay," and headed to breakfast at 3AM with the most beautiful woman to ever place a spell on him.

******

The foursome – Denai, Dell, Treena and E-Man – enjoyed their hearty pancakes and bacon-heavy afterparty meal, trying their hardest to soak up as much of the alcohol as possible so they could get back to functioning like normal adults. It was not an easy feat, but the coffee, water and carbs truly made a world of difference.

The whole time they were at the table, each of the ladies seated next to the man their intrigue requested, there was laughter and great conversation. They learned that Dell and E-Man were really more like brothers than cousins, having spent much of their youth living together at their grandmother's house and going to all the same schools.

Even after Dell's mother married his step-father and they moved to Detroit when he was in high school, he and E-Man remained close over the years. So, when E-Man requested his favorite cousin be there to celebrate his thirtieth birthday, Dell wasted no time booking a flight from Detroit to Chicago. He was just sad it had to be such a short trip, but family demands back home dictated his early return.

As the group gathered in the nearby parking garage, preparing to part ways for the evening, or early morning rather, Treena's inner naughty girl with zero inhibitions kicked in and she decided to go for it.

"Hey, girl," Treena started as she pulled her best friend to the side. "So, listen...I think I wanna give the birthday boy my gift, if you catch my drift."

"Girl! What the hell?!" Denai gasped with a laugh.

"Look, he is fine as hell and you know he's just my type!" Treena emphasized as she cut her eyes at E-Man, who was standing with Dell by his rental car.

"Oh, you mean hella cute, covered in tattoos and probably bad for you? Definitely." Denai replied sarcastically.

"Exactly! So, you good getting back home? I'll even give you my keys and you can go to my house since it's closer." Treena said with a raised brow.

"Treena!" Denai exclaimed, her eyes wide.

"What?! I mean I'm sure Dell wouldn't mind a bunk buddy, if you're feeling up to it?" Treena hinted, smiling with the tip of her tongue sticking out.

"Oh, yeah? I bet," Denai said, rolling her eyes before stealing a glance at Dell, who just happened to be looking her way, as well.

Denai had to admit the idea did sound tempting, but she couldn't do it. She often admired Treena's fearlessness, and sometimes reckless abandon, in a given situation. She was never afraid to go after what she wanted. Whether it was a career move or a man, if Treena Thompson wanted it, there was really no stopping her. So, Denai didn't even try. Just begged her to please be safe, in every way, and to share her location as soon as she got in the car with E-Man.

"If I gotta come look for you, I will hurt you *and* that nigga, understood?" Denai said in a stern tone.

"Yes, ma'am," Treena said dryly.

The two hugged and kissed on the cheek before Treena happily skipped off in E-Man's direction. Seeing her come over to them as Denai began walking towards her car, Dell's eyes narrowed and darted back and forth trying to discern what was going on. Once he overheard Treena's proposition to his cousin, Dell quickly stepped away to catch up with Denai.

"Hey, uh, is my cousin safe in her hands this late at night?" he called out.

"Probably not," Denai laughed as she turned to face him.

"Hell, he probably likes that kinda shit," he said, exhaling a laugh of his own.

"Looks like it," she said, looking around Dell's shoulder at the exchange between the two flirty deviants.

"Are you good to drive home?" he asked, his voice sounding serious now.

"Yeah, I'm good. I actually didn't drink as much as everyone else because I knew I'd be stuck as the DD."

"Ha! Same here. I wanted him to enjoy his night without any worries. Well, Ms. Denai, it was an absolute pleasure spending my Friday night with you. Truly."

"I have to say the same. Even being in a club, it was really great hanging out and holding hands with you tonight."

"If only we had more time."

"If only, indeed."

Dell took Denai's hand in his, stroking her knuckles softly once again and placed a tender kiss in her palm. She blushed as her heart fluttered at the touch of his lips, even if it was just her hand. He cuffed her chin with the knuckle of his index finger, looking longingly into her eyes that glimmered even under the dull fluorescent lights of a city parking garage. Dell stroked her cheek with the pad of his thumb, and softly whispered, "Goodnight, gorgeous," before turning to walk back to his car and waiting passengers.

Denai stood there at her own car door as she watched Dell's retreating silhouette. *How is it possible to look that good walking away?!* she mused to herself. She let out an exasperated sigh as she opened the door and slid behind the wheel. She looked in the direction Dell went once again, but could no longer see him for the tinted windows on the rental. Denai shook her head at her own propensity for bad luck.

Of course, she would meet what could possibly be the most amazing man of her dreams and he doesn't even live in the same state! What are the chances? If she were somewhere traveling abroad and this happened, then Denai would've just shrugged it off as "It was nice while it lasted," and jet-set back home without a care. But, in this case it was Dell shrugging it off and she was the one left behind.

"This some bullshit!" Denai huffed as she cranked the engine and yanked the gear shift down to "Reverse."

Her tires screeched angrily through the parking structure as she rounded each corner, descending down one level after another, until she sped out the exit onto the street. She tapped her fingers in anxious annoyance every time she came to a red light, trying hard to just accept the situation for what it was...some bullshit.

The streetlights cascaded across the windshield, bathing Denai's face in soft yellow-orange light as she navigated the Dan Ryan Expressway, headed towards Treena's Hyde Park townhouse. Despite how late, or early, it was, Denai felt wide awake. It was probably the cocktail of raging hormones and just flat out rage that was hitting her harder than caffeine ever could.

Just as Denai was rounding one of the many curves of the expressway, she heard the chime of her cell phone notifying her of a new text message. She tapped the screen of the phone cradled in the vent clip and opened the message. It was a voice note with a website link from Treena. Confused by the message, Denai hit the play button.

Hey, Toots! I know what you said, buuuut I'd be a terrible friend
if I didn't say this. So, E-Man had a room down here
at the Westin for the weekend. Perfect, right?!
Well, guess who also happens to have a room here too?
That's conveniently right across the hall?
Now, I ain't saying nothing, but I'm saying something.
Get it, girl! Room 1106, just in case you care. K, byeee!

The attached link was Google Maps directions to the hotel. Treena was in full support of Denai popping up on Dell, because why not?! What harm is there? People have one-night stands all the time, right? Hell, Treena was literally in the middle of one right now. And in Denai's case she'd be getting off easy because Dell lives in a whole other state. Spend the night together and then never see each other again. Just a one and done kind of thing.

Besides, she was single now. So, she really could do whatever she wanted with whoever she wanted, and right now every inch of her wanted every inch of him. *This is crazy! I can't do this. I don't even know him, and that's not like me. Nope. No!* Denai mused and mumbled to herself as she kept driving. Fighting hard to remain sensible in the midst of her tipsy horniness.

******

"I cannot believe I'm doing this," Denai chastised herself.

She anxiously watched the red numbers flash at her as the elevator ascended one floor after another. The moment it came to a stop at the eleventh floor, Denai's stomach knotted up and she quickly considered sending it right back down to the lobby with herself in tow. Who did she think she was just showing up to some man's hotel room without invitation? *That's exactly what he'll say when I get there,* she thought as she nervously navigated the carpeted path leading to the potentially most mortifying moment of her life.

When she arrived at the door to room 1106, Denai just stared at the brass number plate and peephole like she was looking down the barrel of a gun. She took three deep breaths, stood up straight and rotated her neck until she heard a few light cracks.

"Oh, well. Shooters shoot, as Treena would say," Denai mumbled before softly knocking.

She could hear movement coming from behind the door, but wasn't sure if it was in Dell's room or someone else's. After waiting about thirty seconds, Denai knocked again, trying not to disturb anyone else on the floor. The sound of the lock clicking on the other side made Denai jump a little. It sounded so loud to her, or it could've just been her nerves playing tricks.

The door opened slowly and there stood a barefoot and shirtless Dell Hewitt looking like a model on the cover of a 1980s romance novel. Denai felt like she was really just seeing him fully for the first time, and *oh,* the beauty of what she saw.

Dell was tall and lean with muscles everywhere. His entire torso and arms looked like they were chiseled out of stone. His arms were long and would no doubt feel perfect wrapped around her body. His abs were firm but not hard, and looked like well-placed cobblestones leading a path directly to the v-cuts of his pelvis that disappeared into the waistband of his Calvin Klein underwear peeking out of jeans. Jeans that clung to his thighs and calves the way Denai wanted to.

He had half-sleeves of tattoos on both arms from right above his elbows up to his shoulders and connecting to a larger piece that covered his chest just below his collarbone. It was all black and gray-tones with a variety of images from biblical to tribal. Though it was beautiful, the work of art covering his body was no match for the body itself. Especially not the face.

Dell's thick, curly, dark hair was cut in a semi-mohawk with lightly faded sides and neat sideburns that connected to the most beautiful beard Denai had ever seen. It was full, but not too bushy; it was dark and contrasted perfectly against his skin tone. Skin so golden it looked like honey was blended with caramel and poured over him. *I wonder if he tastes as sweet as he looks?* Denai wondered silently.

"Denai?" Dell called to her, curiosity in his voice. "Wha...How...?"

"Uh, Treena told me where to find you. I hope that's okay," Denai answered shyly, hoping he couldn't tell what she was thinking.

"Is it okay that you were trying to find me? Or that Treena gave up my location?" he asked, lifting his brows.

"Well, uh, I guess both," she said, exhaling a nervous laugh.

"Yeah, that's perfectly fine," he replied with a smirk and tilt of his head.

Dell invited Denai inside his room that was comfortably warm and bathed in the soft light of two bedside lamps. The bathroom was the first door to the right and Denai wondered if she had interrupted him showering. Picturing Dell soaking wet in the shower was a delicious thought she gladly let play out in her imagination.

A few steps past the bathroom was a king-sized bed still neatly made, a coffee table in the middle of the floor and a long sofa in front of the large windows overlooking downtown Chicago. On the table was an open gray and black Kenneth Cole duffle bag with clothes inside.

"Sorry, for interrupting you," Denai offered, realizing he must have been in the middle of packing when she knocked on the door.

"No, you're not," Dell said, grinning sheepishly.

"Yeah, not really," she said with a devilish grin of her own.

Dell walked towards Denai standing in front of the sofa. He stopped just as his toes touched the tips of her burgundy pumps. He looked at her, studying every inch of her face and then his eyes traveled lower, drinking in her entire body. Dell became hypnotized by the rise and fall of Denai's breast with every quick breath she took. He traced his finger along the asymmetrical neckline of her shirt, while lightly grazing the skin of her chest and collarbone as he went.

Dell noticed her skin flush red like his finger was leaving a sensual trail of fire along its trek. He slipped his left hand beneath the hem of her leather jacket and clutched her hip tightly. Then he slid his right hand up her neck, gripping the side and pushing his thumb against her chin to turn her head, making the right side of her neck fully accessible.

Denai began panting in heated anticipation when she felt Dell's thick lips brush against her neck as he inhaled the sweet scent of her skin. The moment he pressed them fully to her pulse, Denai melted in his hands. Dell tightened his hold on her hip and neck, drawing her in closer as he traced the side of neck with the tip of his tongue.

A throaty moan escaped Denai's mouth, which drew Dell's attention straight to it. He moved his hand to cup her face, pulling it close until any gap between them no longer existed. He rubbed his lips against hers, inhaling every ragged breath she released as he teased her.

"Would you be mad if I kissed you the way I wanted to?" Dell breathed against her mouth.

"I'd be mad if you didn't," Denai replied as she grabbed his face with her left hand, pulling him down to her.

The kiss Dell and Denai shared was deep and passionate with the hungry longing of two long-lost lovers. There was no part of their lips that they didn't explore on each other. They nipped at the corners, and licked and sucked bottom lips in between their tongues tangoing together. Dell began peeling off Denai's jacket while simultaneously undoing the button of her pants. He brushed his fingers against the skin of her hips and pelvis until she stopped him.

"I'm sorry," Dell apologized immediately, afraid he may have offended her.

"No, no. You...it's fine," Denai assured him. "It's just that, well after a long night of dancing, I'd like to freshen up first. You know?"

Dell searched Denai's hinting eyes for clarity, until he finally understood what she meant. He exhaled a soft laugh and placed a tender kiss on her forehead before taking her hand and leading her to the bathroom. He flipped the light switch, bathing the bathroom in a perfect soft glow. He slid the glass door open and turned on the showerhead. The doors and mirrors became covered with steam as the water heated up.

Dell slipped his fingers beneath the fabric of Denai's shirt, brushing his knuckles against the softness of her skin before pulling it over her head. He turned her around and kissed the back of her neck and shoulders as he unhooked her strapless bra. Letting it collapse to the floor and replacing it with his hands, he cupped her supple breasts in his palms. Dell assessed Denai's reflection in the mirror and loved everything he saw.

From the beauty of her body to how good he looked with her, it was all truly a sight to behold. He slid his fingers inside the waistband of her pants and underwear and pushed them down her smooth legs, placing a trail of kisses from her buttocks all the way to her ankles. Denai's knees buckled at Dell's delicious assault on her body, and this was only the beginning.

Once they were both naked, Dell pulled Denai into the shower and stood her in front of the steaming, hot water. The pulsating stream pelted the front of her body while Dell massaged the back. He grabbed a towel, soaked it in water and shower gel until it formed a foamy lather and began washing Denai's back. Dell noticed what looked like a slight bruise, or maybe a birthmark, on her lower back and right hip, and he purposely made his touch more gentle as he wiped there.

He continued on until he had washed and massaged her entire body in the shower, and then in a pleasantly surprising twist, Denai returned the favor. While she had gotten used to staying in the bathtub until the water went tepid, doing it in the shower now was a much more welcomed change. Especially, with the company she had.

Dell and Denai wrapped themselves in large plush bath towels and exited the bathroom. Taking Denai completely by surprise, he turned her around and pushed her down on the bed, lying flat on her back. He unfolded the corners of her towel, revealing round, hazelnut-brown breasts adorned with chocolate nipples and a tiny heart-shaped beauty mark on her right breast. Seeing it, he leaned down and kissed it softly.

Narrow waist with soft curves called to Dell and made him ache in all the right places. He kissed his way down Denai's torso, stopping for a moment to draw circles around her belly button with his tongue. The feel of his warm lips against her skin sent shockwaves through her entire body. Every kiss from his lips and gentle nip of his teeth gave her goosebumps. Dell knelt down next to the bed and pulled her towards him until her hips rested at the edge.

When Denai felt the heat and wetness of his tongue meet the heat and wetness between her thighs, she swore her lungs would burst from the sharp intake of breath that sensation caused. Dell's tongue licked and stroked against her clit with slow agony that continuously snatched the air from Denai's lungs. The way he kissed and licked her center from top to bottom, felt like he was making love to her with his mouth.

Denai whimpered and moaned as she clawed at his shoulders with one hand and massaged the back of his head with the other. Just as Denai felt the pulsing build up of an orgasm coursing its way through her pelvis, she rested her feet on his shoulders and clenched the sheets, holding on for dear life. The closer she came to release the more she squirmed, writhing around in pleasure and agony.

She made the mistake of whispering, "Oh, my God, I'm about to fucking cum," and Dell heard her. He gripped her hips, digging his fingertips into her buttocks, and pulled her closer to his mouth. The harder she squirmed and tried to fight it, the tighter his grip became.

"Dell...please...Dell...FUCK!" Denai's orgasm tore through her entire body as she screamed from her soul in ecstasy.

She gripped the sheets so hard they ended up getting wrapped around her hands. Her toes curled and thighs tightened around Dell's head, a feeling he welcomed happily. He moved back up her body, encircling her chocolate nipples with his tongue and sucking them passionately.

Dell brushed his lips against hers before kissing her mouth almost as intimately as he had her womanhood. Then he walked over to his open duffle bag on the coffee table to retrieve a condom. Denai, still wrecked with bliss, sat up on her elbows and watched his every move, enjoying the sight of his naked form.

Dell came back and stood at the edge of the bed between Denai's open legs. The sight and feel of his rock hard erection that curved slightly to the left brushing up against her calf, only made Denai wetter with each passing second. Dell massaged her luscious thighs as he looked in her eyes and asked, "Can I keep going?" She nodded eagerly and said, "Absolutely."

He pulled her closer so that her butt and hips hung slightly off the bed, and then eased himself inside of her warm and welcoming core. Dell bit his bottom lip and inhaled sharply as he felt every muscle of her womanhood engulf him. Once he was fully inside, he had to rest his head on her shoulder to get his bearings. After several deep breaths, Dell began to move his hips against hers, driving his hard penis in and out in a perfect rhythm.

He stood up and pushed Denai's knees towards her shoulders while pressing her feet against his chest. Dell quickened his pace as he bucked against her, the sound of their skin slapping together echoed throughout the room. Denai held on to the back of her knees and pulled her legs wider, giving Dell deeper access to her core. The feeling of him inside of her drove her crazy. The sounds of their lovemaking turned her on in ways she'd never felt before.

"Shhhhhit!" Dell groaned as he penetrated her.

"Fuck! Fuck! Fuck!" Denai moaned through gritted teeth as she dug her nails into her thighs.

Just as Dell switched to longer, deeper strokes, Denai felt a very familiar, strong sensation in her lower body. However, before she could gain control, she came so hard she squirted. The powerful stream sprayed Dell across the stomach and hips and rained down his thighs like torrential downpour. Denai immediately covered her face with her hands.

"I'm sorry," she groaned, her voice muffled.

"Why are you sorry?" Dell asked as he kept thrusting.

"I...uh...oh, fuck!" she screamed as another orgasm rushed through, making her squirt again.

"Mmmm," he moaned, smiling and biting his lip.

"Oh, shit! S-sorry."

"Baby, look at me."

Dell narrowed his eyes as he watched Denai's hands slide away from her face. Her eyes were wild and glazed over with passion and the bangs of her short hair were now completely sweated out. Her pouty lips were parted as one sensual cry after another passed through. Dell saw the exact moment another orgasmic wave crashed through her body and washed over him, and once again she apologized.

He didn't understand why she was apologetic for something so amazing, but after tonight he'd make sure she wasn't anymore. Dell laid his body over hers until their bare chests were pressed together. Cradling the back of head and neck in his hand, he rested his temple against hers, putting his mouth right next to her ear.

"Don't say that. You hear me?" Dell breathed against her neck and ear. "You keep apologizing and I'm gonna keep making you squirt, and I'm not gonna stop. You hear me?"

"Oh, my God! Oh...my...God! Dell!" Denai cried as she raked her nails across his back.

"Yeah, there you go. Give it to me. Give me what I want," he commanded.

Denai locked her ankles together behind Dell's back as her thighs pressed hard against his ribs. She bit down on his shoulder, trying to muffle her screams as she felt her dam break once again. Dell growled in her ear as he clawed at the sheets above her head. The feel of her body literally erupting against him over and over sent him over the edge.

Dell thrusted harder into her, his rapid breaths keeping pace with his pelvis. He felt all of the blood rush to the center of his body as he released. Dell moaned Denai's name and gnawed at her neck as his entire body shook and jerked on top of her.

Dell soon collapsed on top of Denai, trying to catch his breath. She rubbed his back and kissed his bicep softly as she tried to regulate her own breathing. Slowly, Dell pulled away and rolled over to lay next to her. He draped his arm across waist and pulled her into a spooning position. The sounds of birds chirping and cars going by played an early morning lullaby as the pair drifted off to sleep, floating on a cloud of euphoria.

{ three }

The repetitive screeching of the alarm clock next to the bed jolted
Denai awake as the bright morning light burst through the opened
curtains and hit her directly in the eyes. Slamming her hand on top of
the clock to shut off the blaring sound, Denai sat up in the unfamiliar
bed. As the sheet fell away revealing her naked torso, she slowly
remembered exactly where she was and how she'd got there.

The creases where her hips and inner thighs met were tender and
sore, and flashbacks of last night's exploits began to play like a highlight reel in her mind, causing a naughty smile to form across her face.
Denai looked around the hotel room for signs of her coitus companion,
but saw none. His duffle bag was gone, as was his wool coat and shoes.
For a brief moment, she felt a twinge of sadness in her chest until she
saw a note written on hotel stationary lying on the nightstand next to
the clock. Denai picked it up and saw it was from Dell.

> *Good Morning, Sweetness.*
> *You were sleeping so peacefully, I didn't want to wake you*
> *before I left for the airport. I loved every single second*
> *that I was privileged to be near you and with you.*
> *I only wish we had more time.*
> *One night with you was simply not enough for me.*
> *I look forward to more soon.*
> *P.S. I booked the room for another day so you could sleep in.*
> *Enjoy a little breakfast in bed on me.*

At the bottom, Dell had signed his name and written his phone number. All signs pointed to the possibility he had full intentions of continuing this beyond the parameters of a one-night stand. Not that Denai was opposed to that idea, but the fact that they lived in two separate states did give her pause. She had never done long distance dating before, and honestly didn't think she ever would because consistent in-person quality time was very important to her.

Deciding she didn't have to figure out the rest of her romantic life right this minute, Denai flipped the covers off her body and swung her legs over the side of the bed. She tossed the note and let it float back down onto the nightstand. Looking over at the clock, Denai saw it was 8:30AM Saturday morning. *Oooh, maybe I can still get breakfast through room service*, she thought to herself.

Finding the menu on the desk across from the bed, she called down to order a veggie omelet, a side of mixed fruit, cinnamon raisin toast and coffee. Since Dell offered breakfast on his dime, she was certainly going to take advantage. While waiting for her food to be brought up, Denai shuffled groggily to the bathroom for a much needed shower and to splash cold water on her face.

Standing in the shower under the spray of hot water, she was hit with another flashback of last night's tryst. Dell's touch was so gentle and full of care and affection, even though they were practically strangers. He was so attentive to every square inch of her five-foot, four-inch frame. Who knew something so simple as washing someone's back could be so intensely intimate.

Denai's thoughts briefly switched to her ex-boyfriend, Ryan. She tried to remember had he ever been anywhere near as soft and self-less when it came to her? She could recall a few times over the last three years where they had in fact been in the shower or a jacuzzi tub together, but Ryan Lattimore had never once taken the time to wash Denai's body.

The act itself was so holy and healing. It was an ultimate act of service that involved the most intentional level of physical touch anyone could do to show they cared about someone, and Ryan had never done anything like it. Hell, it was like pulling teeth just to get a massage from him when she was in pain.

It was crazy how often Denai would be forced to beg him for the bare minimum things that seemed to just be a given, but not with Ryan. He always put her in a position to have to ask, and then would only provide whatever was requested on his own terms. His arrogance and selfishness was at an all-time high some days, and ultimately that's what drove Denai away. Well, part of it.

Just as Denai stepped out of the shower, she heard a knock at the door. She quickly toga-wrapped a large bath towel around her body and trotted on her toes to answer the door. As she was letting the server in with the dining cart, Denai saw the door directly across from hers open up. It was Treena tip-toeing out of what presumably was E-Man's room.

Trying to pull the door closed as gently as possible and holding her breath the entire time, Treena almost squealed when she turned around and saw Denai standing half-naked in Dell's doorway. Once the server was done delivering Denai's food and exited the room, Treena darted inside.

"Well, well, well!" Treena exclaimed in a high pitched voice with a huge grin.
"Well, shit!" Denai said with a soft giggle.

"Well, shit, indeed," Treena replied. "So, are we gonna talk about it or take it to the grave?"

"Depends. You wanna talk about yours?"

"Not really."

"That bad, huh?"

"Oh, no ma'am! Anything but!"

"Say what?!"

"Giiiirrrlll!"

Denai and Treena sat down on the sofa, basking in the bright morning light and sharing Dell's sponsored room service. The twosome eventually ended up sharing all the juicy details of their risque exploits. It's amazing how what began as a girl's night out for them to just hang, as well as to get Denai's mind off her breakup, ended with them completely throwing caution to the wind and sleeping with two random men.

Now for Treena, this wasn't necessarily habitual, but it wasn't exactly unheard of either. Denai, on the other hand, had never done anything like this, and was still reeling from the fact that she actually went through with it.

"Soooo, what are you gonna do? Are you gonna use the number? Add him to the roster?" Treena asked inquisitively, sliding a piece of sliced strawberry off the end of her fork with her teeth.

"Honestly, I don't know," Denai replied with a sigh. "Am I wrong if I don't?"

"You're wrong if you start something up with this man when you really don't want to. Because then you become the one stringing someone along and we both know that's not cool."

"Yeah, you're right. I mean it's not that I don't want to. It's just I don't think I'm in a good place to start up anything with someone new right now. The wounds are still kinda fresh, ya' know?"

"Exactly. And, not that it's any of *my* business, but something tells me that Dell is so much more than just rebound, booty call material."

"T, he washed my feet."

"*Bitch, marry him!*"

Denai and Treena fell out laughing. They agreed that Dell seemed like a great guy or at least a guy with great potential for Denai, but the timing of their meet-cute could not have been worse. She was right. The wounds from her fallout with Ryan were literally only five days old now, and she knew she needed more time to get over them.

At the end of the day Ryan Lattimore was not without his faults and flaws, but Denai would be lying to herself and everyone else if she said she didn't still love him immensely. On the other hand, those steamy flashbacks of her night with Dell Hewitt offered up a great distraction to take her mind off her recent heartbreak. Not to mention the free breakfast and hotel stay were an excellent added bonus.

******

Monday morning arrived on the wings of a violent rainstorm with lightning that cracked and lit up the sky brighter than the sun, and thunder that shook the windows. With each pass, Denai was startled and nearly jumped out of her skin. She was sitting in the corner of her mother's red sectional sofa with her legs folded and laptop resting on her knees. Denai suddenly felt a renewed energy within her after the previous weekend's excitement.

Following Friday night's sexy exploits and Saturday's free breakfast courtesy of Dell Hewitt, she and Treena left the hotel and went home to change before setting out to run some errands. Treena was a luxury residential and commercial realtor and had some showings and open houses coming up that she wanted to prepare for; and since Denai had nothing but free time now, she decided to tag along.

When they stopped at *Yolk Cafe* at the Chicago Riverwalk for lunch, Treena decided to address the proverbial elephant in the room that had been bugging her for a while.

"Sooo," Treena started as she took a sip of her iced caramel latte. "I haven't heard much outta you. How's this last semester going, ma'am? When's graduation? You know how much I hate last minute invites."

Denai put down her fork and fell silent for a moment. She averted her gaze to look anywhere but in Treena's probing eyes. It wasn't until Denai heard her friend clear her throat, that her attention snapped back to the conversation at hand.

"Uh, that's a bit of a long story," Denai finally replied softly.
"Well, good thing we got time," Treena said sweetly with a smile.
"You're not gonna like it."
"Try me."
"*My* semester ended two weeks ago."
"What? I thought it was sixteen weeks? You just started in January."
"Yeah, I know. But it's over for me. And I'm not graduating."
"And why not?"
"Because I can't finish out the semester."

Treena sat back in her chair and looked across the table through narrowed eyes at her best friend. Nothing she said made sense. Denai was attending Kendall College for their eighteen month Culinary Arts Certification program because she wanted to get her license and start a catering business.

She had dreamed of being a chef since high school, but her mother wouldn't have it. So, Denai agreeably attended the University of Illinois-Chicago to study Criminal Justice so she could get a "real job" – "A good paying job," that her mother, Claudette constantly preached about. She went to school, studied something that guaranteed employment, did her internship and got offered a job as an Executive Administrative Assistant and Law Clerk at Dempsey, Little and Rowe Law Firm downtown. Just like her mother wanted, but her culinary dreams never wavered.

Then Denai met Ryan while working at the firm, and when they started dating she shared those dreams with him. He encouraged her to follow her heart and go for it and he'd be the ultimate supportive partner. And everything was going great, until it wasn't.

"I'm sorry?" Treena said, blinking fast. "What do you mean you can't finish?"

"The only reason I was able to start school in the first place was because Ryan promised he'd pay for it. The whole thing," Denai said in a hushed tone, her eyes lowered.

"Okay?" Treena responded with a slow nod.

"Ryan convinced me to quit my job and go to school full time so I could complete the program in eighteen months instead of twenty-four, and he'd pay for every semester as long as I was serious about it," Denai continued.

"I respect that. So what happened?"

"I guess I was too serious about it."

"What does that mean?"

"It means Ryan waited until my last semester, ten weeks from graduation, to stop paying. So, I can't finish because I can't pay for it and he refuses to."

"What the fuck?!"

"Yeah."

"Did he say why?"

"He said he was done paying for me to be anywhere but at home."

Denai offered a saddened shrug in response to Treena's explosion of expletives that flew across the table. She was livid and demanded to know just what the fuck that was supposed to mean? Denai went on to explain that she had registered for and was attending classes like normal from the moment the semester began in mid-January. Then one day, she received an email from her professor saying they couldn't input her grade for a test because she wasn't showing up in the system.

After getting the runaround from multiple people, it was discovered that Denai was locked out of the system and essentially dropped from all of her classes because her tuition had not been paid. No matter how hard Denai argued with the financial aid office and everyone else, the numbers didn't lie. Her balance was past due and there was nothing that could be done until it was paid in full.

Denai immediately called Ryan and told him about it and he said he would take care of it, and then three weeks went by without a word. Every time she asked, he'd just say "I'll handle it," until one day he had finally gotten tired of her asking. She had received an email from the school basically saying too much time had passed and she had to redo the semester at another time. She had gotten so close and now it was too late.

When Denai showed Ryan the email his only response was, "Good. Now I don't have to hear about it anymore." And then the fight started. She was enraged by his flippant attitude and seemingly broken promise. Ryan told her she had wasted enough time *and* his money and he was over it. If she wanted to cook, then cook at home where she needed to be anyway.

Regardless, he wasn't paying Kendall College another dime and he didn't want to hear anymore about it. So, she made sure he didn't. Just as flatly as he ended her educational journey, Denai ended their relationship.

After sharing her sordid tale of heartbreak and woe, Denai tried to reassure Treena that she was okay with it all. "No, you're not. But, you will be," was Treena's firm response as she raised her glass of peach bellini in a toast to her best friend. The one she knew would rise up victoriously and defy defeat at all costs. Treena believed it so much that she challenged Denai to write up a business plan for her catering venture as if she were readying to pitch it on Shark Tank.

"I want to know everything," Treena said. "And I want it by the end of next week. If you're as serious as I think you are, then I know you'll do great and I'm already excited to see it."

So, here Denai sat curled up on the sofa on a Monday afternoon, sipping coffee from a Advocate Christ Medical Center mug her mother had brought home from work, trying her hardest to write up an acceptable and professional business plan. Luckily, one of her classes from the Fall semester was centered around this very thing, so the information was still pretty fresh in her head. Also, still having a trunk full of old textbooks, didn't hurt either.

Denai was in the middle of adding some photos of plated dishes she had made to her portfolio when her phone vibrated with notification of a text message. It was facedown on the cushion beside her in an effort to avoid distraction, but it wasn't really working. She turned the phone over, glanced at the screen and saw it was a text from Ryan. It just said "Hey." She flipped the phone back on its face and muttered, "Boy, fuck you."

About an hour later, she was leaning on the kitchen counter staring at her laptop screen intently as she proofread what she had written in the business plan so far. Her mother, Claudette, came in through the side door drenched and breathing hard from running inside to get out of the pouring rain. She was also carrying two large Aldi paper sacks full of groceries, which added to her struggle. Denai stepped away from the computer to help her mother with the bags.

"Hey, Ma," she said as she kissed her mother on the cheek.

"Hey, Baby," Claudette sighed heavily as she wrestled off her soaked wool cardigan.

"I didn't know you were going swimming after work," Denai said with a wink.

"Shit, me either," Claudette replied with a chuckle.

Claudette Powell was a short woman with an even shorter fuse. She had brown skin with sandy-brown hair cut into a bob. With the exception of their eyes, Claudette and Denai looked just alike, but they were radically different. Where Denai had dreams and goals of being a chef and caterer, Claudette thought the whole idea was ridiculous.

She emphasized the importance of stability that a steady pay-check from a "good job" could provide. Her biggest pride and joy was being employed as a registered nurse for over twenty years – a career that afforded her the luxury of fierce independence. Especially since, "I could never depend on a man for shit!" as she would always say. A notion Claudette tried hard to instill in her only daughter, until Ryan Lattimore entered the picture. She had been his biggest cheerleader from day one, much to Denai's detriment.

Denai unloaded her mother's groceries without prompting and noticing the ingredients in one of the bags, she knew Claudette was making her highly requested chicken chili. Denai immediately became giddy, but was soon shot down when her mother said she was making it for a potluck at work tomorrow. After a short bout of pouting, Denai wore her mother down and she conceded to making a little extra for the house.

"I'll get everything chopped and prepped, if you wanna go get out of those wet clothes," Denai offered as she grabbed the wood cutting board hanging on the wall above the sink.

"Thank you, Baby. Yeah let me go, 'cuz it'd be just my luck I wake up sick as hell tomorrow," Claudette replied, shaking her head as she walked out of the kitchen.

A few moments later, Claudette came back downstairs in an old, tattered red and blue U.I.C. t-shirt Denai had given her during her undergrad days, a pair of black leggings and some bright pink fuzzy footies. Denai had chopped up the veggies and prepped the whole chicken her mom bought. She was grabbing a large stock pot from the cabinet under the island, when her mom noticed what was on the laptop screen.

"What's all this?" Claudette asked, eyeing the laptop suspiciously.

"Something I'm working on for Treena," Denai replied matter-of-factly.

"Since when is Treena tryna get in the food business?" Claudette asked, cutting her eyes at her daughter.

"Since now, I guess," Denai answered in a dodgy tone.

"Girl, this is all you. Don't lie. I thought you were done with all this foolishness?"

"It's not fo...it's not for me."

"Mmhmm."

An uncomfortable silence fell over the kitchen as Denai continued to get the ingredients ready for her mother. Claudette's words stung a bit, but that was nothing new. She was often very curt and off the cuff, sparing no ones' feelings. Not even Denai's. Claudette said whatever was on her mind without care or concern of consequence or impact.

"Folks don't like to hear the truth," was always her response when someone disapproved of what came out of her mouth. Sometimes the harshness was a bit too much for Denai, and this was one of those times. She knew her mother didn't really approve of her culinary aspirations, but that didn't stop her from pursuing them. If anything, it just stopped her from sharing her plans with her mother.

Denai learned very early in life to keep personal things like hopes and dreams to herself, and to only share them with Claudette when they were successful. Otherwise, everything was always "foolishness" or "a waste of time." Denai just silently shook her head at her mother's predictability on full display.

"I'm just saying, hell," Claudette grumbled as she opened the refrigerator to grab a carton of chicken stock. "What's Ryan got to say about all this?"

"He ain't got nothing to say. We broke up, remember?" Denai replied dryly.

"Exactly!" Claudette exclaimed. "You lost a damn good man chasing some wild ass dream, instead of listening to reason. Now, look at ya! Single, jobless and nowhere to live. You need to be using that thang to find a job and an apartment, instead whatever the hell this is."

"Damn! Wore out my welcome already and it's only been a week. That's gotta be a new record."

"If you're gonna be wasting your time on this, then yeah!"

Denai let out an exasperated sigh as she slammed her laptop shut, snatched it off the counter and walked out of the kitchen. She headed upstairs to what was now officially deemed the "guest room," since she clearly no longer had a place reserved for her here. Denai had to remind herself, just like Claudette used to do so often, this is her mother's house and hers alone. "You eat, sleep and shit here, but until you pay a bill, *this* is *my* house!" was the running motto throughout Denai's entire youth, and it seems nothing had changed.

She lamented on her mother's words, "Now, look at ya! Single, jobless and nowhere to live." It was so sad how true her words were at the moment. *My, how the mighty have fallen,* Denai thought to herself as she surveyed the bare walls of what used to be her childhood bedroom. Bare walls with dusty shadows where her framed diploma, degree and certificates used to hang. She really didn't have a place here anymore.

Denai grabbed her car keys and wallet off the dresser, slid on her black, patent leather rain boots and her satin-lined beanie and headed back downstairs. Without uttering a word, she walked out of the front door, intentionally letting it slam behind her. The rain had since eased up, and thunder and lightning had stopped completely. The sky was still gray and hazy as daylight fought to stick around a little longer these days.

Denai sprinted to her car, sloshing through sidewalk puddles as she went. She got inside, turned the key and fought with every muscle in her body not to succumb to the emotions laying bricks in her chest right now. She pulled away from the curb, inhaling and exhaling one shaky breath after the other as she made her way down the block.

******

Denai froze in place with the moving box in her hands the second she heard keys in the front door. After leaving her mom's house, she stopped by Walmart to get some moving boxes and drove over to Ryan's. Though Denai hated to admit it, even to herself, Claudette was right. She needed to find somewhere to stay sooner rather than later, and when that time came she didn't want to have to come back to Ryan's house for anything. So she figured she'd grab the rest of her things and at the very least put them in storage until she found a place. As long as they weren't here anymore.

When she pulled into his driveway, she breathed a sigh of relief seeing his car gone. Denai wasn't sure where he was, and she still hadn't responded to his text from earlier. She was hoping she could get her things and be gone before he got back, but no such luck. She was carrying one of four boxes down the stairs when she heard Ryan put his key in the lock on the front door. She just kept saying "Shit!" to herself as she tried to decide if she should hide or not.

Before she could decide, Ryan was standing in the doorway looking up at her with a crocodile leather duffle bag in his hands. He dropped it to the floor in shock at the sight of her in his house.

"Denai? What are you..." Ryan started but lost his words momentarily.
"Just grabbing the rest of my stuff," Denai replied shakily. "No sense in prolonging my occupying your closet."
"You don't have to do that," he said quietly.
"Yeah, I do. That's what people do when they break up. They move out," she said, still sounding nervous.
"True, but we didn't break up. So, you don't have to do that."
"What are you talking about, Ryan? Yes, we did, and it was ugly."

Ryan walked towards Denai as she made it to the bottom step. He took the box from her hands and sat it on the floor. He then took her hands in his and guided her across the open foyer over to the charcoal gray, suede sofa. Denai's steps were hesitant and uncoordinated by her uncertainty to follow Ryan anywhere at this point. Especially since the last time she was seated on this sofa, her whole world had come crashing down.

"Ryan, what are you doing?" Denai finally asked as she sat.

"I want to talk to you," Ryan replied calmly.

"There's nothing to talk about, Ryan. Everything that needed to be said has been. So..."

"Actually it hasn't."

Ryan pulled his hand from Denai's and went over to his duffle bag by the front door. After rifling around in each of the pockets, he found what he was looking for and came back to the sofa. When he sat back down beside Denai, he held out a small midnight blue-colored velvet box.

He opened it, revealing a sparkling pear-cut halo diamond engagement ring. Denai gasped and covered her mouth with her hands. Her eyes darted back and forth from the ring to Ryan's face. She was completely in shock.

"Ryan! What...what are you...what," Denai stammered, but couldn't gather her words.

"Denai, I want you to marry me," Ryan said plainly.

"What?!" she exclaimed.

"Is that hard for you to believe? I love you, Denai," he replied, still holding the open box.

"*We broke up, Ryan!* You made a promise to me and you broke it. So, I broke up with you. Why do you keep ignoring that fact?"

"I'm not ignoring it. I'm trying to fix it."

"And you think *this* is going to fix it?!"

"It's a start."

Denai threw up her hands in frustration and bolted from the couch. She began pacing circles around the foyer. Every few steps she'd look over at Ryan still sitting on the sofa and shake her head in disbelief. None of this made sense, and him thinking an engagement ring was an acceptable quick fix just aggravated her more.

"Ryan..." Denai started but was cut off.

"No, Denai. Let me say something first," Ryan said as he stood up. "I'm sorry."

"For what?" Denai asked as she folded her arms and narrowed her eyes skeptically.

"I'm sorry for breaking my word to you," he started. "I promised you a certain kinda life and that I'd give you anything you wanted in the world, and then in a weak moment of jealousy I betrayed you. I took your dream and all your hard work and trashed it because, I don't know, I guess I just felt like I was competing for your time and attention and I didn't like that."

"What?" she asked with a confused glare.

"I know how crazy it sounds, but I swear that's all it was," he continued. "I'd come home and you wouldn't be here or you'd be locked away somewhere studying and working on recipes. You'd make these elaborate dishes, but say they were for school and I'd have to fend for myself. I could say that I was feeling neglected, but really it was just petty jealousy. I was being unfair instead of supportive like I promised, and for that I am sorry."

"And what about the other thing?"

"What other thing?"

Denai raised her sweater to show a fading bruise that covered her right side and hip. The night she and Ryan had their blow up about him not paying her tuition, he got so mad that he pushed her. As if that weren't bad enough, Denai happened to be standing at the top of the stairs. So, when Ryan pushed her, she took a nasty, painful tumble down five of the ten hardwood steps. The only thing that saved her from going down all ten was her grabbing hold of one of the vertical bars that connected the banister to the stairs.

She was in so much pain and positive something was broken or fractured, but luckily she was just badly bruised. Denai will never forget how terrified she was during that fall, or how violated she felt by Ryan putting his hands on her like that. Even in the moment, he had rushed to her side to see if she was okay, but the damage was already done.

Denai found the strength to pull herself up and fight off a suddenly overly concerned Ryan. First it was him shattering her dreams of graduating from Kendall with her culinary certification like she had planned and hoped, and now he compounded it by pushing her down some stairs. That was enough for Denai to wash her hands of the entire relationship.

"Denai, I will never forgive myself for what I did," Ryan said. "So, I don't expect you to, but I will gladly spend the rest of life making up for it."

Ryan walked towards Denai, who had finally stopped pacing. He stood in front of her and cuffed her chin with his finger. Tilting her head backwards, he leaned down and placed a kiss softly on her lips. The tenderness of his kiss made Denai's knees weak for a split second, but she regained her wits and placed her hand on his chest, pushing slightly. She pulled her lips away from his and let out a ragged deep breath.

Denai could feel the tightness forming in her throat as the tears threatened to spill from her eyes. Ryan grabbed Denai's left hand and held it tightly. He called her name to make her look at him.

She hesitated, wrestling against her better judgment, and then looked into his brown eyes. Denai wasn't certain, but something about this moment made her feel like she could trust Ryan at his word.

Considering who and how he was, it's very rare for him to be apologetic about anything. One of the curses of being a brilliant lawyer, maybe – always believing you're right and justified in everything. Yet, here he was apologizing, asking for forgiveness, a second chance, and her hand in marriage. Ryan got down on one knee and held up the velvet box, the living room lights flickering across every diamond.

Tears began streaming down Denai's face as she watched him slide the ring on her finger. He told her how much he loved her and how she made him a better man. He said he wanted to spend the rest of his life with her by his side.

At that moment, Denai was more scared than she'd ever been in her life. She wanted so badly to believe him, to trust him, but something deep down stirred up doubts. Doubts that were hard to ignore when the stings of Ryan's betrayals could still be felt.

"Denai Renee Powell, will you marry me?" Ryan asked earnestly with a smile.

Denai placed her free hand on her chest and swallowed her doubts. She closed her eyes and exhaled a "Yes" as she was overcome with emotion. Ryan kissed her knuckles as he rose from the floor. He cupped her face in his hands and pulled her in for a deep kiss. Silently, Denai prayed she was making the right decision. Praying that this was it – for real, this time.

{ **four** }

September '22

Denai winced a little as she patted foundation along her left cheek-bone and jawline, trying diligently to cover up any discoloration from probing eyes. She finished applying her makeup – a soft, neutral look with bold brown lips and contoured cheeks – and raked her fingers through her hair.

She had grown out her pixie haircut into a blunt mushroom cut that framed her beautiful honey-green eyes nicely. Assessing her reflection in the vanity mirror, Denai forced a smile that she really didn't feel, because today was definitely a "put on a brave face" kind of day. She threw on a dark denim, mid-length jacket on top of a simple black turtleneck, paired with a beige corduroy skirt and mid-calf black leather boots.

Denai grabbed her purse and a purple three-ring binder off the bed, headed out of her bedroom and down the stairs. She took each step gingerly, trying to quiet her descent. She could hear Ryan in his office upstairs on what sounded like a heated work call, which was great because that meant he'd be busy for a while.

Denai slipped out of the front door, closing it softly, and quick-stepped to her burgundy 2022 Hyundai Elantra in the driveway. It was one of Ryan's many "I'm sorry" gifts she'd received for one infraction or another over the last six months. She had never been more grateful for how quiet the engine was than at this moment.

Backing out of the driveway, Denai commanded the Bluetooth to send a quick text saying, "Be there soon," before putting her phone on Do Not Disturb. She turned up the radio, blasting V-103's Saturday Afternoon mix and made her way down rain-soaked 47th Street towards the expressway.

Denai arrived at *Beatrix*, a restaurant and cocktail bar on Clark Street in Chicago's River North district, in record time. Just as she stepped inside, she heard her name being called out across the restaurant. Treena was seated to the right side of the dining area at a table near a window. She was waving her arm feverishly in the air, her gold bangles rhythmically clinking together.

Denai laughed at the unnecessary gesture because Treena was certainly not hard to spot. She was seated directly in front of a daylight-flooded window, wearing a canary yellow three-quarter sleeved blazer with a bright pink curly mohawk.

"Hey, girl, heeeyyy!" Treena squealed as she stood up to hug her best friend.

"Hey!" Denai excitedly greeted in return as she squeezed Treena tightly.

"You look amazing, as per usual!" Treena complimented.

"Looking at you, I feel underdressed," Denai teased.

"Don't hate!" Treena replied, sticking out her tongue.

The two friends shared a giggle as they took their seats. Shortly after, the waiter came over to take their orders, beginning with their starter drinks – Honey Cinnamon and Lavender Honey Lattes. Then the ladies got down to the nitty gritty of their planned lunch date.

"So, I know it's like six months late," Denai began. "But, it's better late than never, right?"

"Only for people who aren't as impatient as I am," Treena replied sarcastically with a raised brow.

"Yeah, yeah. Here."

Denai handed Treena the purple binder. Inside was the portfolio and business plan for her catering business that Treena asked for months ago. Denai had dreamed of starting it once she graduated from Kendall College, but after that went bust due to Ryan's own selfish reasons he still had yet to truly atone for, Denai decided to take matters into her own hands. She told Treena that after spending the Summer sulking in her disappointment and seeing all of her classmates posting their graduation photos on social media, she decided to write her own ticket to success.

Denai had over a year's worth of formal education learning the business side of running a food service establishment under her belt. Coupled with her existing culinary skills that could be honed and perfected along the way, she figured she had everything she needed to at least get her started. So, she put together a professional portfolio complete with photos and recipes of dishes she'd made in school and at home. Then, she wrote a full business plan, courtesy of tutoring from YouTube University, and put everything together for Treena to look over.

Treena had been an entrepreneur for years and was well-versed in what a solid business plan and strategy looked like, and the importance of looking and sounding like you know what you're talking about at all times. From running her own luxury real estate brokerage to managing herself and two other semi-professional models in the city, as well as multiple other ventures, Treena's eyes were perfect for reviewing Denai's handiwork.

"This looks really good, girl!" Treena complimented as she flipped through the perfectly curated and laminated pages.

"Really?!" Denai asked nervously.

"Girl, yeah! It looks so pristine and professional. You'd be surprised what some folks try to pass off these days. But this?! This is top notch."

"Oh, my God! Thank you! I was so nervous putting that together."

"That just means you really care about what you put out there with your name on it."

"Absolutely!"

As Treena closed the cover of the binder, she flagged the waiter down to request two glasses of the most expensive champagne they had. When Denai tried to protest because of the cost, Treena casually said, "Oh, girl, one of my client's owns this place. I don't pay for shit." Denai shook her head and laughed at her friend's colorful candor that went perfectly with her ensemble. Once their drinks arrived, Treena prepared a toast to celebrate and express how proud she was of her best friend.

"Cheers to you," Treena started. "For being brave and defiant enough to take control of your future. For creating your own opportunities and building your own tables right in front of those who've tried to stop you. I'm proud of you, Toots."

"Thank you, Toots," Denai said, her voice cracking a bit from getting choked up.

"We're also toasting to you securing your first client," Treena added as she clinked their glasses together.

"I did?" Denai asked with a furrowed brow and sipping her champagne slowly.

"Yup. You're looking at her."

"What?"

"We're about to enter peak buying season in this crazy ass market and I have some very big spenders for clients. Which means a lot of upcoming open houses and new build presentations for ya girl, and my clients are just like me. They like to spend money and they like to eat. So, you are now my official caterer."

"Treena, are you serious?"

"*Deadly*. Ever since you mentioned being remotely interested in becoming a chef, I've been waiting for this day. You are my best friend. I will be the first one showing up to support any and everything you do, and I respect you way too much to not put you on my payroll. So, I give you the dates, you quote me a price and I pay you every dime you're worth. That's just how serious I am about you, Toots."

Denai buried her face in her hands as she burst into tears. All Spring and Summer, she had been wrestling with the fear that no one would be in her corner. Between her mother, Claudette, constantly shooting her down any time she even mentioned the idea of being a chef; and her own fiancé pulling the financial plug on her education goals, Denai automatically assumed that she'd be alone in her cheering section. Yet, here was Treena Thompson in all her vivacious and vibrant glory, singing Denai's praises louder than anyone else ever could. It truly left her speechless.

The duo concluded their emotional and celebratory lunch date and exited *Beatrix* just as the afternoon rush was beginning to file in. They stood outside the restaurant saying their goodbyes and simultaneously fishing car keys out of their purses. Before they parted ways and headed towards their cars, Denai made one final request.

"Girl, listen, I really, really appreciate you and all your support with this," Denai said, still beaming.

"Of course!" Treena exclaimed as she held Denai's hand.

"I just need one last, small favor."

"Anything."

"Keep this between us for now. I'm not ready to go public with it, just yet. And *please*, whatever you do, don't tell Ryan."

"Girl, I wouldn't tell Ryan's ass the time! Let alone share *your* good news with his wannabe jealous ass. I got you covered."

"Thank you, girl. Love you, Toots."

"Love you, Toots."

The two of them embraced, holding on tightly and rocking side-to-side. They squealed in excitement for what their future held and planned to talk later in the week.

******

Denai slid the purple binder under the lining in the trunk of her car and pushed around all the other miscellaneous items in the trunk so that they sat on top of the lining to keep it down and looking undisturbed. After closing the trunk as quietly as she could, Denai headed in the house, carrying just her purse. The second she stepped across the threshold, she was under rapid fire from a very pissed off Ryan.

"Where the hell have you been and why the hell weren't you answering the phone?!" Ryan barked as he stomped towards her barefoot and shirtless.

"Why are you shouting?" Denai asked shakily as she cowered against the closed front door.

"Do not make me repeat myself, Denai. Answer the goddamn question," he demanded through gritted teeth, now standing in front of her.

"I just went to lunch with Treena," she said, trying not to flinch or sound as scared as she felt.

"Lunch with Treena, huh? Dressed like that? Yeah, Treena and who else?"

"What exactly are you implying, Ryan?"

"That birds of a feather tend to flock together, and we both know Treena's willing to flap her lil wings for anybody."

"Okay, now you're going too far! *Do not* talk about her like that. And don't you talk about *me* like that either. We went to lunch at Beatrix. Don't believe me? Subpoena the security cameras if it'll make you feel better, *Counsellor.*"

With that, Denai pushed away from the door and brushed past a still heaving Ryan. She began to ascend the stairs, when he gruffly called her name. She stopped just at the middle step and turned slightly to look over her shoulder and down at her crazed fiancé. It never ceased to amaze her just how angry he'd get at the mere mention of Treena's name, let alone the fact that Denai was still hanging out with her so often. Ryan swore Treena was some kind of bad influence, as if Denai were some impressionable little girl instead of the grown woman she actually was. It was all maddening.

Ryan's bare chest continued to rise and fall rapidly as he tried to steady his breathing and calm his anger. He loosened his fingers that had folded into fists when he was standing in front of Denai at the door. He shoved his hands into the pockets of his gray sweatpants as he looked up at her in frustration. Ryan had decided a while back to let Denai carry on her unsavory friendship with Treena until they got married, and then he'd be implementing some serious changes that she could not and would not be allowed to fight him on.

"Well, since you got so much time to be running the streets with Treena the Tramp," Ryan said, his disgust evident. "Then you won't have no problem making food for this Bears watch party I'm throwing on Sunday."

"Excuse me?" Denai huffed with agitation.

"No, you're *not* excused. You like tinkering around in the kitchen right? Well, here ya go. Fifty or so people made up of a few friends, colleagues and potential clients will be here on Sunday to watch the Bears game and they'll need food."

"And you're just springing this on me now?"

"You going out making plans without telling me shit. Figured I didn't have to tell you shit either. Especially about what *I'm* doing in *my* house."

"*Seriously*, Ryan?!"

"Yeah, *seriously*, Denai. The menu for what I want is on the kitchen counter. Familiarize yourself with it, and do not stray away from it either."

Denai stared at Ryan in stunned silence for a long while before shaking her head in disbelief and continuing her ascent to the bedroom. Just then she heard Ryan go, "Uh, tut! Tut!" She turned around at the sound and saw him pointing towards the kitchen. As if saying that's where she needs to be headed before deciding to do anything else.

Denai attempted to explain she was going up to change into more comfortable clothes, but Ryan wouldn't hear of it.

"It was good enough for you to traipse around Chicago in, then let it be good enough for you to traipse around that goddamn kitchen like I told you to," he barked.

* * * * * *

Denai slid the glass shower door open and stepped out on the plush floor mat as she reached for the large bath towel hanging from the porcelain hook on the wall. She wrapped the towel around her body and tucked in one of the top corners to hold it in place as she moved toward the double sink. She swiped her hand across the large steamed up oval mirror to reveal her slightly distorted reflection.

The streaks and water droplets created a fractured image in the mirror and Denai was intrigued by what she saw. Probably because it so accurately reflected outwardly how she truly felt inwardly. She had been feeling very broken lately and was trying hard to push through and put herself back together one jagged piece at a time.

She heard a light knock at the door and exhaled a heavy sigh before telling Ryan to come in. He pushed the door open and surveyed Denai's half-naked form standing at the sink cleansing her face. Just as she patted her face dry with a crisp white face towel, Ryan could fully see the bruising left behind by his very own hands three days ago. He dropped his head, feigning shame for what he had done to her once again.

He had gotten to the point where he no longer even tried to explain why or what caused him to get angry enough to hit Denai. Ryan would wholly acknowledge he was wrong and that nothing should ever make him mad enough to hurt the woman he loves. And every time he failed at keeping his hands in check, he'd spend hours upon hours and days upon days repeatedly apologizing.

Tonight was no different. Just another leg of his apology tour, and it was a double feature because now he was trying to make up for three days ago and the way he spoke to her this afternoon when she had returned home.

Ryan walked towards Denai, coming to stand behind her. He pressed his pelvis against her backside and slowly dragged his knuckles through the water droplets gathered along her spine. He leaned down and kissed his way along the back of her shoulder to the nape of her neck.

Ryan trailed his lips along her pulse as he lightly blew on the water trickling down her skin. Denai shuddered slightly and Ryan slipped his left arm under hers and wrapped it around her waist, pulling her closer to him just as he kissed along her ear and whispered, "I'm sorry, baby."

Denai watched Ryan's reflection in the mirror as the words left his mouth and snaked through her ear. Every time he said them, they sounded so sincere, and she wanted so badly to believe them, but Ryan had a bad habit of not matching his words with his actions. So, she stopped putting so much weight on his words and watched what he did very closely. And right now all Ryan was trying to do was fuck her until she forgets. Typical.

Ryan slipped his hand beneath the bath towel and between Denai's thighs. He caressed her lips with his middle finger, parting them just enough to get to her clit. The second the pad of his finger made contact with her sensitive flesh, Denai slammed her hands against the sink counter and released a gasp wrapped in a moan. Ryan pressed the middle of her back, bending her slightly forward, giving him more access to her wet and waiting flesh.

He put his middle and ring fingers together and slid them inside of her, pushing them in and out until they were covered in her wetness. Denai's coral-colored nails scraped wildly against the brown marble countertop and her body bucked against Ryan's fingers, driving them deeper inside each time she met his thrusts. She closed her eyes and bit down on her bottom lip as her passion began to build.

When she felt her release getting closer, Denai reached back and grabbed Ryan's wrist. He knew she was just trying to stop him because it was getting intense, and the mere fact she was trying to hold back just turned him on more. Ryan pulled his fingers out and flipped the towel up onto Denai's back, pushed his sweatpants and boxers down to his knees and pulled her hips towards him.

Gripping her waist tightly, Ryan entered Denai in one swift thrust, causing her to yelp softly. A smirk formed on his face at the sound as his desire heightened. *Slap! Slap! Slap! Slap!* The sound of Denai's butt and thighs bouncing against Ryan's pelvis as he pounded, and his grunts mixed with her moans echoed throughout the bathroom.

"Fuck! I'm about to cum, baby," Ryan said through gritted teeth as he thrust faster.

Denai pressed her forehead to her forearm resting on the counter and exhaled heavily against the cool surface. She felt the moment Ryan pressed his fingertips hard into her flesh, signaling he was close to release. He gave a few more hard thrusts before he pulled out, slapping his manhood on her butt as his seed landed on the towel draped across Denai's midsection. Ryan playfully smacked her butt as he pulled his boxers and pants back up.

As Denai stood up straight, he kissed the back of her neck once again. Then he grabbed her face by the chin and tilted her head back and kissed her deeply. Just before he pulled away, he repeated, "I'm sorry, baby," in a breathy whisper and kissed her bruised jaw. Denai offered a half smile and nodded her acknowledgment of his apology as she leaned into his kiss. Ryan smacked her butt again before turning and heading for the shower. Denai grabbed her teal plush bathrobe off the back of the bathroom door and walked out into the bedroom.

She dropped the towel in the wicker basket next to the closet and gathered the belt on her bathrobe, tying it loosely in front of her. Denai walked out of her bedroom and headed downstairs. She was on her way to the kitchen for some ice cream, but stopped short when she passed the first floor bathroom right outside the kitchen.

Denai darted inside and quickly closed and locked the door. She pulled open the counter drawer closest to the wall filled with towels and miscellaneous items. Rifling through the contents, reaching towards the back of the drawer, Denai's fingers grazed what she was looking for and she quickly pulled it out.

She twisted the base of her silver bullet and turned it on, the quiet hum of the vibrator was music to her ears. Denai sat down on the bathroom floor with her back against the wall and her feet pushed against the bottom of the door. She reached up and grabbed a towel out of the drawer and bit down on it to muffle her sounds.

Denai pressed the vibrator to her womanhood and immediately moaned, "Oh, my God!" into her terry cloth gag. In that moment, she was so glad for Ryan's incessant need to always shower after sex. It bought her all the time she needed to reach her actual peak. And reach it, she did...twice. The intensity of her orgasms rocked her body so hard, she kicked the door.

Denai sat on the floor listless and breathless in her very own passion puddle. She came so hard the second time that she squirted all over the floor. The euphoria of her orgasm had her giggling like she had taken an edible as she struggled to stand back up. Just as she made it to her feet, Denai could hear Ryan turning off the shower in the bathroom right above her.

She took the towel she used as a muzzle, soaked it with water and rang it out over the floor. Then she used two more towels from the drawer and swiped them across the floor with her feet to wipe up the water and her essence. When she picked up the damp towels from the floor, Denai caught a glimpse of her engagement ring and a thought occurred to her.

"Is this really what I'm signing up for?" she wondered out loud. "A lifetime of getting my own rocks off, because he can't stand what happens when I do?"

Denai huffed in frustration as she cleaned her vibrator and shoved it back in the drawer. *Now, about that ice cream,* she thought as she exited the bathroom.

{ **five** }

The melodious chime of the doorbell broke through Denai's intrusive thoughts while she was going over the menu for today's watch party. Thankfully, Ryan yelled out, "I'll get it!", so she could stay focused on today's mission. In just four short days, Denai was able to not only put together a full menu to satisfy a variety of appetites, but she was also able to get all of the shopping and pre-prep done sooner than she thought. She even sweet talked Ryan into letting her make a few changes to the menu he had created, and surprisingly he agreed.

"This is your wheelhouse, after all. Have at it, but make it good," he had said.

Since it was mid-September and still rather warm out, Ryan decided he wanted to grill, which was a big help to Denai's workload. He was in charge of grilling the chicken, shish kabobs, cobbed corn, hot dogs, polishes, and burgers that she had seasoned and marinated the night before. To compliment them, Denai was making potato and macaroni salads, spaghetti, deviled eggs, and a seven layer salad.

Then this morning she had the bright idea to add a few sandwiches, fruit and veggie platters for people to snack on while they waited for the grilling to be done. *Yeah, Denai. Just make more work for yourself,* she silently fussed. Denai had just started slicing up some kiwi for the fruit tray when she looked up and saw it was Ryan's parents who had been at the door and just walked in the kitchen.

Isaiah and Iris Lattimore looked like the epitome of classic Black Hollywood. Isaiah bore a striking resemblance to Harry Belafonte with a slightly darker complexion and the dark, wavy cropped hair of Smokey Robinson. Iris, on the other hand, carried the features of Lena Horne with all the poise and grace of Phylicia Rashad.

They were the dream power couple. Isaiah was a Circuit Court Judge for Cook County out in Country Club Hills, a quaint suburb south of the city. Iris was a Family Lawyer and Adjunct Professor at the University of Chicago Law School. Ryan was definitely the product of what some might call "good breeding," and Denai adored them both. She beamed at the sight of them.

She fell in love with Ryan's parents the first time she met them. They were so warm and welcoming, making anyone in their presence feel right at home. Denai's smile widened the second she felt Iris's arms wrap around her and squeeze tightly. They gave each other a quick peck on the cheek, before Denai made her way over to Isaiah for one of his bear hugs.

After all the greetings and pleasantries were exchanged, Isaiah announced he'd be going outside with Ryan because, "My son knows nothing about grilling." To which Ryan playfully protested and tried to reassure everyone that he did know what he was doing. Then the two men went out the sliding patio door to the backyard.

"Okay, Baby Girl, what can I help with?" Iris offered while looking for a spot in the refrigerator for her platter of cupcakes.

"Oh, uh," Denai stammered as she went back to slicing fruit. "You know I love you, Ms. Iris, and I sure appreciate the offer. I really do."

"Uh huh. But?" Iris asked with a smirk and her hands on her hips.

"But, I'm a chef. So, anything you'd be doing to help will really just feel like you're in my way."

Iris clapped her hands and cackled loudly. She knew Denai would say that, because anytime Isaiah tried to help in the kitchen she'd eventually shoo him away for that same reason. So, she completely understood and took no offense. Denai did, however, ask Iris to make a pitcher of her popular Sassy Sangria.

"You're welcome to use anything in this kitchen," Denai explained. "As long as you fill this glass for me. *Immediately.*"

She grabbed a large thirty-one ounce red wine glass with embossed frosted white roses imprinted on the bowl and sat it in front of Iris with a loud clunk against the countertop.

"Now *that*, I *can* do," Iris said with a wink and went over to the sink to wash her hands and get started.

A short while later, Denai was humming and two-stepping around the kitchen as she sipped away. Iris had blended red and peach wines, triple sec, orange juice, club soda and a mixture of fresh fruits like strawberries, blueberries, pineapple and kiwi slices and made the most divine sangria Denai had ever tasted. She was on her second glass filled to the rim when she heard a familiar voice call out from the living room.

"Hey, girl, heeeyyy!" Treena greeted as she walked through the house looking for Denai. She had let herself in when she realized the door was unlocked.

"Heeyy!" Denai sang as she handed Treena a glass.

"Oohh! Sangria? Ms. Iris here?" Treena asked excitedly, taking the glass.

"Mmhmm!" Denai replied as she sashayed to the stove to stir her homemade barbecue sauce and still sipping away.

Denai asked Treena to help her carry the platters of fruit, vegetables, and miniature sandwiches out to the patio since many of Ryan's guests were starting to arrive. He had invited several people from his office, including the partners he was trying hard to impress. There were also a few of his past clients and college friends he was still close to. When Denai told Treena about Ryan springing this impromptu shindig on her out of left field, her friend gladly decided to crash it.

Not only to be the help she knew would be needed in entertaining all these people on short notice, but also because she knew just how much it would irritate Ryan. The group gathered on the patio instantly cheered when Denai and Treena walked out with the platters.

The outdoor patio was covered with a wood awning. There was a variety of seating from a four-seater glass-top table, wicker love-seats with decorative cushions and matching individual seats spread around. A metal grate fire pit stood in the middle of the patio area with a wooden ledge that went around the outside so people could sit their drinks on it.

A 72-inch mounted TV with great surround sound hung down from the awning, and Ryan's large grill was positioned perfectly to the left of the TV so he could easily watch the game while tending to the food. Denai lined the platters up along the top of the outdoor bar and brought out paper plates, napkins and plastic utensils so everyone could help themselves.

Once back inside, Denai pulled the foil pans of marinating chicken out of the refrigerator and sat them on the counter for Ryan. Treena came in from the patio to refill her glass with more sangria and to grab a glass for Ryan's mother. She was pulling the pitcher out of the re-frigerator and telling Denai about having acquired two new potential real estate clients while she was outside socializing with the guest. As Treena was pouring, she noticed Denai hadn't said a word.

"Damn, girl! You look like you just saw a ghost. You alright?" Treena asked as she eyed her friend worriedly.

"Ah..." Denai muttered but couldn't get her words out.

"D, what's wrong?"

******

"Hey, man! Glad you could make it," Ryan greeted his new guest as they walked through the back gate.

He walked over and shook their hand. They thanked him for the invitation and handed him a bottle of Uncle Nearest 1884 Small Batch Whiskey as a show of appreciation. Ryan thanked him cheerfully and ushered them over to the patio with the rest of the guests. When he offered food, they asked if there was somewhere they could wash their hands.

"Yeah, sure. Follow me," Ryan said as he walked towards the door leading into the kitchen, with his guest following close behind. "You can come meet the little lady, as well."

"Oh okay, cool."

******

Denai was standing with her mouth slightly agape, blinking rapidly. She was breathing hard like she was hyperventilating and her hands were shaking. No matter how hard she tried, the words would not come out as her eyes quickly darted back and forth from Treena's face to the patio door. Just as Treena was about to ask again if everything was okay, the door opened.

"Dell, that's my fiancée, Denai," Ryan stated as he pointed across the counter at a still stunned Denai. "Babe, this is Dell. He just moved here and started at the firm about a week ago."

Denai managed a weak wave and soft "Hello," while still struggling to catch her breath. She was hoping her face didn't show the utter shock and sheer terror she was feeling right now. Behind the counter and out of everyone's sight, Treena squeezed Denai's hand to signal that everything was fine and she had her back. Then Treena stepped forward and cleared her throat as she tilted her head to look at Ryan with a furrowed brow.

"Oh, yeah. That's Treena," Ryan said dryly and rolled his eyes.

"You know," Treena started. "You'd think with all that education and fancy career, that manners would be a given. Guess not. Nice to meet you, Dell."

"Yeah...yeah, nice to meet you too," Dell stammered as he tore his eyes away from Denai and shook Treena's extended hand.

"So, you're new in town, huh?" she asked, trying to keep his attention on her, and maintain the ruse.

"Sort of. I was born here and moved away about fifteen years ago. Just got back about a month ago."

"Oh, relocation. Have you found a place to live yet?"

"No, not yet. Still looking for the right fit."

"Well, that just made you one of my new favorite people. I'm a realtor, and the perfect one for you."

"Oh, yeah, Treena Thompson. You come *highly* recommended with *raving* reviews."

Treena narrowed her eyes in suspicion at Dell's statement until he smirked and winked at her. Just then she remembered who his "source" was, and quickly turned her head away to cover her smile and blushing. Dell chuckled quietly to himself before returning his attention to Denai who had now turned her back to the group so she could pretend to be washing the dishes. Ryan beckoned for Dell to follow so he could show him to the bathroom to wash his hands.

When Ryan came back in the kitchen, he asked Denai if the chicken was ready to go out on the grill? She told him it was and he said, "Alright, well bring it out," before walking towards the door. Annoyed by Ryan's flippant attitude, Treena responded.

"Uh, is something wrong with your hands?" she asked in a gruff tone with her hand on her hip.

"Excuse you?" Ryan said over his shoulder as he held the doorknob.

"You're going outside. So, take the pans with you. Why does she have to bring it?"

"Treena, I strongly advise you to mind your business."

As he walked out the door, Treena turned to Denai and said through gritted teeth, "I fucking hate that nigga!" Then, she stacked the three pans of chicken on top of each other and took them out to the grill. Denai shook her head and laughed because she knew Treena was so serious about her dislike for Ryan, but she always appreciated her best friend coming to her aid. Whether it was telling him off or carrying a pan of food, Treena was more than willing to show up with a helping hand.

Dell rounded the corner into the kitchen and saw Denai loading the dishwasher. How could she make something so mundane look so sexy? Maybe it was the way her light blue t-shirt clung to her breasts as her chest rose and fell with each breath. Or maybe it was the way she brushed her bangs away from her forehead with one perfectly manicured fingernail as she sighed heavily. He noticed how much her hair had grown out since last they'd seen each other.

Just like the night they met at the club, Dell could not tear his eyes away from her. Her every move had him hypnotized. And also like that first night, Denai could feel Dell's eyes roaming across her skin like fingertips. She turned slowly to face him, to truly take in the sight of him after all this time.

He had bulked up a little over the last six months. The way his thin wool sweater wrapped itself around every muscle in his chest, back and arms. The brown and tan stripes decorated his torso beautifully. His dark blue jeans hugged his thighs and calves like an intimate lover; like the way Denai's own thighs did once...

"Hey," Denai said, trying to sound casual.

"Hey, Denai," Dell replied in a lowered tone, his eyes drinking her in.

"Dell, I..." she started but was interrupted.

"You know, I thought about this day for months," he admitted. "Imagining what I'd do...what it would be like to see you again."

"Yeah, me too," she confessed.

"But, I gotta admit, you being the fiancée of a guy I work with at my new job was definitely not on my bingo card."

"Ha! Yeah, this isn't how I pictured it either. To be honest, I never thought I'd actually get to see you again."

"I guess not. Since you never called."

"I wanted to. I really did, but it just wasn't the right time."

"Yeah, me and bad timing go together like suits and ties. A perfect fit. Oh well, I'll cherish the time we did have together. Even if it was just one night."

"That one night meant alot to me, though."

"Oh, you have no idea."

With that, Dell flashed her a sexy grin and headed towards the door, back out to the party on the patio. Denai dropped her eyes to the floor and gnawed at the corner of her lip, trying to hide a grin of her own. Dell gripped the doorknob and paused, turning to look at Denai once more.

"Ryan's a lucky son-of-a-bitch. I hope he knows that," he stated, still smiling as he walked out into the backyard.

Denai placed her hand on her chest as if trying to rub away the stinging she felt as reality set in. Dell Hewitt, the man of her wet dreams, was back in town to stay...and there was nothing she could do about it.

"Shit!" she exclaimed as she slammed the dishwasher door closed.

******

Dell leaned against the oak bartop trying hard to pay attention to the game playing on the suspended television. He had already made his rounds of polite conversation with the partners and coworkers from Dempsey, Little and Rowe Law Firm, as well as with Ryan's family and friends, but now his social battery was spent. Not to mention he was still feeling winded from the blow of being reintroduced to Denai as Ryan's now fiancée.

At this point, Dell was just trying to figure out how soon he could leave without it being seen as rude – or worse, obvious. The sound of the patio door opening caught Dell's attention and so did the sight of Denai emerging through it carrying a tray of what looked like football themed cheesecake bites. He watched as she sat the tray on the table in front of Isaiah and Iris.

The sound of Denai's sweet laugh tickled his ear even over the loudness of the television and everyone's excitement at a big play by the Chicago Bears. None of that mattered to Dell, because all he cared about was the woman in front of him. The woman of his dreams. The woman he could not have.

Dell found himself staring as Denai walked over to Ryan and leaned into him, still smiling as he tilted her head back to kiss her. The sight made Dell feel nauseous, but somehow he couldn't look away, just like the trainwreck his life had suddenly become. Luckily, at that moment Treena slid directly in front of him, blocking his line of sight.

She eyed him with suspicion as she tucked in her lips to keep from smiling. Realizing how he must look to her, Dell smacked his lips and exhaled a heavy sigh before breaking the seal on the bottle of whiskey he had gifted Ryan earlier.

"Okay, I just gotta ask," Treena started in a hushed tone as she leaned against the bar. "You do get how this looks right?"

"Like I'm pathetically pining away for my coworker's girl after he so graciously welcomed me into his home and introduced me to her less than two hours ago? Oh, yeah. I know," Dell grumbled as he poured himself a second shot and gulped it down hard.

"Well, yeah that too," Treena shrugged, still eyeing him skeptically.

"Wait! You don't think I planned this? What kinda stalking ass nigga do you think I am?!" he whispered loudly, holding up his hands defenselessly.

"I don't know! That's why I said you know how this looks?" she said, trying to hold in her laugh.

"No, no, no, no. Nothing like that. I swear. We haven't spoken since that night."

Dell explained he had left his number with Denai the morning he flew back to Detroit, but he never heard from her. No calls or texts. He didn't even try to find her on social media, because he felt if she wanted to be found and contacted she would've made it known from the beginning. So, Dell just cut his losses and chalked up their impromptu meeting as one amazing night to forever be imprinted on his memory, and just let that be enough.

He then told Treena about him making several trips back to Chicago over the Summer to visit friends and family celebrating milestones and reunions, and in those moments he realized how much he missed home.

"So, I started putting things in motion to make the move back," Dell continued. "I figured all I had to do was land a job, and everything else will fall into place. Just so happened that while in Detroit, I had worked on a case partnered with Dempsey, Little and Rowe and made a pretty good impression. When they heard I was relocating, they immediately offered me a job with a full relo package."

"Well, damn!" Treena exclaimed, both impressed and intrigued.

"Yeah, it was an opportunity I couldn't pass up. Who knew that shit would land me at the same firm and on the same team as this dude," Dell huffed as he rolled his eyes and gestured towards Ryan.

"You were dealt a helluva hand, brotha," she said softly.

"Tell me about it."

"So, what are you gonna do?"

"What any self-respecting Black man would do. I'm gonna finish my drink, pack a to-go plate and get the hell outta here."

Treena chuckled as she watched Dell down a fourth shot of Uncle Nearest and neatly tucked the bottle back behind the bar. She shook his hand, but held on a few seconds longer, trying to reassure him that everything will be okay. Appreciating the selfless gesture, Dell gave her a quick kiss on the temple and bid her goodbye.

Thankfully, Denai was now back inside the house when he made his way over to Ryan. Dell shook his hand and thanked him for the invite, saying that he had enjoyed the evening's festivities.

"Hey man, thanks for coming," Ryan said cheerfully. "And feel free to help yourself to some more food on your way out. We have plenty."
"Yeah, yeah. Thanks, bruh. I'll do that," Dell replied politely.

Dell looked through the opened blinds and stole one last glance at Denai moving around in the kitchen. Knowing this may be the last time he saw her made his heart ache, but such is life, and this was hers. Dell quietly slipped out the gate, and walked around to the front of the house without taking anything to-go. Even something as trivial as a plate of food would be too harsh of a reminder of today's tragic turn of events.

Walking towards his car parked across the street, Dell felt something in his gut tell him to turn around. When he did, he saw Denai standing just outside the front door, looking right at him. She had thrown on a brown and beige tribal print cardigan sweater to shield her from the late afternoon chill in the Fall air. She pulled the sweater closed and folded her arms across her chest, still silently staring out at Dell.

So badly Dell wanted to run to her. To pull her in his arms and kiss her as ferociously as he had dreamed of doing all Spring and Summer. To press their hot bodies against each other, fitting together perfectly like puzzle pieces. How he had longed to recreate their special night at the Westin Hotel over and over, but Dell knew that would never happen.

He knew that his window of opportunity had closed, and that all his hopes, wants and dreams shall never be. The pain of that truth was very hard to accept, but not as hard as it was for him to walk away from her right now. Suddenly, Denai turned back towards the open door because someone was calling her name. That break in eye contact was just the reprieve Dell needed to find the strength to get in his car.

Hearing the car door close made Denai's head swivel around, her eyes searching the empty street for Dell's face. The sound of tires screeching and engine roaring down the block was deafening and disheartening, but Denai knew it was necessary. Dell was literally driving off into the sunset towards his own life, and now she was walking across the threshold back into hers.

As Denai pushed the front door closed, she heard the rumble of thunder outside. She wondered if the noise would mask the sound of her heart breaking with disappointment?

{ six }

October '22

"Aye, bro, I need you to come with me to look at this new spot this weekend," E-Man said with a mouthful of pizza.

"What new spot?" Dell asked as he flipped the top of the box open to survey for a slice of his own.

"I'm going to look at this property."

"Property? Property for what?"

"I'm going to look at a condo."

"A condo?!"

Dell had just gotten in from the office when E-Man said a family-size meat lover's pizza from Lou Malnati's was en route. After the day he had, Dell was happy to hear it, especially since he had grabbed a six pack of Coronas on his way home. Dell had been staying with his cousin, E-Man, since moving back to Chicago at the end of August. E-Man was so excited to have his cousin back home, that he gladly let him move in until he found a place of his own.

Honestly, he enjoyed sharing his bachelor's pad with Dell. Pizza, beer and ESPN on a constant loop with one of his favorite people and frequent partner-in-crime was the dream. And right now a partner-in-crime was just what E-Man needed.

"Yeah, man. A condo," E-Man answered in a high-pitched tone.

"Bruh, you already have a house! What the hell do you need with a condo?!" Dell asked, taking a swig of his beer.

"Maybe I'll get one and rent it out. Tryna dip my toe into the real estate game."

"Dip your toe in the *what*?! Normal people get a single apartment and sublease it to get started. You're talking about spending 2-300k on a condo to *dip your toe in*?"

"Why you being a hater?"

"I'm not being a hater, nigga! I'm being logical!"

The two of them burst into laughter as E-Man tried to explain his rationale for wanting to go look at condos this weekend. There was a two-day open house Saturday and Sunday for some luxury units in the Gold Coast neighborhood, and he wanted to take a look at them.

"An open house?! Man, them shits take all day!" Dell groaned.

"No they don't!" E-Man groaned back, rolling his eyes.

"Aight, fine. We can go Saturday. I'm not giving up my Sunday for you."

"Saturday's cool. It starts at noon. We can go early. Get in and out."

Just as Dell headed towards the kitchen to put the half-empty pizza box on the stove, he had a thought and quickly turned on his heels to face his cousin who was still seated on the couch.

"Aye, man! If you want me to move out, just say that," Dell barked in annoyance.

"What the hell are you talking about?" E-Man asked with a confused tone, the beer bottle halted at his lips.

"I've been living outta your guest room for over a month, and now you're suddenly talking about going to look at condos on the opposite side of town. So, I'm just saying."

"Nigga, shut up!"

Dell howled with laughter and continued to the kitchen. He could still hear E-Man in the living room cursing him out about the foolishness he just said. Although his cousin never impressed any kind of urgent timeline on him, Dell knew he had to find a place of his own soon. He hadn't had a roommate since college and he hated it then.

Thankfully, Dell and E-Man kept somewhat similar schedules that had them out of the house most of the day, and in the times they were home together, they had a lot of shared interests. Not to mention, having grown up practically living together at their Granny's house, made doing so as adults that much easier. So, it all worked out perfectly.

However, bachelor or not, Dell had no interest in making his cohabitation with E-Man permanent. Besides, pizza and beer nearly every night was becoming hell on his workout plan.

******

"Girl, you looked amazing tonight!" Denai cheered as she tightly hugged a smiling Treena.

Denai had come to see her walk in a fashion show for Freddie J and another local designer. Among her many other hustles and talents, modeling was Treena's first love. She owned every catwalk and runway she stepped foot on and whether it was couture or a shower curtain, Treena made it look damn good.

Tonight's theme was "Real Housewives of Halloween," honoring many of the prominent female idols in Hollywood horror and villain culture. Treena was still in her Cruella Deville leather catsuit and red lipstick, but had taken her two-toned wig off by the time Denai came backstage.

"Aww, thank you, girl! And thank you for coming," Treena said as she pulled back from their embrace.

"Of course! Gotta support my Toots!" Denai exclaimed.

"Ya know, even though I hate his ass, Ryan could've come too," Treena said, rolling her eyes.

"Ha! Girl, it's not even that. He's actually out of town for work this week," Denai said, giggling.

"He travels more than any damn lawyer I've ever met."

"Well, when you're on that Partner track, you gotta make certain moves, or in his case, trips."

"Mmhmm, I guess."

"But he's back on Sunday. Which is why I'm making everything and dropping it off on Saturday."

"That works for me."

Now that Denai was really trying to get her catering business off the ground, she took Treena up on her proposition to cater events for her. Treena was having an open house for some pretty well-to-do clients, and for them, she always went all out. There would be food, libations and vendor presentations, and she wanted Denai to take full advantage of such an audience to put her delicious food in front of – and take advantage, she would.

Since Ryan was out of town for the whole week, Denai could save herself a little time by prepping and cooking at home. Knowing he still wasn't fully on board with her pursuing this career path, despite all the flowery promises laced in his proposal six months ago, Denai created a system.

When she booked catering jobs, she'd be sure to schedule them either around times when Ryan was out of town or when he had big cases that kept him so busy he practically ignored her. She would stash all of her professional cooking and serving equipment in the garage at her mother's house, because Claudette never went in there. She always said it gave her the creeps, especially because it faced the alley.

Denai also took full advantage of her mother's recently remodeled miniature chef's kitchen, courtesy of Ryan as a Mother's Day gift to his future mother-in-law; as well as another apology gift to Denai. Claudette had a habit of working long sixteen hours or more shifts at the hospital, and when the cat's away, the mouse sure did play.

Denai would go to her mother's house to prep, cook and package her catering orders for delivery. Then she'd clean up any evidence that she was ever even there. Leaving both naysayers, Claudette and Ryan, none the wiser.

Sometimes to cover her tracks even more when it looked like she'd be getting home later than anticipated, Denai would go to *Target*. Ryan never questioned her whereabouts or timeliness when he saw a *Target* bag in her hands. He understood Denai in *Target* was like a gambler in a casino – you just let them go until they can't anymore, and then they'd eventually come home.

She had created a foolproof system for herself to finally have the career she wanted and on her terms. Denai was done waiting for Ryan to come through on his promises, or for her mother to offer any real support for anything besides her just being a trophy wife. That's simply not the life Denai wanted.

"So, I'll come by early on Saturday to set up everything," Denai explained as she walked with Treena to her car. "And it will be easy to break down and set up again for Sunday. So, all you gotta do is grab the food out of the fridge and sit it back on the counter. Done and done."

"I mean it sounds easy enough. Now, why can't you come back on Sunday?" Treena asked suspiciously while fishing for her keys in her purse.

"Because Ryan gets back on Sunday, and I have to pick him up from the airport."

"That's what Uber is for, girl."

"Not when he has me. His words, not mine."

"Ugh! Have I told you I hate that nigga?!"

"Every day, twice a day for the last three years."

"Good. As long as you know."

"I do indeed."

******

"Uh, dude! Why are we here so early?" Dell griped as they pulled into the parking garage.

"Whatchu mean?" E-Man asked as he rounded another level in the structure.

"You said the open house starts at noon. It's not even eleven o'clock!"

"Early bird gets the worm, right?"

"Yeah, you are a bird ass nigga."

"Aye, fuck you, fam!"

Dell cracked up laughing as he exited the car. The chill of the lake-front air rushing through the openings of the parking garage made him quickly zip up his leather bomber jacket, before shoving his hands in his jean pockets. He and E-Man jogged down the three flights of stairs and burst through the ground floor door, making their way to the circle drive in front of the high-rise they were prospecting.

The sound of Saturday morning traffic whizzing by on Lakeshore Drive and the icy cold waves of Lake Michigan crashing against the barricades below echoed all around them. Dell took another look at his watch and voiced his confusion to his cousin.

"Yeah, really not understanding why we're here so damn early. Realtor's probably not even here yet," Dell mused, shaking his head.

"If you're early, you're on time, my guy," E-Man said matter-of-factly.

"Oh, nigga, whatever!" Dell groaned.

"What?! I'm serious!" E-Man quipped.

"No, you're full of shit!" Dell barked as they approached the front doors of the building.

When they were just a few feet from the automatic doors, Dell spotted Treena emerging from them. He shoved E-Man in the back when he realized he had been duped into coming to the open house.

"What I do?!" E-Man asked, trying to sound innocent.

"You know damn well wha..." Dell's voice trailed off when he caught sight of who Treena was talking to.

Denai was parked curbside at the front of the high-rise, unloading her car into two green collapsible vinyl wagons. She came to set up the refreshments for Treena's open house and was placing foil pans and covered platters into the wagon while waiting for further directions on where to go. Treena stepped back inside to confirm if they could use the service elevator, leaving Denai outside alone momentarily.

Denai had just grabbed a twelve pack of Sprite from her trunk to place in the wagon when she heard male voices coming up behind her and one sounded very familiar. She shook her head dismissively at the possibility of what she thought she heard and turned to sit the case down in the wagon. As Denai straightened up, she saw Treena walking back through the lobby towards the doors, and then she turned to the right, seeing her suspicions had been confirmed.

Dell stood frozen in place as he locked eyes with Denai. It had been weeks since they'd seen each other at Ryan's watch party, and this moment felt just like that one, with all the same angst as their last six month separation. Even though he never broke eye contact, Dell saw all of her. The way her black North Face fleece jacket fit every inch of her torso perfectly, and how her black leggings accentuated her hips and thighs beautifully. Even the way her lips parted slightly at her surprise to see him made Dell crave her in that moment.

"Hey, you," Denai said breathlessly, trying to hide her nervousness.
"Denai," Dell exhaled, his eyes narrowed slightly.
"Denai?" E-Man asked from behind Dell, as he couldn't see her at first. "Oh, shit! Hey, lady!"
"Hey, E-Man! How are you?" she greeted.
"I'm good. H..."
"Okay, I secured the freight elevator. We're good to go," Treena unknowingly interrupted as she stepped outside.

Treena didn't see Dell and E-Man initially, but when she spotted two figures in her peripheral view, she quickly turned to her left. She was surprised to see Dell there and said as much.

"Dell?! I didn't know you're looking at condos?" she said questioningly
"Oh, I'm not. He is," Dell said, gesturing towards E-Man with a head jerk.
"Emmanuel? Well, well, well," she said, biting the corner of her lip trying not to smile.
"Hey, mama," E-Man said in a flirty tone.

"If you're here for the open house, you're too early," she said, smirking.

"That's exactly what I said," Dell chimed in, cutting his eyes at his cousin.

"Well, since I have you, I'll take advantage. We need help with this stuff," Treena ordered, pointing to the wagons on the sidewalk.

"Uh, no we don't. I got it," Denai piped up in protest.

"Denai, you have help. Take the help," Treena whispered through gritted teeth.

"I don't need the help, Treena," Denai snapped through her own gritted teeth.

Denai angrily yanked the 48-count case of water out of her trunk and turned to sit it down in the wagon, but bumped into Dell before she could. Standing nose-to-chest with him, she involuntarily inhaled his Spice Bomb cologne. It smelled just how she remembered him tasting – spicy and sweet like horchata with a dash of cinnamon. Denai mumbled her apologies as she tried to step around him, but he grabbed hold of the case of water, attempting to hoist it out of her hands.

A small game of tug-o-war ensued until Dell's fingers brushed against the backs of Denai's hands, causing her to look at his face. He was looking down at her, biting his bottom lip. He exhaled a frustrated sigh, making his nostril flare. Dell had this look in his eyes that was both commanding and pleading, and it sent the butterflies in Denai's stomach in a tizzy.

Between the smell of his cologne, the look in his eyes and the feel of his skin touching hers, it was all enough to make her melt into the cold asphalt. Denai tilted her head and closed her eyes, trying to get her nerves to calm down. She conceded and let go of the case of water and went back to grabbing the rest of the serving utensils and platters out of the car.

After both wagons were loaded up, Dell took hold of one handle and E-Man took the other and they walked through the automatic doors behind Treena. They passed through the luxurious lobby with a front desk concierge and fireplace, went by the main elevators carrying tenants and visitors up and down, and headed down the hall to the service elevator.

Denai went to move her car to a better semi-permanent parking spot, then headed upstairs to meet the rest of the group. Just as she exited the main elevator on the penthouse floor, Denai heard Treena's voice coming from the other end of the hall as she swiped a keycard to enter the penthouse apartment through the backdoor that led directly into the kitchen.

"Thank you, gentlemen," Denai said politely as she entered the penthouse. "You can just park the wagons right over here and I'll unload everything."

"Where do you want these? I'll put them up so you don't have to lift the cases," Dell offered, gesturing to the cases of water and soda in his wagon.

"In the freezer drawer so they'll chill faster, if you don't mind."

"No, I don't mind."

The feel of Dell's leather sleeves brushing against Denai's arm as he walked towards the refrigerator made her clench her fists, trying to fight the urge to touch his skin again. Denai cracked her neck and took a deep breath as she snatched down the zipper of her jacket, peeled it off her body and tossed it on one of the kitchen chairs. Then she went to work pulling out her supplies and setting up the multiple food stations she had mapped out.

Dell watched in awe as Denai moved around the kitchen with immaculate precision and focus. It was amazing how many things she could carry or move in one fluid motion and not miss a beat. He tried his best to stay out of her way, but his soul wouldn't let him leave the kitchen completely, because he couldn't take his eyes off her. The meticulous professionalism that went into her presentation of something as simple as a cheese plate or veggie tray was so impressive to him.

"So, how long have you been doing this?" Dell asked, almost sounding entranced as he studied her every move.

"Oh, uh, I'm still pretty new at it," Denai said offhandedly as she situated foil pans over burners.

"Yeah, I doubt that," he murmured.

"I was in culinary school but didn't finish. And I've been cooking all my life. So, I just took what I did learn and mashed it together with what I already knew, and viola! Caterer."

"You make it sound easy, but I know it's more than that."

"Eh, not really."

Dell pushed off the wall he was leaning against and moved towards Denai. She could feel the heat of his body radiating against her back as he stood behind her. She turned slightly to look at him over her shoulder and swore she saw a flicker in his eyes. Was it annoyance or adoration? Frustration or flirtation? Denai couldn't tell.

"You shouldn't do that," Dell said softly, his breath brushing against her neck and ear.

"Shouldn't do what?" Denai asked, her eyebrows knitted together as her eyes darted back and forth.

"You shouldn't minimize how dope you really are," he replied. "Not everyone can do what you do, and those who can, can't do it like you. Own that. You'll have enough people breeze into your life just to talk down on you. Don't add your own voice to the noise."

Dell pulled a toothpick from the dispenser on the counter and skewered two barbecue meatballs out of the pan Denai had just set up. She scoffed and laughed before pushing past him to take the charcuterie and veggie platters into the living room. As she did, Dell caught a glimpse of her left shoulder blade that was visible through her black racerback tank top. There was an odd yellow and purple-ish discoloration that stoked his curiosity.

"What happened there?" he asked, following her out of the kitchen.

"What happened where?" Denai tossed over her shoulder as she continued hustling around the apartment.

"Here," he asked again, lightly grazing the spot with his fingertips.

The sensation gave Denai such chills, she actually jumped. She looked back at Dell's hand, then up into his eyes and just said, "Kitchen cabinets and countertops be getting in the way," with a casual shrug. Dell eyed her skeptically because the bruise didn't look like something you'd get by bumping into counters, but he didn't press the issue. Just simply said, "A clumsy caterer sounds like a walking contradiction," making them both laugh.

******

"Damn! This view is crazy!" E-Man exclaimed as he looked out the bedroom window, surveying the view of Chicago's lakefront.

"That it is," Treena replied absentmindedly as she skimmed through text messages on her phone.

"Hope that's not how you plan on selling it," he said sarcastically.

"Well, I'm not selling it to *you*. So, no sense in wasting a perfectly good pitch," she quipped.

"Damn, I'm not worth an actual sales pitch?"

"No. Especially when I know you're not even in the market for a place like this."

"Are you saying I can't afford it?"

Treena looked up from her phone at E-Man, but didn't say a word. Her silence was loud enough. He huffed and turned back towards the window. The two of them stood in silence for a short moment, with nothing breaking through but the muffled sounds of Denai and Dell moving around in the other room. The sound of Treena's cellphone dinging with a new notification made her finally speak up and say she needed to get ready to greet her actual clients. A statement that sent ice through E-Man's veins.

"Right and I'm clearly not one of them," E-Man said, clicking his teeth and turning to face her.

"My clients know to make appointments for my open houses, sir," Treena said flatly.

"Yeah, you're right. It was wrong of me to just show up here without booking time on your precious calendar."

"If it's not on the calendar, it's not happening."

"I see. Well, considering I've been trying for the longest to get in contact with you and, oh, I don't know, *schedule* some *personal time* with you. I figured an open house would be the easiest way to at least see your face beyond your IG page."

"Why do you care about seeing my face, Emmanuel?"

"Because I *miss* your face, Treena."

"Sir, it was *just* one night."

"It could be a lifetime, but I guess I should schedule an appointment first."

E-Man shrugged his shoulders as he shoved his hands in his pockets. Stealing one last look in Treena's eyes, he walked out of the bedroom. He saw Dell sitting on the sofa and signaled to him that it was time to go. They said their goodbyes to Denai as they swiped a few cookies from one of the platters set up in the dining room. Treena watched E-Man's retreating back as he disappeared through the kitchen to head out of the condo. As she ruminated on his last words, she felt an odd sinking feeling watching him leave.

{ **seven** }

Dell walked out of the Circuit Court of Cook County and the brisk Chicago wind sweeping through downtown greeted him on the steps. He pulled his scarf tighter around his neck, then buttoned his tan wool double-breasted trench coat to protect from the autumn elements that felt more and more like an early winter every day. Dell picked up his briefcase from the ground and began descending the courthouse steps when he heard someone call his name.

He looked back and saw it was Ryan Lattimore, his team colleague and new secret archnemesis, though he was trying hard to shake off the latter and remain mature. It had been over a month since Dell was blindsided by the revelation that the same woman he had pined over for six months was not only engaged now, but to a man he had to look at every day, inside and outside of the courtroom.

The desire to be cold and jockish towards Ryan was so strong, but Dell resisted and tried his best to accept defeat gracefully. *But, why does this dude always wanna talk to me?!* he thought to himself as he forced a smile he didn't really feel.

"Hey, Ryan. What's up, brotha," Dell greeted him with a handshake as they met in the middle of the staircase.

"What's good, man? What'd you have going on today?" Ryan asked, patting Dell playfully on the back.

"Deposition for this acquisitions thing with CPS school district," Dell said with a huff.

"That good, huh?" Ryan joked.

"Aw, man, you know how shit with the City can be. It's never as simple as just sign here and let's go."

"Don't I! Murph passed that one to you?"

"Hell yeah! Talking about it'll be a good way to build my client books here. I would take a gang of pro bono cases over this shit."

"Yeah, I feel you. Unfortunately, we all gotta pay our dues. Come on, I'll buy you a drink to help drown your sorrows."

"I wish. I got a meeting on the other side of town in like 45 mins, and I'm hoping to beat traffic. But, thanks, though."

Dell shook Ryan's hand again as they parted ways – he headed towards the parking garage and Ryan towards the subway. Dell almost felt bad for rejecting another one of his invitations for like the fifth time, but as mature as he wanted to be, it was still way too soon to become drinking buddies – all things considered.

He chucked his briefcase in the back seat, no longer needing to mask his frustration, and flung his coat right in behind it. Dell peeled out of his parking spot, his tires screeching and squealing with every bend and turn he made descending the parking levels until he was out in the throng of his fellow city commuters.

When he got to a stop light, he sent a text message to Treena letting her know he was on his way to her office as planned. They were meeting up to view three houses she believed would be perfect for him. Dell had decided that if he was going to entrust his home buying journey to anyone, it would be her.

"Better the shark you know than the one you don't," he said to E-Man when he told him about it.

Exactly forty minutes after leaving the courthouse, Dell arrived outside of Treena's realty office in Wicker Park. The area was alive with the hustle and bustle of Northsiders with their boots and shoes crunching through the leaves riddling the sidewalk. However, it was much quieter and settled than downtown where he worked or the Southside where he lived with his cousin.

Just as he was grabbing his coat from the backseat, Treena came out of the front door. As usual, she was impeccably dressed in a cream pantsuit, fuchsia silk blouse with a ruffled collar, and matching fuchsia pointed toe pumps. She had her cream and brown tweed coat draped over her left arm and her brown Michael Kors purse dangling from her right wrist.

Treena strutted towards Dell with all the prowess and power of Naomi Campbell, but with a smile as sweet as pecan pie. He offered a smile of his own – one much more genuine than the way he gave Ryan earlier. The two hugged and exchanged pleasantries.

"You ready to do this?" Treena asked excitedly.

"As ready as I'll ever be fresh outta court on a Tuesday," Dell said with a lazy shrug.

"Uh, perk it up, sir! We are embarking on the journey of a lifetime. Imma need more enthusiasm."

"This all I got."

"Ugh! Come on, then. I'll drive."

Dell followed her to a chrome-colored Jaguar F-PACE SUV parked across the street and joked about being in the wrong business as he looked back at his own car – a simple black-on-black Infiniti Q50. Treena laughed as she cranked the engine and pulled out of her parking spot. She expertly navigated the neighborhood streets, not even needing GPS, until they came to the first property on the list.

It was a beautiful, newly restored Cape Cod three bedroom home in the Norwood Park neighborhood. Even with the restorations, something about the way it looked on the outside alone, made Dell not even want to go in, but he humored Treena anyway. They spent about ten minutes walking through the house before he decided against it. They got back in the car and headed to another property in Rosemont, where Dell griped that the only selling point for it was the close proximity to the train station so he could take public transit to work.

Treena resisted the urge to yell at him for being a downer, because she understood choosing a home wasn't something done lightly. After they had seen the third home on the list, she got an idea for a last minute addition to the schedule. It happened to be a property one of her existing clients was selling, and she thought it might be suitable for Dell.

It was a beautiful three-story structure in Oak Park. The outside was painted a cool, steele blue color, and the front yard was neatly manicured. The minute he stepped inside, Dell got a great feeling about the house.

He and Treena walked through each of the bedrooms upstairs, and he even voiced his approval of the closet space. Once they came back down to the first floor, Treena let him survey the property unsupervised but still remained close by in case he had questions.

"You know I'm surprised you're looking at single-family homes," Treena said as she leaned against the doorjamb between the living and dining rooms.

"What do you mean?" Dell asked as he examined the kitchen and laundry room.

"I just assumed a single bachelor like you would want something smaller, like a townhouse or condo," she explained.

"You clowned me when I was at your open house for a condo, though," he smirked, cutting his eyes at her.

"I wasn't clowning you. Just offended you were potentially looking at properties and hadn't booked with me."

"I respect that."

Dell told Treena, even though he was currently a single bachelor, he was preparing for the life and future he truly wanted. He hoped to someday have a woman to share his life with and he wanted to be able to offer her something besides his winning charm. Dell proudly thought of himself as a family man and wanted to be able to provide for the people he loved. So, whether it was his parents coming to town for a visit or another relative who fell on hard times and needed somewhere to go, he wanted to be in a position to provide that. A trait he fully credits his Grandmother for instilling in him.

"That's actually really honorable. I had no idea," Treena praised.

"Thanks. Plus, living with E these last few months kinda inspired me too," Dell said as he checked around the windows in the living room.

"Inspired you how?" she asked curiously.

"E has a house. Three bedrooms and everything. He said he bought it because it was time to grow up and he wanted to make room in his life," he explained.

"Really? Wow."

"You sound shocked."

"I guess I am. But, now so many other things make sense."

"Yeah, like what?"

Treena told him about the heated exchange she had with E-Man at the open house and what he had said about "a lifetime."

"I don't get it, though. Nobody has a one-night stand with a person and actually expects more to come from that," she scoffed.

"Yeah, that's not true. Not at all," Dell replied with a scoff of his own.

"Dell, come on. We met at a club. Got pissy drunk on complimentary birthday shots. Went to a hole-in-the wall for breakfast and back to his hotel room at 4AM. Don't get me wrong. We had a bomb ass night together. But that's all it was. One night."

"If you say so, Treena."

"What do you mean? He and I had the same night you and Denai had. How could it be anything other than one good ass night?"

"No. *You* and *Denai* had *one* good ass night with zero expectations to follow. Me and E had one good ass night with a great ass woman – one that we would've loved to repeat every night with for the rest of our lives, if possible. *Y'all* had one great night. We've had a miserable six months. Not the same."

Treena stood at the bottom of the stairs looking up at Dell dumbfounded as he reached the top landing and disappeared around the corner headed towards the owner's suite one more time. She dashed up the stairs to press him further about what he had just said. When Treena entered the bedroom, she cornered Dell inside the walk-in closet and demanded he expound on what he meant.

"I don't know all the details," Dell began. "But, I do know he tried to find you or a way to contact you for weeks after his birthday, and when he couldn't he decided to leave it up to fate. If y'all saw each other again, he'd make his move. If y'all didn't, then he'd let the memory of that one night be enough."

"He knows Freddie J. Why not ask him for my contact info, huh? Don't sound like he tried that hard," Treena said, sounding annoyed.

"Freddie J gave this whole speech about how and why he don't give out other folks' numbers. He wouldn't help him," he replied with a shrug.

"Aw, what the fu...Okay, and what about you?"

"What about me?"

"Why opt for a miserable six months instead of reaching out to Denai? Make it make sense, Sir."

Dell exhaled a heavy sigh and shoved his hands in his pockets. He leaned against the back wall of the closet, pressing the bottom of his foot against it like a kickstand. He told Treena he had left his name and number for Denai before leaving to catch his flight back to Detroit the next morning. Because she was dead asleep, he didn't want to wake her up just to get her number.

So, he opted to leave his and wait to hear from her. Unfortunately, that never happened. Just like E-Man, Dell waited anxiously for weeks, hoping she'd call or text or anything. The silence was excruciating and totally unexpected.

After about three weeks, Dell just accepted that maybe it was just a one-night stand for Denai and she had no desire or intention for it to be more than that. After all, he did live in a different state and they were complete strangers, despite having spent a wildly intimate night together. So, he forced himself to move on and forget about her as best he could, until he got the opportunity to relocate back to Chicago.

Dell immediately set his heart on finding Denai and pursuing her like the Queen he thought her to be. Nothing could prepare him for the reality that steamrolled over his life the moment he saw her again.

"Trust me, I thought of nothing or no one since I met her, but I guess the feelings weren't mutual," Dell said, dropping his gaze to the tan carpet beneath his feet.

"Oh, Dell," Treena said with sadness in her voice as she placed her hand on her heart.

"It's cool. I can accept my losses like anyone else, but don't ever think I didn't try," he said strongly.

"I know you did," she replied softly.

"And don't think E-Man didn't try either. You were so much more than just some random blip on the radar for him. Do with that what you will, but don't say you didn't know."

Dell pushed off the wall with his raised foot and walked out of the closet past a stunned Treena. He told her he had seen enough of the house and was ready to head back to the office to make an offer. She mumbled a response as she tried to gather her thoughts. Treena slowly descended the stairs, meeting Dell at the front door. He held it open and waited for her to walk out. Before closing it, he took one last look around the empty house and immediately began picturing what his life would look like inside of it.

This was definitely the next big step he needed to make on his quest for maturity and stability, and it felt really good to do. Dell closed the front door and headed toward Treena's running car.

******

As Dell stuck his key in the front door of E-Man's house, his cell phone started ringing. "Shit!" he exclaimed as he wrestled it out of his pants pocket. Looking down at the caller ID, he saw the familiar number and rolled his eyes before hitting the "Ignore" button.

"You alright out there?" E-Man asked jokingly when Dell finally entered the house.

"Why your bum ass ain't come see?" Dell spat back sarcastically.

"'Cuz I knew you had it," E-Man said plainly, raising his beer in salute.

"I hate you so much," Dell chuckled.

Dell sat his briefcase down on the bottom step and went to hang up his coat in the hall closet. Just then his phone rang again. Checking the caller ID, he cursed and hit "Ignore" once more. E-Man laughed and asked who was he dodging? Dell told him it was his ex-girlfriend, Destiny.

Ever since word had gotten out that he was back in town for good, she had been calling incessantly. They had broken up nearly four years ago, and it made no sense why she was calling him so much now. Especially since the last time Dell saw her, she was in bed with someone who wasn't him, and he explicitly told her they had nothing more to say to each other.

E-Man huffed and rolled his eyes at the mere mention of her name. If he lived the rest of his days never hearing her name again, that would be heaven for him. He didn't even like Destiny while she was dating Dell. So, she certainly didn't have a friend in him now. When Dell's phone rang again, E-Man said, "Give me the phone. I bet she won't call no more after I'm done." Dell cackled and said it was actually his mother calling.

"Hey, Mommy!" Dell greeted sweetly when he answered.

"Hey, my baby! How are you?" Annette Denton's cheerful voice wafted through the speaker.

"I'm good, actually. E-Man's here and you're on speaker." he told her.

"Hey, Auntie!" E-Man yelled from the couch.

"Hey, Butterscotch!" she yelled back, calling him by his childhood nickname.

"Come on, Auntie! I'm too old for that now."

"Not to me. That's who you'll always be. My Butterscotch."

"Just cuz it's you, I'll allow it."

Dell laughed loudly when he saw E-Man pouting on the couch. He told his mother about it and she laughed just as loud. He grabbed his briefcase and took the steps two at time heading up to his bedroom. Once inside, he asked her what was new in Detroit and what he was missing. "Child, these church folks are something else!" is what she always said.

Annette had met and married Randall Denton, a semi-truck driver and Pentecostal Pastor when Dell was fifteen. Randall was really the only father Dell ever had, and never once did they let the matter of genetics come between them. Dell knew of his biological father, but when asked about his "Dad," he would always refer to Randall Denton.

The two of them clicked instantly and developed a great relationship. So much so, that when Randall said they would be moving to Detroit for a new opportunity to pastor his own church, Dell respected the decision even though he didn't want to leave. He was just about to start high school and wanted to do so with his friends and family he was close to, but he just asked if he could stay in Chicago for the Summer to say his goodbyes, instead.

The only reason Dell never went as far as changing his last name to Denton was because Hewitt was his last tie to his maternal grandmother, who helped raise him and passed away while he was in college. That was one of the few things Dell regretted most about not coming back to the city when it was time for him to attend college.

He had fully planned to move back in with his granny for the whole four years, but instead opted for school in Michigan because it was more feasible for his parents. So, four years at Michigan State, two and a half at the University of Michigan, passing the Michigan Bar Exam on the first try, and beginning his law career immediately after graduate school, Dell owed it all to his mother and step-father.

When he announced he was ready for a change and wanted to move back to Chicago, his parents were certainly sad to see him go, but were excited about the new possibilities that awaited him.

"Ma, don't let them people drive you crazy. Not even in the name of the Lord," Dell said with a chuckle.

"I'm really just tryna keep from flipping over a pew or two, because these folks will take you there!" Annette said through gritted teeth. "But, anywho, enough about them crazies. What's new with you, dear?"

"Well, I'm kinda house hunting at the moment," he said shyly.

"You're what?! Oh, that's great! Where have you been looking?"

"Honestly, I've preferred looking outside the city just because the quality and pricing have been better. I think I found one today, though. Fingers crossed."

He described the house to his mother, who exclaimed her pleasure and excitement at how it sounded. She told him how proud she was and that she couldn't wait to see it.

"So, since you're house hunting, I guess that means you're not coming home for Thanksgiving?" Annette questioned.

"And miss out on your dressing? Are you crazy?! Even if I gotta drive to save money, I'm coming home," Dell said bluntly.

"Dang it! Here I thought I could get out of it," she giggled.

"Hey, all you gotta do is make me some dressing. I don't even need a whole meal," he joked.

"Good luck getting your daddy to agree to that."

"Oh, well that's when he goes back to just being your husband and your problem."

Annette squealed over the phone and Dell burst out laughing. They carried on their conversation for a little while longer, before hanging up. Annette made him promise to let her know when his closing date was coming up so she could be there.

"There is not a single milestone achievement you've had that I wasn't present for. Buying a house will be no different," she fussed. To which, all Dell could say was "Yes, ma'am."

When Dell came back down the stairs, he spotted E-Man on the couch staring at his phone with a bewildered expression. Without saying a word, Dell sat next to his cousin and peered over at the screen. It was a text message from an unsaved number, but the context let it be known exactly who it was.

> *Since I spent your birthday with you,*
> *it's only right that you come spend mine with me.*
> *I'm hosting a fashion show & brunch for my birthday next weekend*
> *and I would love for you to come. Please say you'll come for me...*

Dell quickly averted his eyes when he read the last line and covered his mouth with his hand to stifle his laugh. He looked over at E-Man, whose eyes were still wide as saucers and mouth was partly open. Dell pushed his cousin's chin up to close his mouth, snickering the whole time. He had never seen E-Man rendered speechless before, and the entire ordeal was hilarious to him.

Dell patted his shoulder three times before getting up from the couch, his own shoulders still trembling from laughter as he headed into the kitchen.

"Bruh!" E-Man screamed, finally coming out of his stupor.

"So, whatcha gonna wear?" Dell teased as he flicked on the tab of a soda can with his middle finger.

"I...shut up! But, *bruh!*" E-Man screamed again, now standing up and anxiously pacing the floor between the couch and coffee table.

"I'm gonna go to my room and let you panic in peace. Congrats, by the way," Dell grinned as he walked by and patted E-Man's shoulder again.

"Huh?! For what?"

"It's now your turn to freak out over a woman you like. Consider it a rite of passage, my dude. Proud of you."

"Shut up!"

Dell let out another hearty laugh as he climbed the steps and headed up to his room. Right before he closed the door, he heard E-Man shout, "You're going with me! Fuck that!" from the bottom of the stairs. Dell guffawed again as he swung the door closed. He plopped down on his bed and popped the top on his soda. As he took a hefty sip, the sting of envy pierced his throat worse than the carbonated bite of the cola drink.

He began coughing slightly, choking on the blend of emotion and soda mingling in his throat. Suddenly, the reality that his favorite cousin could soon become another person he'd be envious of was too much for Dell to bear. He was glad Treena heeded his advice from earlier and reached out to E-Man. If only Dell, himself, could be so lucky, but naturally, that's not how his universe worked.

{ **eight** }

November '22

Denai stepped back to assess her handiwork. She had been tasked with crafting a sweets table for Treena's birthday brunch and fashion show event, and she happily welcomed the challenge. Since today's festivities were supernatural/fantasy themed, Denai went with a whimsical look for the table. She took inspiration from both *Tinkerbell* and the Elves from *Lord of the Rings* lore. The colors were varying shades of blues, greens, silvers and golds with glitter dusted everywhere.

Denai made two cupcake towers with chocolate, vanilla and marbled cupcakes, topped with more of the "fairy dust" edible glitter and miniature wands, crowns and fairy wing-shaped adornments. There were also platters with an assortment of fresh baked cookies and handmade pixie candies. Additionally, she made Treena a custom, three-tiered birthday cake.

It was teal, aqua and emerald green blended marble fondant with a glossy glaze and streaks of gold that made the cake flicker in the venue lighting. On top of the cake was a halo of an edible mixed bouquet, made of Iris and Dahlia flower buds draped around a large cursive "T" standing in the center.

When Treena mentioned having this shindig for her birthday, she quickly and strictly assigned Denai "The Best Friend Only" role and not the caterer, because she wanted them to enjoy the day together.

However, Treena still wanted to give her an opportunity to shine in this new lane of a culinary entrepreneur. So, she outsourced the brunch buffet to another company, and tagged in Denai for desserts. A request not taken lightly. With her growing confidence over the last few months, any chance Denai received to showcase her skills in hopes of gaining new clients, she was all over it.

She stepped back from the table to take some photos of the spread. The catering crew was on the other side of the room setting up the brunch buffet. Those helping with the fashion show were setting up tables and chairs for the attendees. Treena walked the room, surveying everything with a sharp eye to ensure it was all perfect. When she made it over to Denai, who was still snapping photos, she commented on how beautiful the dessert table looked.

"What would I do without you?" Treena gushed while resting her head on Denai's shoulder.

"Probably be suffering through some dry ass, pre-made grocery store cake and hating yourself for it," Denai teased as she swiped through the pictures she had taken.

"Ew!" Treena gagged.

"Exactly," Denai giggled.

"So, how did you pull all this off, Secret Agent Powell?"

"Ryan's traveling again this weekend and Mama's out of the house working doubles. Plenty of unsupervised time for me to create magic."

"I still think it's crazy that you can only work in peace when they're not around, but I'm glad it always works out for me."

Treena stuck out her tongue and laughed before skipping away to go check on the models in the back. Denai shook her head and smiled as she began placing stacks of disposable dessert plates and cutlery at the end of the table where the serving line would start. As she did, she mulled over Treena's words. It was hard enough revealing that Ryan had outright refused to continue paying for her education, resulting in her not graduating the first time. She certainly couldn't reveal that she had once again fallen for his empty promises of investing in her future, and he *still* hadn't.

Denai also couldn't tell her the reason why her window of creative opportunity was only open when Ryan and Claudette were M.I.A. was because neither of them supported her goals of running her own catering business. Anytime she mentioned anything about it, she was pummeled with disparaging remarks and criticism. Neither her fiancé, nor her mother saw any point or value in Denai wanting to cook for a living.

Just last week, Claudette said, "If you're so hell bent on cooking for the rest of your life, then you stay your ass at home and cook for the man taking care of you. That's the only person you should be worried about feeding anyway." What made it so bad is they were sitting at the dinner table with Ryan, who raised his glass in salute to Claudette.

Denai let out an exasperated sigh recalling that moment, but shook her head, arms and hands to expel any negative energy trying to invade her space right now. She was going to enjoy today, no matter what.

About two hours later, the event space was filling up with guests and spectators ready for another one of Treena's extravaganzas. The DJ was spinning R&B jams from the 80's to the 2000's – providing the greatest soundtrack to the Saturday mid-morning brunch.

Denai had changed out of her sweats into a fitted burnt orange sweater dress, with gold faux buttons down the left hip leading to a mid-thigh split and low v-neckline. She had on flesh tone stockings and brown knee-high boots with a short heel. She finished off the look with brown and gold faux wooden dangle earrings and matching neck-lace; as well as a brown, yellow, dark orange and maroon geometric patterned headwrap that was situated across the middle of her head and knotted at the back, leaving just her bangs exposed and swooped across her forehead.

Denai helped fill in as hostess while Treena finished prepping and getting dressed for the fashion show. Whether it was directing attendee traffic, checking on the DJ and catering staff, or just making sure everything and everyone was where they were supposed to be, Denai was all over it. Just as she was pointing a guest in the direction of the gift table, she heard Freddie J's booming voice over the speakers, which meant he had been allowed to find a microphone and the event was about to start.

Guests were still milling about finding their seats when Freddie J introduced himself as the emcee. He explained there would be three sections to showcase three different designers; but before the show kicked off, everyone should get in line to grab food so they could sit still and enjoy both together.

People began lining up at the buffet station. The room echoed with the sounds of multiple conversations carrying on at once, while being threaded together by the upbeat tunes of New Edition. Denai was standing in the doorway, scanning the room to make sure things were moving along seamlessly, when a cold breeze hit her back, sig-naling someone had just opened the first set of doors leading into the building.

She turned around and spotted E-Man and Dell walking towards the second set of doors where she stood. Denai's stomach immediately knotted up and her heart began to race. No matter where she saw Dell or how long it had been, it always felt like she was seeing him for the first time and his attractiveness was always startling each time.

Dell showed signs of a freshly trimmed beard and mustache, as well as a freshly tapered faux hawk glistening in the sunlight that shone through the doors. He wore a burgundy two-piece Dashiki pant suit with a Mandarin collar and gold tribal patterns down the front and around the cuffs of the sleeves. The color looked magical against his caramel complexion, and Denai swore she felt drool running down her chin as she watched him. Even his walk was sexy with his long, lean legs carrying him in her direction.

E-Man reached Denai first and greeted her with a quick one arm hug and peck on the cheek. She noticed his wardrobe was quite different from the last few baggy ensembles she'd seen him in. Today he was rocking a well-fitted navy blue blazer over a crisp white v-neck t-shirt and slim fit dark blue jeans with chocolate brown loafers. His long black hair neatly pulled up into a top knot. His dark beard and eyebrows made his gray eyes sparkle. Denai complimented him and noticed he was holding a bouquet of deep red roses.

"Yeah, I brought these for the birthday girl. I hope she likes them," E-Man said shyly.

"I know she will," Denai confirmed with a sweet smile. "She's in back with the models. You should take them to her."

E-Man's eyes lit up with excitement as he thanked Denai for the tip and headed towards the dressing rooms she pointed to. When he walked away, Denai turned to her left to see Dell watching her intensely. She nervously twisted her mouth to keep from smiling.

"You not speaking to me?" Dell asked, his voice husky and thick like smoke billowing over each word.

"Hi, Dell," Denai said dryly, still trying to hide her smile.

"Now that hurts," he said, clutching his chest.

"Aww, poor baby. You want a hug?" she asked playfully, poking his chest.

"I'd love one, actually," he replied, holding his arms open.

Denai stepped into Dell's arms, scooping hers under his and wrapping them around his waist. His heavy arms draped around her neck and shoulders like a weighted blanket, and the feel of them was so soothing and warm. As Denai laid her head against his hard chest, she inhaled his masculine scent and became engulfed by the heat of his body. This was the first time their bodies had touched since that one fiery night at the Westin Hotel eight months ago.

Swimming in euphoria from the feel of their bodies pressed together, Dell's hand caressed the nape of her neck as he hummed his satisfaction in her ear. Denai gently rubbed her hands along his back, her fingers tracing the lines of every flexed muscle as he tightened his hold on her. She knew if they didn't pull away soon, they'd fuse together like a melanin mosaic and never want to part. Denai was the first to loosen her hold on Dell, and he slowly but begrudgingly followed suit.

Denai stepped back and looked him up and down, no longer trying to stifle her smile. She complimented his outfit and told him it was a perfect choice for Treena's party. Dell thanked her for saying so and expressed love for her outfit, as well. He took her hand and spun her around. Denai giggled as she turned slowly, letting him appreciate every angle, and he was glad for it.

For a brief moment, Dell continued holding her hand, loosely intertwining their fingers and looking into her eyes. While stroking the back of her hand with his thumb, he brushed against the ring decorating her finger, and his heart sank as reality invaded his temporary fantasy. Dell released Denai's hand and shoved his lonely ones into his pants pockets. Denai clasped her hands together in front of her, trying to stave off the empty sensation washing over them. She guided Dell into the room, showing him where the buffet line started and where the available seating could be found.

Dell wanted to prolong their closeness for as long as he could, so he stood beside her at the back of the room as she surveyed the crowd of brunchers and Freddie J Go-Go dancing in front of the DJ booth. He asked Denai if she catered this event, as well, and she explained how she ended up just doing the dessert table and birthday cake instead.

Dell praised her creativity, saying how impressed he was with the table and proud of her for continuing the pursuit of her catering dreams any way she could. Denai bashfully thanked him, then attempted to change the subject to keep from blushing.

"You know I'm a little surprised to see you," Denai quipped. "Since you haven't been around much lately."

"Whatchu mean?" Dell asked, eyeing her curiously.

"Well, there have been a lot of Dempsey, Little and Rowe associates at the house watching football the last few Sundays, and *somebody's* been noticeably M.I.A.," she said plainly, cutting her eyes at him.

"Oh, yeah, that. I'll probably never come around for that again."

"Why not?"

Dell turned his body to face hers and leaned down until his lips were inches away from her ear. The feel of his breath against her skin, made Denai shudder.

"Because I'd spend the entire time picturing your naked body on every surface of a house you share with another man I just happen to work with. And frankly, I'd rather not spend my Sundays that way." Dell explained, his voice deep and sultry.

Denai's mouth suddenly went dry and her eyes widened at Dell's confession. She angled her face to look up at him, to see if he was being serious, and everything in his expression said he was indeed. Denai licked her lips nervously as Dell seductively bit down on his own, never breaking eye contact.

"Behave yourself," Denai chastised in a breathy whisper, trying to maintain her composure.

"This is as tame as I get, Baby," Dell replied with a wink as he slipped past her and headed towards the buffet.

Denai simply shook her head and exhaled a laugh as she listened to Dell's retreating footsteps. She looked up and spotted E-Man coming towards her. It was the first she had seen of him since pointing him in Treena's direction earlier. He had a different swagger in his step as he strolled across the room, rubbing his palms together and flashing a sinister grin. He could see Denai looking at him curiously, so he made a beeline for her.

"Hey, Romeo," Denai said jokingly.

"Ha! What's up?" E-Man chuckled, shoving his hands in his jean pockets.

"Is that lipstick?" she squealed, leaning in for a closer look.

E-Man wiped the pad of his thumb across the corner of his mouth and laughed when saw the bright red smudge.

"I take it she liked the flowers?" Denai giggled.

"I'd say so," E-Man said with a wide grin.

"I'm glad you came. She really wanted you here," she confessed. "But, don't tell her I told you that."

"Ha! Girl Code violation?" he asked.

"Huge!"

"It's cool. Your secret is safe with me. What'd you do with my boy?"

Denai pointed at the buffet where Dell stood third in line. E-Man gave a thumbs up and headed that way. By the time he made it there, Dell was moving along, having food piled onto his plate. E-Man stood closely and covertly next to him, hastily looking around the room before speaking.

"My nigga, we got a problem!" E-Man exclaimed in a whisper.

"We do?" Dell asked over his shoulder, snorting out a laugh.

"Yeah. *We* do," E-Man confirmed, his eyes still darting around the room.

"Okay, and what's that?"

"Bruh, Destiny's *here*!"

Dell stopped cold in his tracks and nearly dropped his plate at the mention of his ex-girlfriend. He turned his head slowly to look at E-Man who was now staring at him wide-eyed and panicked.

"She's what?" Dell asked through gritted teeth, his jaw tight and eyes narrowed.

"She's *here*! She's one of the models in the fashion show. I saw her in the back when I went to see Treena," E-Man explained.

"Aw, what the fuck!" Dell huffed.

"Bro, we can dip right now, if you want," E-Man offered earnestly.

"What?! No, we came so you could be with Treena for her birthday."

"I know, but I saw her. I gave her flowers, told her happy birthday and everything. We don't have to stay, if you don't want to."

Dell paused to give it some thought but shook his head. They came there specifically to celebrate Treena's birthday with her because that's what she wanted, and he refused to let Destiny ruin this perfect reunion E-Man had been longing for since March.

"Nah, we're not leaving," Dell proclaimed.

"Bro, Destiny is twisted! She *cannot* see you," E-Man emphasized.

"If she does, I'll deal with it, but we're not leaving," Dell murmured.

"Okay, and what about her?" E-Man asked, gesturing towards Denai.

Dell looked longingly at the beautiful brown skinned woman who had shaken up all his senses and sensibilities the moment he laid eyes on her. Even now, he could still feel her small hands rubbing his back from their hug earlier. He was so jealous of the way her sweater dress wrapped itself around her petite frame, touching all the places he yearned to touch but couldn't.

Though they weren't together, and had no option to ever be, Dell felt extremely protective over Denai in every way. He wouldn't let anyone or anything be a potential threat to her peace. Especially not some cheating ex-girlfriend from forever ago.

"I'll take care of that too," Dell replied to E-Man's question. "Here. I need some air."

He passed his untouched plate to E-Man and walked off angrily, heading for the double doors. It took everything in Dell not to barrel through them like an angry bull, but he didn't want to draw any attention to himself. He pushed one side open with his hip, to keep from punching the door like he wanted, and walked out into the hallway.

Denai watched Dell closely when she saw him going out the door and looked at E-Man questioningly, who just shrugged his shoulders. Before she could go after him, Freddie J and the DJ announced the start of the main event: the fashion show. Treena strutted from the back wearing a mint green tulle tutu dress and gold stiletto heels with bejeweled butterflies on the back. She danced her way to the front of the room to take the microphone from Freddie J.

Treena thanked everyone for coming to celebrate her birthday and partake in something that meant so much to her. Shortly after her speech, the parade of fashions began. All the pieces were whimsical and fantasy inspired with butterflies, fairy wings, foliage appliques and the like. Continual thunderous applause, whistles and cheers radiated throughout the room.

All the women looked stunning as they took to the catwalk, prancing and twirling with impeccable confidence. It was truly a glamorous sight to see and a raw representation of who Treena Thompson is at her core.

******

Denai was helping Treena pass out slices of her birthday cake when she spotted Dell in her peripherals. He was sitting at an empty table looking down at his phone. Everyone else was mixing and mingling, partaking in the plethora of sweet and savory treats, and imbibing on the open bar that started at noon. The revelry was alive and kicking, and Dell wasn't bothering with any of it.

She grabbed a plated slice of cake and a fork and began making her way over to him, but stopped short when she saw another woman doing the same. This mystery woman wore a beige catsuit and black spiked pumps. She had reddish orange hair flowing down her back and sweeping across her voluptuous butt. Her waistline was nonexistent beneath very large breast spilling out of the scoop neckline of her one-piece. Her makeup was flawless and she oozed sex appeal like a vintage pinup model.

She sashayed over to Dell's table and slid the plate in front of him as she placed her dainty hand on his shoulder and leaned in to whisper in his ear. Denai's fingers clenched around the plastic fork in her hand so tightly that her knuckles turned white and the plastic cracked. She felt a pang in her chest she couldn't explain as she watched this woman tuck a few fiery strands of hair behind her ear as she continued her flirtatious assault near Dell's.

Denai couldn't stomach the sight anymore and threw the plate of cake in the trash can nearby before storming out of the room right past Dell's table. E-Man saw her go by in a furious blur and snapped his head around to look over at Dell, who was still sitting at the table. Because she had changed her hair from earlier, it took him a second to recognize the woman sitting with his cousin was none other than Destiny.

E-Man shook his head in disgust and huffed in frustration at the sight. He then got the sneaky desire to go over and interrupt whatever was happening, just because he knew it would irritate her. So, E-Man grabbed a handful of cookies from the dessert table and headed straight for them.

Dell continuously rolled his eyes and scrunched his face each time Destiny spoke or touched him. The aggravation made him antsy, clenching his jaw and rapidly tapping his index finger on the table next to the untouched cake. The more Destiny talked, the more Dell's rage bubbled inside him like lava. He looked across the table at a smirking E-Man, who dramatically pulled out one of the chairs and plopped down in it.

"Well, this looks cozy," E-Man said sarcastically with his mouth full.

"Go away, *Emmanuel*," Destiny fumed, whipping her head around to glare at him across the table.

"Girl, I do not fuck witchu. You don't get to call me that," he said, sending a glaring look of his own right back to her.

"Whatever," she said dismissively, rolling her eyes. "Now, back to you, Boo."

"Destiny," Dell said through gritted teeth as he turned to face her for the first time. "*Stop* fucking touching me. *Stop* fucking talking to me. *What...the...fuck...do...you...want?*"

"Ooh! I forgot how sexy you looked with your face all frowned up like that," she said playfully as she stroked his chin.

Dell grabbed her wrist and yanked her hand away from his face. Destiny gasped and scoffed at the act.

"You'd think after all these years, you'd be happier to see me," Destiny pouted.

"And why the fuck would you think that?" Dell asked dryly as he went back to scrolling on his phone.

"'Cuz she dumb as hell," E-Man mumbled from his side of the table.

"Fuck you, E-Man!" Destiny snapped back at him.

"Nah, I'm good on that," he grimaced.

"Destiny, we have nothing to say to each other. Nothing's changed," Dell said flatly.

"Seriously, Dell! It's been long enough!" she cried, flailing her arms in a tantrum.

Dell slowly turned his head to look at her. He stared in stoic silence, completely unmoved by her tantrums and pleas. He shoved her plated peace offering to the center of the table as though he were pushing her away, as well. For a split second a flash of what looked like hurt feelings flickered in her eyes, and still Dell was unfazed. He pushed his chair away from the table and stood to leave. Just as he did, E-Man called out to him.

"Uh, fair warning. If you go outside, you might wanna keep your head on a swivel," he said, reaching for the rejected piece of cake.

"And why is that?" Dell huffed with his back still turned.

"Because a certain green-eyed goddess is not too pleased with you, my nigga," E-Man mumbled after shoveling a hefty piece of cake in his mouth.

"Fuck!" Dell groaned as he headed towards the doors Denai had stormed through.

"Who are you talking about?" Destiny asked E-Man as she watched Dell's retreating back.

"Someone you'll never be and can never compete with, sugar tits," he said before standing up and leaving her at the table alone.

Destiny frowned in offense at E-Man's eerie words and quickly got up from the table to follow Dell's path outside. When she stepped into the hallway, she could hear heated voices coming from the other end of the hall to her right. Without hesitation or shame, Destiny strutted her way towards the voices when she recognized one as Dell's. The closer she got, the bigger her grin became and her eyes laser focused on the side profile of her prey.

******

Dell put his hand on the wall, his outstretched arm blocking Denai's path as she tried to walk away from him. She pushed against his chest, trying desperately to move him out of her way. He had cornered her in the hallway when she emerged from the bathroom. There was a soft pleading in his eyes she had never seen before, but she was also too enraged to care about it. More than anything, she was angry with herself for reacting at all to what she had seen between Dell and Destiny.

"Dell! Dell! I don't care!" Denai fumed as she tried tirelessly to walk around Dell.

"Okay, but I do! Please just let me explain," Dell pleaded, as he kept cuffing her chin to make her look at him.

"Explain for what? You don't owe *me* an explanation. Who the fuck am *I*?" she raged on.

"You're *you*, and that's enough for me. I owe you this," he said softly.

"Baby! There you are. I was wondering where you disappeared to," Destiny said melodically as she laid her back against the wall and flashed a devilish grin.

Denai looked at the woman boldly standing in front of her, calling Dell pet names so freely. So badly she wanted to take off her headwrap and strangle this woman just for the audacity she possessed. Denai could feel Dell's arm tighten around her waist and realized it was because she was unconsciously trying to lunge at this unknown woman. The fact that she was feeling this way at all, considering there was nothing going on between her and Dell, actually made Denai feel embarrassed. There was no reason for any of this.

"Dell," Denai quietly called his attention to her.

"Yes, Love?" Dell asked in a nervous, heavy breath.

"Let go of me," she said pointedly without blinking.

Dell pulled his arm away from her side and took a step backward to give Denai room to gather herself. She tugged at the hem of her dress to pull it down and ran her hands over her body to smooth out any bunched material. She craned her neck left and right to release any tension that had crept up, and stepped around Dell to walk away.

Instinctually, he grabbed her wrist to halt her steps. Denai turned around and took two steps back towards him, bringing them nearly face-to-face.

The sternness of her expression and darkening of her golden-green eyes made Dell loosen his grip on her wrist. He knew right then, this was not a look he ever wanted to see again. It was gut-wrenching. Heartbreaking. Painfully unbearable. The feel of her small fingers sliding through his palm was a harsh, realistic reminder of just how she had slipped from his grasp once before. The emotional pain of that experience was bad enough, but just now it became tangible. Excruciatingly tangible.

Denai spun on her heels and walked away from Dell. As she passed by Destiny, she locked eyes with her like a lioness with a gazelle. No words were spoken. There was nothing to say. Not to Destiny. Not to Dell. Not to anyone. Denai had her own life with enough of its own problems. She was not about to make room for anymore. Especially not for a man that wasn't even hers. Hell, the one she already had was troublesome enough. This shit here was for the birds.

Denai breezed past E-Man who held the banquet hall door open when he saw her coming. He could tell by her face that something was wrong, but decided it was better not to ask. He looked back down the hall where she just came from and spotted Dell and Destiny. That sight told him everything he needed to know.

E-Man shook his head and went back into the room to find Treena and say his farewells so he and Dell could make a break for it before things got too atomic. Treena thanked him for coming and said she wanted to see him again, sooner rather than later. He told her how much he'd love that, but suggested she check on Denai first, then they'll talk. E-Man was certain once Treena heard the details of today's fiasco, she'd probably never want to see him or Dell ever again.

Just the possibility of that happening made him furious. E-Man angrily pushed the double doors open and stepped out into the hallway. Dell walked up and said he wanted to go inside to speak with Denai once again before leaving.

"Nope! Nope! *Hell No!*" E-Man exclaimed as he grabbed Dell's arm, pulling him to the exit.

"Whatchu mean?" Dell asked, struggling to pull his arm away.

"Now is not the time, bruh. Trust me," E-Man advised through pursed lips.

"E, I need to fix this."

"Not right now, you don't. Going in there now will only make it worse."

Dell looked longingly at the doors of the banquet hall, catching a quick glimpse of Denai when someone pushed the doors open to come out. She was breaking down the sweets table and helping Treena pack up. She had a smile on her face that looked forced and hollow, as if she were trying to put on a brave front for her friend.

Dell wanted so badly to go to her. To explain further. To kiss her pain away. Hell, he'd even let her hit him if that's what she needed, but E-Man was right. She needed time and Dell had to give her that, but Lord knows he wanted to do anything but.

{ nine }

"Denai, we're hosting Thanksgiving at the house this year," Ryan announced absentmindedly as he walked by staring at his phone screen.

"I'm sorry, what?!" Denai exclaimed from her blanket cocoon on the sofa.

"We're hosting Thanksgiving. Mama needs a break from a bunch of people being in her house," he replied, still not looking at her.

"And I don't?!" she fumed as she sat upright and flung the covers off.

Ryan stopped in his tracks and finally looked at her. He walked up to the sofa, stopping short to perch his knee on the armrest. He pursed his lips and squinted, contemplating his next words carefully.

"What the hell do *you* need a break from exactly?" Ryan asked smugly.

"Are you serious?!" Denai asked, sounding frustrated.

"Very," he said, his tone unchanged.

"Like you don't have an ass-load of people here every fucking Sunday?! I've been shackled to that kitchen for *weeks*! *Months*! Cooking for a bunch of people you don't even fucking like for real, but insist on playing host to. And you think I don't deserve a break?"

"You're the one with these asinine dreams of being a cook. Now, when you're being asked to cook, it's a problem?"

"It wouldn't be such a problem if I thought you were actually *asking*?"

Ryan dropped his knee from its perch and started to walk away when his cellphone rang. He looked down at it and suddenly his expression softened. Before he answered the call, Ryan looked over at a frowning Denai.

"I'm not asking, and it's not up for debate. You're cooking," he said flatly and walked away before she had a chance to respond.

The sound of his jovial laughter coming from the kitchen as he answered the phone made Denai's blood boil. She didn't know what angered her more. How happy he sounded on that phone call or how he basically just issued an executive order to her about cooking for the holiday. Never mind the fact that he was once again springing his last minute plans on her with less than optimal time to prepare. His blatant disregard and disrespect for her time was currently at an all-time high, and Denai had no idea why. What she did know was that Ryan Lattimore was working her last damn nerve like a part-time job, and she was over it.

Denai angrily flailed her arms and legs, throwing the fleece blanket off her and onto the floor. She snatched up her cell phone from the coffee table and sprang from the sofa. She shoved her feet into her fur-lined Ugg slippers, pulled up the zipper on her hoodie and walked out the front door. She was so heated with rage that the chilly air of mid-November barely fazed her as she paced up and down the driveway.

Denai dialed Treena's number and waited with bated breath as she counted the rings. When the voicemail picked up, she growled in annoyance and hung up. It took all her strength not to hurl the phone across the front yard. Denai sat on the trunk of her car, pulled her hood over her head and shoved her hands into the pockets of her sweater.

She looked up at the sky, watching the thick clouds float across the blue expanse, passing one another like familiar strangers. Denai felt the heaviness forming behind her eyes as she tried to swallow the tightness growing in her throat. She closed her eyes, her face still aimed at the clouds. Then as if on cue, the sky opened up and watered her sorrows. Denai took advantage of the moment and released the hold on her tears.

She sobbed openly into the evening air, releasing everything she had bottled up. She was so exhausted just from holding her head high in the face of adversity, carrying on from day-to-day like everything was okay. Some days were better than others, but today it all became too heavy to bear and the dam finally broke. The weighted feeling in her chest made it hard to breathe as she gasped for air between sobs.

Denai covered her eyes with one hand and put the other on her hip as she tried to slow the flood of emotions and regulate her breathing. When her phone started vibrating in her pocket, Denai took a deep, shaky breath and wiped her face, even though a few stray tears continued to fall. The rain slowed to a steady drizzle, once again matching the flow of her tears.

She pulled the phone from her pocket and frowned at the caller ID flashing an unknown number. Denai had been doing more secret freelance catering and wondered if this was someone calling to inquire about her services. She inhaled deeply and let out one more heavy sigh before answering the call.

"Hello?" Denai answered, trying her best to sound professional.
"Hey, you," a familiar husky baritone replied.
"Dell?!" she asked, jumping down off the trunk in shock.
"Guilty," he said slowly.
"How..." she started but couldn't find the words.

"I...uh...swiped one of your business cards at Treena's birthday party. Sorry," he confessed.

"I see. Well...uh...wh-what do you want?"

"To talk."

Just hearing Dell's voice had Denai struggling to find even the simplest words, but him seeking an actual full conversation right now rendered her totally speechless. She looked over her shoulder at the front door to the house, and worried about how Ryan might react to her missing in action for too long. Especially when she had walked out of the house without a word right after their heated exchange. It was only a matter of time before he came charging out that front door like a mad man.

"I...uh...don't think that's a good idea," Denai nervously whispered into the phone, still staring at the door.

"I won't take up too much of your time, I promise," Dell replied in a gentle tone. "There's just something I need to say to you."

"What?" she asked, still in a throaty whisper.

Dell took a moment to respond, but she could hear his heavy breaths as he searched for his next words. He wanted to choose them carefully because he was sure this would be his one and only chance to get them out.

"I wanted to apologize," Dell started. "And to explain myself."

"I don't understand," Denai said.

"Yeah, I know. Okay, here goes," he said, exhaling a heavy sigh.

Dell opened with a heartfelt apology for having upset her at Treena's birthday event two weeks ago, as well as for waiting so long to reach out to her.

"Honestly, I was afraid to," he confessed. "Everything in your eyes said you hated me, and I was too much of a chicken to face the possibility of that being true."

"I didn't hate you," she told him. "I still don't. Truthfully, I feel silly getting so upset seeing you just sitting with another woman. I had no reason or right to. So, I'm sorry too."

"You have every right to feel how you feel. Don't apologize for that. And that's the other thing I need to say to you," he said.

Dell explained to Denai that Destiny was his ex-girlfriend, who he had not seen since grad school, and never had any plans to ever see again, if he could help it. He had no idea she would be there and was completely blindsided by her presence. Dell really wanted to leave before she saw him, but chose to stay because he was there strictly to celebrate Treena's birthday, and to hopefully see Denai.

"Seeing you was the highlight of my day," Dell said sweetly. "And seeing her was just one big ass dark cloud. You and I spent most of the afternoon celebrating your best friend and enjoying the closeness of each other's company. Then you look up and see some other woman practically feeding me cake right in front of you. I'd be pissed too, if I were you."

"Yeah, but I had no right to be," Denai pressed.

"I had no right to be pissed seeing you with Ryan, but that doesn't change the fact that I was and wanted to flip some shit over," he said plainly.

"Dell!"

"I'm serious."

Denai leaned against her car in stunned silence. The earnestness in Dell's voice caused a soothing heat to settle in her chest, butterflies to flutter in her stomach, and throbbing in the most intimate places. She pulled the corner of her hood into her mouth and bit down on it to muzzle herself. Hearing Dell profess even a twinge of jealousy when it came to her, made Denai want to admit all the things she felt for him, as well, but knew she couldn't. So, she bit down harder.

"I know I shouldn't say it, but it's true," Dell continued, breaking the silence between them. "I feel the same way about you today as I did the night we met, and I doubt that will ever change. And it's because of those feelings, that I had to call you and apologize. I had to call and explain. I would never do anything to hurt or upset you in any way, *because* of how I feel about you. I'm sorry, Denai. For everything."

Denai finally regained her ability to speak, and told Dell she appreciated his apology and all was forgiven. She wanted to tell him how much the other things he said meant to her, as well, but decided against it. She didn't want to blur the lines of their association with one another and risk them growing any closer together. She was engaged, after all, and highly doubted the two of them could ever just be friends. Cordial in each other's presence? Sure. Put on a good face in front of certain company? Probably. Strictly platonic friends? Not likely.

She ended the call with Dell and went back into the house. There was a sudden renewed bounce in her step and air of peace in her mind. When Denai stepped inside, Ryan was coming down the stairs, wrapped in a bath towel. He watched her suspiciously and she looked at him with a blank stare, as if he didn't even exist. Ryan asked where she had been, and Denai simply said, "Getting some air."

She climbed the stairs and walked past him without another word. Ryan called after her to announce he was going out for a bit to meet a client for drinks.

"It's eight o'clock at night on a Wednesday, and you're meeting a *client* for *drinks*?" Denai asked skeptically with a raised brow.

"Is that a problem for you?" Ryan tossed over his shoulder sarcastically.

"Nope. Have at it," she replied dismissively with the wave of a hand.

Denai continued up the stairs to her bedroom. She peeled off her damp hoodie and sweatpants and tossed them in the hamper. Standing in front of the floor length mirror in just her bra and panties, Denai examined her half-naked reflection. Something she avoided doing the past few months since moving back in with Ryan. Most days she couldn't stand what she saw – the constant reminders of an unstable love.

She went into the bathroom, stepping in puddles left behind by Ryan, and turned on the shower for herself. Denai closed the door and locked it so she could shower in peaceful isolation. Much like the rain from before, she will let the shower wash away the remnants of the day; wash away the stains of sorrow. Denai stayed in until the water ran cold, like the baths she used to soak in at her mother's house all those months ago.

Eight months can feel like an eternity to some, but to Denai it felt like a constant loop of yesterdays where nothing ever changes.

******

The raucous chatter of family mixed with joyful soul music filled the house as the Thanksgiving festivities got underway. Dell's mother and step-father, Annette and Randall Denton, had come down from Detroit to spend the holiday with their only son and their favorite nephew. Annette even offered to do the cooking because she loved "spoiling her sweet boys," as she affectionately said.

Dell, Randall and E-Man spent most of the afternoon in the backyard drinking and joking when they were supposed to be frying the turkey. Annette commandeered the kitchen pulling the rest of the day's feast together. She was pulling two of her delicious sweet potato pies out of the oven when Dell and E-Man stumbled through the backdoor carrying a golden brown twenty pound, piping hot turkey in a flimsy foil pan.

"What in the world?!" Annette squealed, trying hard not to laugh at the two tipsy turkey handlers.

"We got it! We got it!" Dell yelled as he kept jerking his hand away from the bottom of the scalding hot pan.

"Bruh, I don't think we do," E-Man grunted. "And where the hell are you going?"

"To the dining room. It's going in the middle of the table, right Ma?" Dell asked his mother for confirmation.

"I mean if you don't want this stuffing with it, then yeah, sure," she replied with a smirk.

Dell and E-Man immediately halted their steps in the hallway between the kitchen and dining room and clumsily backpedaled into the kitchen. Annette erupted in a fit of giggles as she directed them to put the hot pan on the counter. She fussed at them for drinking too much before dinner, and being a bad influence on her husband by having him do the same.

"How are *we* the bad influences? *He's* the father figure!" E-Man protested before falling against the wall from laughing so hard.

"Yo! You are so dumb!" Dell guffawed.

Annette ordered both of them out of the kitchen and to not come back until dinner was ready, because she couldn't function surrounded by their silliness. Dell kissed his mother on the cheek and laid his head on her shoulder like he used to do as a boy whenever she started fussing. She swiped at him with an oven mitt that he dodged before darting out the back door to go check on his step-father.

About an hour and a half later, the family was seated around the table, saying a heartfelt prayer of grace and gratitude before digging into the hearty meal Annette had prepared. They told stories and shared fond memories of yesteryear and gave thanks for current blessings. During which, Dell announced that his offer had been accepted on the house he saw in Oak Park and everything was underway to complete the purchase.

The table erupted with congratulatory applause and cheers. Randall raised a glass to his son to express how proud he was and how much he prayed that blessings continue to pour for both Dell and E-Man. The two cousins grabbed each other by the shoulder and rocked back and forth as they smiled excitedly at one another.

"So, Dell, what does this mean?" Annette asked, her eyes glittering in the chandelier light.

"Huh?" Dell asked, looking confused.

"Son, I know you," she explained. "You are very much a checklist kind of guy. Move to a new city. Check. Find a promising career. Check. Buy a house. Check. Sooo, how much longer do I have to wait before the wife and kids show up?"

"Ma!" he exclaimed.

"Uh oh!" E-Man said, snorting from laughter.

"What?! I didn't forget about that young lady you met a few months ago."

"Ma!"

"You went on and on about her when you got back to Detroit. Yet, you've been back in Chicago all this time and I ain't heard one word about her. What's the problem?"

Dell dropped his eyes to his plate. He had really hoped they could get through this weekend without his mother playing the "wife and kids" card. Of course, he'd never be that lucky, though. E-Man cut his eyes at his cousin, as if he, too, were waiting anxiously for a response. Even though he knew all the details of the "Dell and Denai" saga already.

"Uh, that's a little complicated, Auntie," E-Man chimed in after a while of awkward silence.

"No, it's not," Dell interrupted. "She's engaged to someone else. The problem is I waited too long."

Annette sat silently and watched her son's face intently. The way his jaw tightened around his words, and the way he fought the urge to frown around his eyes as he took a thoughtful sip of water. Just as he picked up his fork to try to continue eating, Annette took the opportunity to offer her son some consolation.

"There's no such thing as waiting too long," Annette began softly, gently touching his arm. "You're just waiting for *your* time, and there's nothing wrong with waiting for that."

"Your mother's right," Randall added. "Patience is a virtue, and the payoff is just that much sweeter. Trust me. Your window of opportunity is about to open. Just make sure you're ready."

******

Across town, guests had converged onto Ryan and Denai's home to celebrate the Thanksgiving holiday together. As a man of his word,

Ryan put all responsibilities for the day's meal on Denai's shoulders. Luckily, the last few months of her juggling his Football Sunday shindigs with her secret catering gigs, prepared her for a day just like this. Even though he had only announced his plans for hosting Thanksgiving dinner with less than the optimal two-week-advance-notice, Denai executed the challenge with such skilled precision.

She pulled together an epic four-course meal that consisted of multiple dishes during each course. She presented multiple options for the variety of people coming to her table. No matter what dietary restrictions or preferences were present, Denai had a solution for it. She was simply unstoppable today.

Treena floated into the kitchen carrying three bottles of wine as her contribution to the day's festivities. She learned a long time ago to stay away from bringing food to a chef's house when they're hosting a meal. So, instead she brought libations and shenanigans.

"Hey, girl! Heeeyyy!" Treena sang as she shuffled up to Denai for a hug.

"Hey, Toots! Happy Thanksgiving!" Denai greeted as she embraced her best friend.

"Happy Turkey Day! I see the gang's all here," Treena said sarcastically.

Treena was referring to both of Ryan's parents, Denai's mother and Ryan's boss and his wife. Both sets of parents being present was expected, but he hadn't mentioned the extra guests until this morning. Denai was already feeling outnumbered, because she was positive her mother, Claudette, loved Ryan more, but now his boss was here, too. Which meant Ryan was fully prepared to put on a show in some lame attempt to impress this man and his wife.

What's worse is he expected Denai to play along like a good little supporting character. So, of course, she immediately called Treena for backup. Not only did Treena pull up without hesitation, but she brought reinforcements with twelve percent alcohol content. She quickly poured full glasses for the two of them and toasted to hopes of the night going well. Denai nearly gulped down her entire glass in one sip.

The only reason she stopped was because she heard Iris Lattimore's voice coming towards the kitchen. Denai and Treena started giggling like two teenagers caught smoking in the girls' bathroom.

"Hey, ladies!" Iris greeted cheerfully when she entered the kitchen.

"Hey there, Mrs. Lattimore! You look amazing, as always," Treena complimented.

"Why, thank you, honey! I'm just trying to hold it together," Iris joked as she smoothed out the material of her dress around her waistline.

"And holding it, you are!" Denai said with a wink, as she refilled her glass.

"Uh oh! She's gotten into the wine. What do you need me to do?" Iris asked with a chuckle.

Denai accepted her offer of help this time and had Iris and Treena help transfer portions of the food from pots and pans into ceramic serving dishes. She grabbed the serving spoons from a drawer on the kitchen island, and made her way into the dining room behind Treena and Iris. The three of them went about setting the table while Claudette watched from the doorway, clutching her cocktail of scotch and soda.

She took another long sip as she rolled her eyes at the camaraderie between Denai and Iris. Claudette walked away mumbling to herself as she headed back down the hall to the den where the bar was. Ryan came marching into the dining room shortly after seeing Claudette and asking if she had seen Denai? He was becoming anxious about his boss and wife still waiting so long to eat.

When he entered the dining room, ready to voice his displeasure, he noticed his mother standing there and stopped himself. Instead, he walked up to Denai, feigning the role of affectionate fiancé, and gently asked about an ETA for dinner. Denai eyed him skeptically for his odd behavior, but decided against calling any attention to it. She simply said he could bring everyone in now, if he wanted.

He stepped out and returned a short while later followed by the other four guests and showed everyone to their seats. Denai handed the carving knife to Ryan so he could do the honors of carving the turkey after he blessed the food – a task he quickly deferred to his father. After all the formalities, Thanksgiving dinner was underway, and Denai was thankful for the reprieve of temporary quiet while everyone ate. That moment was short lived, however, once the boss's wife piped up to compliment the food.

"Denai, everything is delicious! I'd swear you were a professional chef, the way you pulled all of this off today," the woman said graciously.

"Oh...uh...thank you. I'm glad you're enjoying it," Denai replied humbly.

"Yeah, I trained her well. Just the first of many holidays she'll be hosting as Mrs. Ryan Lattimore," Claudette chimed in from her side of the table.

"Ryan, you're engaged?! I had no idea. Congratulations, old man," Ryan's boss offered with a smile.

Denai narrowed her eyes in Claudette's direction and shook her head at the comment she made, as well as the awkward mood she'd just created around the table. She could feel Ryan's eyes burning a hole in the side of her face, and she opted not to make eye contact with him. His boss's comment was just the beginning of the proverbial snowball as it began barreling downhill.

"As a matter of fact, they've been engaged for quite some time," Iris said. "And Denai's been keeping us girls in suspense with the plans. Have you two set a date? Have you picked out a dress? What do you need help with? I'd be more than happy to..."

"Mom," Ryan interrupted, visibly annoyed. "No plans have been made yet. Can we just bask in the joy of being engaged first?"

"Not for eight months!" Treena scoffed, looking around Denai at Ryan.

"Has it been that long?" Isaiah, Ryan's father, asked in surprise.

"No, it has not," Ryan grunted, rolling his eyes.

"Yeah. It has," Denai answered, her voice barely above a whisper.

Treena and Iris quickly began laying into Ryan about the length of their engagement, with no moves being made towards planning the actual wedding. Isaiah went as far as asking Ryan if he still wanted to get married, since it sounded like he was hesitating. Even his boss chimed in to say he'd give Ryan some time off from work, if that was the hold up on the wedding plans.

"Okay, everybody relax!" Ryan said sternly. "I literally *just* proposed to this woman. There is no rush to immediately jump into shelling out money planning for a wedding. We're engaged! Let that be enough for now. Geez!"

Denai slipped her hands off the table and folded them in her lap, turning the pear setting of her engagement ring towards the palm of her hand. She sat quietly with her eyes lowered to the table, avoiding eye contact with anyone else. The sound of everyone speaking so cavalier about her life, her future, as if she wasn't even there, felt like a crushing vice grip on her throat. However, her silence didn't go unnoticed.

"You awfully quiet on this subject, lil' girl," Claudette called out across the table.

A hush fell around the room as all eyes went to Denai. She could feel the heat of everyone's watchful glare. She felt Treena's firm hand on her forearm, a sign letting her know that it was safe for her to speak up. However, the harsh sound of Ryan clearing his throat to her left, made Denai tremble slightly. Something she hoped no one else noticed.

"Because now isn't the time to talk about this," Denai said flatly as she lifted her eyes to meet her mother's.

Treena angled in her seat to look at Denai closely. She wasn't sure what she saw in her friend at that moment, but it gave her an uneasy feeling. Not to mention, Ryan's responses about their engagement really pissed her off. How could he be so nonchalant when it came to discussing his wedding to the supposed love of his life? *He's so full of shit*, Treena thought to herself.

Denai quietly stood up and began gathering the empty plates from the table. Treena and Iris both rose to help her, but Denai rejected their offer in a somewhat snappy tone before walking out of the dining room and heading for the kitchen. She overheard Ryan rallying the dinner guests to come back to the den so they could watch the evening football game. She released a heavy sigh of relief as she slammed the stack of dirty plates on the counter.

She reached for the half-empty bottle of red wine they had opened earlier and began drinking straight from it. Denai guzzled the wine so fast, droplets of it spilled over the corners of her mouth and rolled down her chin. As she wiped her face with the back of her hand, she heard her cell phone vibrating on the counter near the stove, notifying her of a text message.

Denai dropped the empty wine bottle into the trash can next to the island, and grabbed another unopened bottle and the corkscrew before retrieving her phone. She tapped the phone screen until it lit up. A smile instantly formed across her face as she read the message. For a brief second, all the anger and anxiety caused by her first time hosting Thanksgiving dinner had dissipated as she stared at her phone.

The warmth filling Denai's chest made her draw her shoulders up to her ears as her smile widened. Something so simple as a message saying, "Happy Thanksgiving, Gorgeous," attached to Dell Hewitt's phone number brought her so much joy in the midst of darkness. It was the sweetest reminder that someone somewhere actually cared about putting a smile on her face – and smile, she did.

{ **ten** }

December '22

"Hey, girl!" Treena's sweet voice floated through the speaker. "Am I seeing you tonight?"

"Not like I really have a choice," Denai groaned with sarcasm as she rifled through the closet for something to wear.

Tonight was the annual Christmas party at the Dempsey, Little and Rowe Law Firm, and as per usual, Ryan was dragging Denai to yet another boring office affair to be arm candy in front of his colleagues and friends. It was bad enough that she had spent nearly every Sunday since September having her house invaded by these same people and being forced to feed them by her popularity-chasing fiancé. Now, she had to get all dolled up to meet them on their home turf to play an endless game of "Who Has More to Brag About?"

Thankfully, Denai had Treena joining her at the party tonight. She was also going at the behest of some former real estate clients and closing attorneys who worked at the law firm. She saw it as a welcomed opportunity to rub elbows with some of Chicago's financial elite who were always looking for an excuse to spend their money on something else they didn't need.

"Well, at least you'll have me and an open bar to keep you company," Treena relied jokingly.

"Thank God, for that!" Denai exclaimed, pressing her palms together and looking up to the heavens.

Denai ended her call with Treena after agreeing to meet at the firm by 7PM. She pulled a black long sleeved jumpsuit with plunging neckline from the closet and a pair of bright red pointed toe stilettos from the shoe rack and tossed the ensemble on the bed. From outside the bedroom, right across the hall, Ryan could be heard pacing around his office on the phone.

He had been holed up in there for most of the afternoon, even though it was Saturday and well outside of his billable hours. Denai wondered if it was even a work call, because his current tone was very different from that of "Counsellor Lattimore." Judging by his octave occasionally dropping to an almost hushed whisper, she knew it was very much a personal call. Denai rolled her eyes and went to the bathroom to finish getting ready. *He doesn't even bother to try to hide the shit,* she thought to herself as she shook her head in disgust.

A short while later, Denai was dressed and closing the clasp on a silver y-neck necklace with a bedazzled charm that rested in the center of her chest when Ryan finally walked into the bedroom. He looked at her and then at his cellphone to check the time – something he had clearly lost track of, but placed the blame on Denai's shoulders instead.

"Why didn't you tell me what time it was?" Ryan asked in a huff as he marched over to the closet to look for something to wear.

"There's a very large clock hanging on the wall across from your desk and you had your cell with you the whole while. Didn't know you needed a timekeeper," Denai said flippantly as she put on a pair of earrings that matched her necklace.

"Watch it, woman," Ryan said sternly, cutting his eyes at her over his shoulder.

"So, who were you talking to for nearly three hours, Ryan?" she asked, turning on her heels and putting her hands on her hips.

"That's none of your business."

"Neither is *you* losing track of time, and yet, here the fuck we are!"

Ryan turned abruptly at the sound of her raised voice. He cocked his head and narrowed his eyes because surely he hadn't heard her correctly. Seeing the steadiness and defiance in her face and stance sent his blood boiling. With a few quick steps Ryan was in front of Denai with his hand clasping her throat and driving her backwards until her back slammed against the wall by the bedroom door. She let out a gurgled yelp on impact and her eyes widened in shock.

Denai clawed at Ryan's wrist, trying to free herself, but to no avail. He tightened his grip on her neck just as his jaw flexed and lips pursed over clenched teeth.

"Who the fuck are you talking to?!" Ryan asked angrily. "Huh?! Who are you getting loud with like you run something in this house?!"

The pressure of Ryan's palm against her windpipe made Denai tear up as she struggled to gasp for air while still trying hard to pry his hand away. Her feet slipped and slid on the carpet as she continued to fight against his rage, but she could feel her body becoming limp. Just as Denai's eyes began to flutter with the threat of losing consciousness, Ryan slapped her to keep her awake.

"I don't know what's gotten into you or who you think you are," Ryan began, his jaw and grip still tight. "But, I strongly suggest you watch your fucking mouth and stop fucking playing with me."

Ryan pushed Denai hard into the wall once again before tearing his hand away from her throat. He ordered her to go "fix her face," so they could go, and demanded that she better not make him late. Tearfully, still coughing for air and shaking with fear, Denai grabbed her makeup bag off the dresser and stumbled out of the bedroom, heading for the guest bathroom across the hall. Denai closed the door behind her, pressed her back against it and slid down to the floor sobbing heavily.

She pressed her hand to her mouth to muffle the sound of her cries as her shoulders shook from the grief and terror tearing its way through her body. Denai put her other hand to her throat and rubbed gently, trying her best to soothe the soreness that remained after Ryan's attack. His violently harsh treatment had ramped up since Thanksgiving a few weeks ago when everyone was harping on him about not prolonging his engagement any further.

He was never a man who liked being told what to do, and the entire ordeal left him brooding for days. Leaving Denai alone to take the brunt of it after all excess company had gone. Since she had accepted Ryan's proposal and moved back in, things turned more and more volatile. It was like every little thing set him off and triggered some angry outburst.

Most times it would be in the way he said things – snarky and undercutting comments that were totally unwarranted. That was coupled with his practically forbidding her to work because, "What more do you need that I'm not already providing, anyway?" In the earlier months, Ryan would come back a day or so later with some half-hearted, hefty gift-laced apology and promises of never again. Seems that lately, "never again" has turned into "more often than not."

Denai mustered up the strength to stand and walk over to the sink. She looked in the mirror and immediately noticed the bruising starting around her neck and redness in her face from being slapped. She slowly unzipped the makeup bag and once again, went to work donning the mask she had tragically become familiar with. Denai covered her eyes with one hand, trying to stave off the new batch of tears brimming in them.

She took one long and shaky deep breath and shook her head, shaking off the influx of emotions coming on. Twenty minutes later, she stood there looking like the glamorous belle of the ball that everyone was used to seeing. Just as Ryan commanded.

******

The chatter of tipsy professionals echoed throughout the foyer and fifth floor lobby of the law firm as the associates and their guests milled about. Waitstaff floated throughout the crowd with trays of filled champagne flutes and customized complimentary cocktails. The live band played one fond instrumental Christmas tune after another and some revelers could be heard singing along in between friendly conversation.

Dell was fighting valiantly to resist the urge of slipping down the hall to his office and hiding out until an appropriate time to leave the party altogether. Even at his old firm in Detroit, he hated office parties and the people his colleagues turned into after one too many visits to the open bar. At least there, the ratio of Black associates was much higher – making him feel a little less out of place. Not at Dempsey, Little and Rowe, however. Black people stuck out like specks of pepper on fine china. He had only been here two hours and was already over it.

One of the partners over Dell's team had cornered him to ask how his adjustment to the new office and city were going for what felt like the fifth time tonight. Before Dell could come up with a clever excuse to get out of that conversation, another one of the partners came over with Ryan in tow. They came to brag about the two "Golden Boys" of the Acquisitions team. *I wonder if he knows calling us 'boys' is kinda racist,* Dell pondered silently as he took a sip of his Cognac.

While the conversation carried on – much to Dell's chagrin – he quietly wondered if Ryan had flown solo to the work shindig or if Denai was with him. As if reading his mind, someone asked Ryan that very question. He dismissively replied, "Nah, she's here somewhere." Dell turned to face the window overlooking the city and rolled his eyes in annoyance. *This nigga here!,* he thought.

"So, Ryan, you two met here, right?" one of the partners asked.
"Yup. She was working as an E.A. and clerk in our department and I scooped her right up," Ryan said smugly.
"How long has it been now?" someone else asked.
"A little over three years. Give or take," he huffed and took a sip of his drink.
"Wait! How long?" Dell asked, trying to mask his surprise.
"Three years."

Feeling like he had just been gut-punched, Dell downed the last of his drink and excused himself from the group, lying that he was going to get a refill. As he quickly weaved through the throngs of people sprinkled throughout the lobby and hurriedly emerged from the crowd, he bumped right into the object of his earlier curiosity – and now his disdain.

Denai placed her hand over the top of her drink, trying to keep it from spilling as she apologized for not paying attention to where she was going. When she realized who it was she collided with, she perked up.

"Hey, you! I was wondering if I'd see you tonight," Denai greeted cheerfully.

"Why you looking for me?" Dell asked angrily, looking her up and down.

"Uh, I don't know. Maybe to say hi. Merry Christmas," she replied with a shrug.

"Well, you said it," he said with a grunt as he brushed past her.

Denai spun on her heels as Dell pushed by, leaving her looking at his retreating back. An act that really hurt her feelings and she made it a point to say as much.

"What the hell did I do to you?" Denai barked at him.

Dell stopped abruptly and stared down the hall in front of him. He could so easily ignore her loaded question and finally escape to his office like he had been wanting to do all night. However, he knew if he didn't get things off his chest he'd regret it forever. Dell turned around and walked towards Denai until they were nearly nose-to-nose. The move made her flinch slightly.

"You used me," Dell said through gritted teeth.

"I did what?!" Denai asked, utterly confused.

"I was just with Ryan," he started. "He said that y'all have been together for over three years. *You* slept with *me* just a few months ago. I know what it's like being the guy sitting at home while his girl is out doing God only knows, and I swore to never be the reason another man felt that pain. So, I really don't appreciate you making me complicit in your infidelity and breaking my word."

Denai jerked her head back like she had been struck in the face by Dell's words. The seething anger in his eyes replaced the tenderness she was so used to seeing whenever he looked at her. Hearing that Dell felt betrayed and duped by the night they shared pained Denai's heart. The last thing she ever wanted to do was hurt him, and she certainly never wanted him to have any regrets about what happened between them. She surely didn't.

"Dell," Denai said softly as she reached for him. "Ryan and I broke up in March. I cried and wallowed in my misery until I got on my own nerves. Then I got up, I got dressed, and went out with my best friend to go drinking and dancing. I ended up at a club where I met the most gorgeous, amazing man. We danced and held hands and had breakfast together. Then I popped up unannounced at his hotel room like a crazy woman."

Dell's eyes softened as he listened to Denai's account of that night and he tried to hide his smile when she mentioned coming to his hotel room. He could see a twinge of sadness in her eyes as she continued to speak, and the sight of it immediately weakened his resolve. He leaned in further, closing the last of the gap between them, but regretfully resisted the urge to pull her into his arms.

"When I came to you," Denai continued. "When you kissed me, when we showered together, and when we made love until the sun came up, I was a single woman. And for one beautiful night, I got to see what it actually felt like to be adored and desired entirely for who I am. I got to see what it felt like to be yours, just in that small window of time, and it was the greatest night of my life. I will never forget it and I will never regret it. I hope you don't either, because you did nothing wrong. I did."

"What did you do?" Dell asked, his voice just above a whisper.

"I never called," he said, her voice cracking. "I made the wrong choice, and now I have to live with that."

Dell reached out to caress her face, but Denai halted his hand with a shake of her head. She laid her palm against his chest, right over his heart and looked into his eyes. The longer she lingered, the more her emotions bubbled up inside her. Denai tearfully mouthed, "I'm sorry," then quickly walked away, disappearing through the crowd Dell had just emerged from moments before.

Dell clenched his hands into fists and let out a heavy sigh before turning and continuing the trek to his office. He angrily pushed the door open and slammed it shut behind him. He paced around his office, trying to get his thoughts and feelings under control. No amount of counting or deep breathing could calm him right now. Unbeknownst to Dell, he had been spotted storming into his office and a light knock on the door interrupted his brooding.

"You alright in here?" Treena inquired when she pushed his office door open.
"Huh? Oh, hey, Treena," Dell replied absently as he kept pacing.
"Is everything okay?" she asked again.
"Not really. I just ran into your girl," he said cryptically.

Treena snorted a laugh and stepped further into the office. She pushed the door up, leaving it slightly cracked. She tucked her satin clutch under her arm and clasped her hands in front of her, waiting for Dell to expound on what exactly happened when he saw Denai. He told her it was a lot to get into and out of respect for the ladies' friendship, he knew better than to have this conversation with Treena.

"Oh, come on!" Treena grumbled as she fixed her gaze on him.

"Look, I know all about Girl Code. It's cool," Dell said with a wave of his hand as he sat down at his desk.

"Okay, because I like you, I'll forgo Girl Code for two minutes. What happened?" she pressed.

"You really don't have to. It's fine."

"Tell me."

Dell gave in to Treena's prompting and told her about what Ryan said and how that subsequently led to him blowing up at Denai for making him the "other guy" in her relationship. He also explained how his ex, Destiny's cheating made him despise infidelity of any form. Treena listened attentively as Dell expressed his disappointment and hurt feelings behind the entire situation, and how it'll make working with Ryan that much harder now.

"So, yeah, it's all fucked up," Dell huffed as he palmed his face.

"Dell, you were not the 'other guy.' I promise," Treena said comfortingly.

"How do I know that?" he said in frustration as he leaned forward on the desk.

"Denai had broken up with Ryan well before y'all met and the only reason she went out that night is because I kept egging her on until she gave in. She was very much single and free to do whatever she wanted. I swear, you are not guilty of anything except bad timing and location."

Treena reassured Dell that Denai did not use him in some nefarious scheme to cheat on her relationship, and everything that happened between them that night was completely by chance.

"I'll be candid," Treena continued. "If I had any say, she would absolutely not be with Ryan's ass. I personally think you're perfect for her in every possible way, but that's not for you or I to decide. Is it?"

"Nah, I guess not," Dell said with a heavy sigh. "My two minutes up?"

"Depends," she replied with a smirk.

"Just tell me this, is she happy? Truthfully?" he asked anxiously.

"She's engaged, Dell," she said plainly with a soft shrug.

Dell nodded his understanding and thanked Treena for entertaining his rant. She said it was no problem, and that even though Denai was her best friend, she fully acknowledged Dell's feelings in all of this. It wasn't lost on her how hurt he must've been coming back to Chicago with hopes of reconnecting, only to find out it's too late.

"I gotta say, I applaud you for respecting her situation, though," Treena added from the doorway.

"Yeah, that's me. Mr. Morality," Dell groaned, throwing his hands up.

Treena let out a chuckle as she pulled the door closed behind her and headed back to the party. She decided she had about one more drink's worth of schmoozing left in her before it would be time to go. Although she appreciated the networking opportunities this party provided, Treena was never more ready to snatch a dress off than she was right now.

While she stood at the bar, scanning the room, she spotted Denai standing with Ryan smiling and being the dutiful fiancée as they conversed with some of his colleagues. Treena shook her head at what her best friend had to endure while dating someone so consumed with his own reputation.

"I bet Dell wouldn't have her dealing with that shit," Treena mumbled to herself as she swirled the skewered olives around in her martini.

She grunted in disgust, taking one last look in their direction before grabbing her drink and walking away from the bar. She found a seat near the lobby's fireplace, giving her a better view of the room. Through a gap in the crowd, Treena saw Dell walking her way with his coat draped across his arm. She noticed how he didn't even bother to say goodbye to anyone. Just pulled his phone out and looked down at the screen as if it was something important.

With a quick glance up, Dell saw Treena watching him closely. He threw up his two fingers in a peace sign and slipped out the door leading to the garage all in one fluid motion. Treena snorted a laugh as she polished off her martini and decided to follow suit. She had seen enough of this dog and pony show for one night.

{ eleven }

"Shit! Shit! Shit!" Denai exclaimed as she pulled into the driveway. She had spent all morning preparing pans on top of pans of food and delivering two catering orders for office holiday parties. However, due to unexpected traffic, she was now running behind schedule. Ryan had flown to Las Vegas again for what he said was a week-long conference and was returning today, fully expecting Denai to pick him up from O'Hare Airport way across town.

It was bad enough she had to go all the way out there to get him, but to do so two days before Christmas was just pure hell. Denai wanted to run home really quick to take a shower so she wouldn't smell like food when she picked him up. Ryan still had no idea she was moonlighting as a caterer, and she preferred to keep it that way for as long as she could. Especially, in light of his recent behavior. The last thing Denai wanted to do was give him another reason to lash out at her.

She planned on telling him eventually, but didn't know when that would be. There certainly was no rush, though. Denai hurriedly unlocked the front door and darted inside. She was moving so fast, kicking her snow-covered shoes off and running up stairs to the bedroom, that she didn't notice someone moving around in the kitchen.

Denai threw her coat and purse on the chair right outside the bathroom door and began peeling her clothes off as she slid the shower's glass door open. She turned on the hot water and as she reached for the knob to add in cold water, something out the corner of her eye made her nearly jump out of her skin.

Ryan stood in the middle of the bedroom with fire in his eyes and his jaw ridgid. Denai let out a short scream at the unexpected sight of him standing there. She placed a hand over heart and laughed at herself for being scared. She smiled welcomingly at him and began walking towards him, wearing only her underwear.

"Hey, babe," Denai greeted, her heart still racing. "You're early."
"Where were you?" Ryan asked gruffly.
"What?" she asked nervously.
"Where did you just come from, that the first thing you need to do is shower when you walk in the house?" he asked, his fist clenching.
"Is it a problem for me to shower or something?" she retorted.

The flames of rage in Ryan's eyes flickered as his eyes widened at Denai's words. He pushed up the sleeves of his gray thermal shirt, exposing veiny forearms. In two quick steps he reached Denai and grabbed her by the arms, dragging her back into the bathroom. He grunted about her indignation and smart mouth as he yanked her arm harder, tightening his grip on her every time she tried to pull away.

Ryan pushed the shower door open wider and threw Denai inside, sending her body crashing hard against the tile wall. She grunted and yelped in pain as her shoulder and knee hit the wall, and the sensation of the hot water meeting the bottoms of her feet made her jump up and down as she tried to hop out the shower. Each time she did Ryan shoved her back in.

"Yeah, you thought you could sneak home and wash off the evidence so I wouldn't know," Ryan barked as he pushed her into the wall again.

"Ryan, what the hell are you talking about?!" Denai shouted as she tried over and over to escape the shower.

"I'm talking about you being a cheating ass whore!" he shouted back.

"I'm not cheating on you! Ryan, move!" she yelled.

"Nah, you wanted to take a nice hot shower, right? Get all squeaky clean, right? Thought the coast was clear, but you didn't bank on me getting an earlier flight and catching your ass!"

Ryan struck Denai hard across the face, sending her reeling backwards into the wall of the shower once again. Then he grabbed the detachable shower head out of its cradle.

"Since you wanted to take a hot shower, let me help you out," Ryan seethed as he turned the shower head's dial to set the water at a steady pulsating stream.

Fueled by his blind rage, he aimed the shower head directly at Denai, pummeling her body with scalding hot water. She released one blood curdling scream after another as she scurried in pain and terror from one end of the shower to the other trying to get away. There was no escape. Ryan wielded that shower head like a fireman with a hose battling a five-alarm blaze.

He aimed the stream at her feet and moved in a sweeping motion, spraying every inch of her body. Denai's skin reddened more and more with the never-ending assault. The only part of her body not sprayed was her face. Though that did not lessen the agony she endured as Ryan continuously blasted her with the blazing water.

He furiously aimed at her pelvic region, breasts and butt - lingering longer on those spots than he did any other areas of her body. The continual array of insults and accusations hurled in Denai's direction, coupled with the scalding water battering her body, made this the first time she actually wished for death. Anything to make this all stop. Once Ryan finally got his fill of degradation, humiliation and horrific abuse, he threw down the shower head and stormed out of the bathroom.

A weakened Denai mustered up all her strength to lunge out of the shower, stumbling into the sink's counter. Even out of the shower, her skin still felt like it was on fire. There wasn't a single part of her body that did not feel scorched. The slightest graze of her fingertips made her yelp in pain. She was barely holding herself up with her palms pressed against the countertop as she panted hard, trying to catch her breath and get her bearings. Her throat hurt from screaming. Her body hurt from being doused with blazing hot water. Her heart hurt because now she truly knew what being hated felt like.

Denai rested her weight against the wall as she walked gingerly out of the bathroom. For a moment, she swore she was going to pass out on the bedroom floor. She braced herself along the edge of the bed, and looked down at her arms and chest and saw signs of her skin beginning to blister. The physical and emotional pain took its toll and she broke down sobbing as she held onto the bed.

This wasn't something that quick-fix makeup could handle. It had officially gone too far, and Denai couldn't just cover this up and ignore it. Taking several deep breaths to calm her sobs and regain some of her strength, Denai pushed away from the bed and stumbled over to the chair. Slowly, she slipped her arms into the sleeves of her knee length parka and grabbed her purse. Wincing with every step, Denai descended the stairs and wrestled her feet back into her boots by the front door. She could hear the television playing in the den down the hall, but didn't see Ryan.

Denai weakly walked out of the front door and shuffled to her car. She slid inside, grimacing and tearing up as she did, because every inch of her body hurt. She cranked the engine and backed out of the driveway slowly, headed to University of Chicago Hospital's emergency room

******

Cheerful laughter echoed throughout E-Man's kitchen as he, Treena and Dell sat around the table playing Drunk UNO. The trio had grown quite close since E-Man surprised Treena at her birthday party. At least once a week, she would come over to hang out with him, and Dell somehow always got roped into whatever they had going on if he was at home.

A heavy snowstorm was predicted to hit the city late in the evening and Treena decided she didn't want to be trapped at home alone. So, she bribed her way into E-Man's house with pizza, beer and her phenomenal good looks. Three things he couldn't resist.

Treena had just slammed a Draw 4 card down on the table and erupted in a giggle fit when Dell shouted, "Motherfucka!" as he was forced to draw cards and take a shot of tequila. Just then her cell phone rang and she jumped up from the table to step away and answer the call, still laughing heartily. When she saw Denai's name flash across the screen, her smile widened with excitement.

"Hey, Toots!" Treena said jovially. "You are missing out on a damn good time. You should sneak out and come meet me."

Treena's smile soon faded when she heard Denai's voice. Instinctually, she knew her friend didn't sound right and could barely make out what she was saying.

"Wait, D, I can't hear you," Treena said, stepping towards the doorway of the kitchen to hear better. "You're where?...Oh, my God!"

The inflection of Treena's tone and mention of Denai's name made Dell's ears immediately perk up. When he noticed the worried look in her eyes, he pushed his chair away from the table and gave her one-sided conversation his full focus. He couldn't say what was going on, but from the sound of it, it wasn't anything good.

"Okay, okay. I'll be right there," Treena confirmed hurriedly as she hung up the phone, her nerves frazzled.
"Treena, what happened?" Dell asked immediately.
"Denai's in the hospital," she replied, her voice shaking.
"What?!" he exclaimed, standing up in a rush.
"Yeah, she took herself to the emergency room at U of C."
"Let's go. I'm driving."

Dell snatched his keys off the kitchen counter and breezed by Treena, heading for the front door. E-Man hopped up, as well, and followed Dell's path, with Treena matching his steps. They each collected their coats and shoes, and she relayed that Denai asked her to bring some clothes, because she arrived at the hospital in just her coat and underwear. Dell said he'd get something from his room and tossed E-Man the keys so he could take Treena out and start the car.

Dell ran upstairs to his bedroom and grabbed an army green pullover hoodie and matching sweatpants from his closet for Denai and a black hoodie for himself. For the first time since overhearing Treena's phone call, he had a moment to process how he was feeling. His stomach dropped as if he were on a rollercoaster. Just the thought of Denai being hurt badly enough to be hospitalized made Dell feel helpless and terrified. The only thing that would settle his nerves was to see her with his own eyes. He darted back downstairs and out the front door to the waiting duo in his car.

The three of them arrived at the hospital in record time and rushed through the automatic doors into the waiting room. Many of the patients and patrons turned their gazes towards the anxious trio, and Treena led the pack as they walked up to the registrar desk.

"Hi, I'm here for Denai Powell," Treena said plainly.

"And who are you to her?" the admissions clerk asked.

"I'm her sister," she replied with a straight face.

"And who are they in relation to the patient? It's immediate family only," the clerk explained.

"Fiancés. Hers and mine."

The admissions clerk looked skeptically at the two men behind Treena. Both stood with their hands in their pockets and a sternness in their eyes that said loud and clear they'd already had enough of her questions. She said she would notify the nurses of Denai's visitors and have someone come out shortly.

Soon after, a nurse named Tammy came out to greet them with visitor passes and instructions to follow her back to the trauma area. They walked down a corridor and into a large open room lined with hospital beds, some shielded by closed curtains and others left open. Nurse Tammy stopped in front of a bed tucked away behind a curtain and pulled it open, revealing an exhausted looking Denai.

The moment she saw Treena, E-Man and Dell, Denai became overwhelmed with emotions. It was hard enough for her to call Treena and say what was going on, but the hospital kept pressing her to notify a next of kin and calling her best friend was the only option that made sense. However, seeing Dell standing there with concern in his eyes, and E-Man with what looked like equal despair in his, made Denai feel even worse than she already did.

"Hey, Toots," Treena greeted warmly. "What's going on with ya?"
"Hey, Toots," Denai replied weakly.

Treena came to stand by her bed, taking Denai's hand in hers and noticed the reddening rashes on her forearms. She asked again what happened and suddenly Denai began to hyperventilate and tears welled up in her eyes. The heart monitor started beeping rapidly, sending Nurse Tammy rushing to her bedside.

"Hey, hey! It's okay. You're okay," Nurse Tammy comforted as she grabbed Denai's other hand and gently stroked her forehead. "We've talked about this, now. I can give you something to help you calm down, honey. All you gotta do is say so."

Denai frantically nodded her head as she continued to heave, trying to catch her breath and calm her anxiety. Nurse Tammy pulled a small syringe from her pocket and injected a liquid into Denai's I.V. Within seconds she was drifting off to sleep and the heart monitors eased back to their steady cadence.

"What did you give her?" Dell asked worriedly from the foot of the bed.

"It's just a sedative," Nurse Tammy explained. "Whenever we've asked her what happened, she immediately goes into a panic attack. So, the doctor suggested a little cocktail to help out until she was ready to talk about it."

"Talk about what?" Treena asked, still stroking the back of Denai's hand.

"Denai came in with varying first degree burns over a lot of her body," Nurse Tammy said, a certain sadness in her voice.

"What?!" Dell exclaimed.

Treena questioned the nurse's statement, as well, because it was so hard to believe. She told the nurse that Denai was a chef and just naturally assumed the burns on her arms were from a cooking accident or something else easily explainable.

"There are burns and blisters on her back, chest, hips, legs and thighs," Nurse Tammy informed the group.

"Jesus! How the hell did that happen?" E-Man asked, reappearing from behind the curtain after having stepped out for a moment.

"Now, I'm no doctor, but in *my* professional opinion, her injuries are consistent with someone who was held under scalding hot water for a long time," the nurse explained.

"Oh my God! Wh...How?" Treena pressed.

"Ryan," Dell said through gritted, as the gravity of the situation hit him.

Treena, E-Man and Nurse Tammy each looked at Dell for clarification of his theory. He said there was no way Denai would have or could have hurt herself like this. Even the fact that she brought herself to the hospital, and only called Treena instead of Ryan, spoke volumes.

"No, that can't be," Treena protested, shaking her head. "Ryan is a lot of things. A narcissistic asshole, sure. But *sadistic*? No."

"I'll admit I don't know him as well as you do, but this absolutely feels like something he'd do," Dell replied.

"Nah. If Denai were being abused by that jackass, she would've told me. She would've said something," she said, waving her hand dismissively.

"Would she?" he asked earnestly.

Treena's eyes widened at his question as she searched her mind for an answer. She knew he was right. Denai always had an incredible ability of keeping hush about what she was going through. A trait that often drove Treena crazy about her. She looked over at Denai who was still knocked out, and her heart broke.

"Aww, Toots," Treena said quietly, her voice filled with pain.

******

Denai awoke a few hours later feeling groggy and confused. She had been moved from the trauma area up to a regular room, and the sedative Nurse Tammy had given her was beginning to wear off. The sound of monitors beeping and the hustle and bustle of the recovery unit right outside the door roused Denai awake. As she blinked her eyes into focus, she could see Treena and E-Man snuggled together as they slept on the small sofa across the room, a sight that made her smile weakly.

She felt a heaviness on her hand and looked to her left to see Dell also asleep in a chair next to her bed, his head resting against his fist. His other hand was wrapped around hers. The weight of it was heavy yet gentle, and the warmth of his skin on hers made Denai's breath catch in her throat, as it always did whenever he touched her.

Seeing Dell beside her like a devoted knight in black Nike armor made Denai's heart swell and she couldn't hold back her tears. To think, after all this time with Ryan being the ever-present wedge between them, Dell's tenderness towards her was the same now as it was that one beautiful night they spent together.

The sound of whimpers and sniffles woke Dell up.

"Hey, hey. Baby, it's okay," Dell said comfortingly as he leaned forward and stroked her hair.

He climbed in the bed next to her, cradling her to his chest as she continued to sob. As they lay there, a new nurse assigned to Denai's care came into the room to check on her patient.

"Hey, you're awake," the nurse greeted sweetly. "Just comin' to check your vitals and see how you're feeling. Per the doctor, if everything checks out, then we can get you discharged."

"Okay," Denai said softly between sniffles.

"Denai, look at me," the nurse prompted, holding Denai's hand and looking deep in her eyes. "Even if everything looks good, if you do not want to go home, all you have to do is tell me, and I got you."

"We won't hold up y'all bed. She's coming home with me," Treena quipped confidently from her spot on the sofa as she stretched and yawned.

"T, you don't have to..." Denai started.

"Girl, don't you even," Treena interrupted, offering up a smile and a wink.

The nurse nodded and smiled at Denai, encouraging her to let her friends be there for her. After checking Denai's vitals one more time, the nurse retrieved the discharge paperwork and the foursome readied to leave.

"I, uh...I need to get some things from the house," Denai stammered as she pulled the hoodie Dell brought over her head.

"What for?" Treena asked, helping Denai stand up from the bed.

"If I'm gonna be holed up at your house for a few days, then I'm gonna need the essentials. You know, like, clothes and underwear," Denai said with a chuckle.

The group left the room and headed out to the parking lot. Once outside, Dell asked Denai for her car keys as he tossed his to E-Man. He said he'd drive Denai to Ryan's house while the others followed in his car. When Denai tried, and failed, to assure Dell that wasn't necessary, he just silently opened the passenger side door and kissed her forehead as he helped her get in.

After a short drive through Hyde Park, the two cars pulled into Ryan's driveway. Denai tried once again to convince Dell he could stay behind while she ran in to grab a few things. To which he simply replied, "Nope," as he turned off the car's engine. When they all walked up to the front door, Dell continued to hold Denai's keys, because he wanted to be the first to walk through the door just in case Ryan was inside.

Denai had been away at the hospital for hours, and now that it was 3AM, she had no idea what to expect where Ryan was concerned. Suddenly, she was flooded with immense gratitude that Dell and E-Man were there. Hell, even Treena made for great backup at the moment.

Before Dell could fully unlock the door, Ryan snatched it open when he heard keys jingling outside. The sight of Dell standing on his doorstep made Ryan frown and ask, "Dell? What the hell are *you* doing here?"

Dell didn't respond. He just stepped forward across the threshold, making Ryan take several steps backwards until the two men were fully inside the house. No words were spoken, but their steady eye contact was full of hostile tension. Ryan looked him up and down, still seeking an answer to his question. Dell's gaze held strong on Ryan's face, as if trying to better understand the man in front of him.

Once they cleared the doorway, Dell beaconed behind him and E-Man was the next to enter, his eyes just as stern and devilish as his cousin's. He came to stand behind Dell and jerked his head, signaling to the ladies that it was safe for them to enter now. At the sight of Denai walking through the door, clearly dressed in men's clothes, Ryan became incensed.

"What the fuck is this?!" Ryan barked as he took a step forward. "You really showing up to my house at three in the morning with a whole other nigga, wearing his clothes? I knew you were a fuckin' whore!"

"Hey!" Dell barked back as he grabbed Ryan by the collar. "You don't get to fuckin' speak to her. Now sit the fuck down and shut the fuck up!"

Dell pushed Ryan backwards towards the couch and E-Man grabbed his arm and yanked him downwards until he practically fell into his seat. Ryan looked back and forth at the two men who were handling him so aggressively and his own anger began to build. Nobody would tell him what was going on or why Denai was with them. She hadn't said a single word since walking in, and the only person she seemed to be listening to was Dell.

Ryan noticed she didn't enter the house until Dell said she could, nor did she head upstairs with Treena until he told her it was okay to do so. While the ladies were out of sight, Dell quietly paced the floor with his hands shoved into the pockets of his sweatpants. E-Man sat on the sofa across from Ryan, his expression unchanged.

"You gonna answer my question?" Ryan asked Dell, agitation in his voice.

"Pretty sure he told you to shut the fuck up," E-Man interrupted, sternly.

"I did," Dell confirmed as he kept pacing.

"You come to my house at 3AM with my *fiancée* in tow and think I'm not gonna have questions?" Ryan pressed, his eyes narrowed. "You doin' a lot for a girl you barely know."

"I'm doin' what you should've been doin'," Dell said flatly as he stopped pacing and looked at Ryan.

"Excuse me?!" Ryan exclaimed as he stood up.

E-Man reached over and shoved Ryan back down in his seat just as Denai and Treena were coming down the stairs, each of them carrying a duffle bag. The tension in the room was so thick, it was like the humidity that hit right before a hurricane. Denai was so nervous watching the standoff between Ryan and Dell, but at the same time, she had never felt safer inside this house than she did now.

"Well, Denai, since Dell won't answer me, maybe you will," Ryan said sarcastically. "Just what the fuck is going on here?!"

"I'm leaving," Denai said plainly, her voice trembling.

"Oh, really? Out of one man's bed and into another one, huh? I knew you were whore," he spat.

"Didn't I tell you not to talk to her?" Dell interjected, his voice full of venom.

"So, is that why you were sneaking back in earlier? Running to take a shower and shit. Because you fuckin' this nigga?!"

The room erupted in shouts and objections as Denai argued against Ryan's accusations and Dell fought every urge to lunge across the room at him for speaking to her in the first place. As Ryan stood up from his seat, so did E-Man and he matched each of Ryan's steps as he moved towards Denai. Dell gently slid his arm across her waist and pushed her behind him, taking the position of her barrier, once again.

"You know," Dell began. "I knew from the moment I met you, there was something about you I didn't like. At first, I thought it's just 'cuz you fit the sleazy lawyer stereotype, but that wasn't it."

Dell took a step towards Ryan, aiming a rigid index finger at his forehead. Ryan squared his shoulders as he watched Dell's movements and listened to his words intently. Treena tugged at the back of Denai's sweater to pull her further backwards in case the three men in front of them came to blows.

"Then, I found out you were engaged to her," Dell continued, gesturing at Denai. "So, I just figured it was an age old case of jealousy, but that wasn't it either. Then, I'd listen to how you talked about her to other people, and the fact that even after three years of being together, you don't have a single picture of her in your office. Everybody else has photos all over showing off their loved ones, but *you*? Nothing but pictures of yourself. Tells me you don't appreciate this woman like you should."

Ryan scoffed at Dell's words as his eyes darted back and forth between Denai and the man advancing towards him. The more intense it became between Dell and Ryan, the more Denai and Treena backpedaled towards the door in case they needed to make a break for it.

"But then, I spent tonight next to her hospital bed, listening to heart monitors in the E.R. she drove herself to because of you," Dell said, his jaw clenched as his rage intensified. "And that's when I knew what it really was about you that got to me. You're an abusive piece of shit."

"Is that what she told you?" Ryan asked smugly.

"She didn't have to," Dell confirmed. "I know pussies like you all too well. So to answer your question, I'm in your house at three o'clock in the morning to get Denai the fuck away from you."

"Is that so?"

"It is."

Dell nodded to E-Man to open the door for the ladies to walk out first. Just as Dell took a few steps back from Ryan and Denai went to walk out the door, Ryan lunged at her. He grabbed the hood of her sweatshirt, wrapped it around his hand and yanked her hard towards him. She gagged and choked as she struggled to fight against his hold. She dropped the duffle bag and tripped over it as Ryan tugged harder, which only strangled her more.

"You ungrateful, whore ass bitch!" Ryan seethed as he yoked her into a headlock.

"You stupid motherfucka!" Dell exclaimed as he pressed the barrel of his chrome .9mm pistol to the back of Ryan's head.

The sound of the gun cocking and feel of cold metal pressed to his skull, made Ryan freeze and tense up. He never loosened his hold on Denai, but he did stop yoking and dragging her backwards. He had been glaring at the side of her face the moment he wrangled her close to him, so he didn't notice that E-Man also had a Glock 19 pistol aimed at his face. When Ryan realized he was caught in the crosshairs of not one but two guns, he released Denai with a forceful shove and put his hands up.

Denai coughed and sputtered as she stumbled towards Treena, who quickly pulled her outside and dashed to the car. Dell ordered E-Man to head out as well and make sure the ladies weren't waiting in the cold. When asked if he was sure he wanted to be left alone, Dell simply nodded, never lowering his gun.

When it was just the two of them, Dell ordered Ryan to turn around and face him. As their eyes met, Dell pressed the barrel squarely between Ryan's eyes. Arrogantly, Ryan told Dell that he grew up on the

South Side too, and having a gun pointed at him wasn't anything new and he was completely unfazed. Dell snorted a laugh and licked his lips as a smirk formed. He told Ryan that very well may be true, because guns don't scare monsters like him, no matter where they're from.

Dell smacked Ryan hard across the face with the gun, instantly drawing blood from his nose and mouth. He hit him four more times before his body fell limply to the floor. Dell stood over Ryan and assured him that his reign of terror over Denai was done. That if he wanted to keep his neatly manicured hands, he had better keep them to himself. Dell stepped over Ryan's fetal body and walked out the front door, slamming it shut behind him.

Denai released a sigh of relief when she saw Dell come into sight, headed to the car. She was also glad she didn't hear any gunshots. Seeing him and E-Man pull guns on Ryan was not something she was prepared for.

As he slid in the driver's seat of Denai's car, Dell looked into her eyes. The silence and assuredness between them made her feel safer than she'd ever felt in all her life. She reached over and stroked the side of his face, quietly expressing her gratitude. Dell kissed the palm of her hand softly, then started the car. Nothing more needed to be said tonight.

{ **twelve** }

Denai was sitting on the bed with her laptop, two notebooks and planner all propped open. It had been a week since she moved out of Ryan's house and started bunking at Treena's. Though the trauma and memories attached to it all were still fresh, Denai knew if she truly wanted to rebuild her life, she needed to start right now. True freedom was well within her grasp, and she was reaching for it with everything she had.

She was hard at work updating her caterer profile across all social media platforms and revamping her portfolio and business plan. Being a full fledged entrepreneur the last few months had been great, but if she was really going to branch out on her own, she needed a little more help. So, one of her many New Year's Resolutions was to secure more funding for her catering dreams.

As Denai began jotting down notes for new concepts and menu ideas for the new year, Treena popped in the room, knocking loudly on the door to get her attention. She said she was just coming up to check in since it's been kind of quiet in the house all day.

"Sorry, I've been M.I.A.," Denai apologized. "You know how much I love putting undue pressure on myself before January 1st gets here."

"I will never understand why you do that to yourself every year," Treena said with a chuckle. "You know what they say about the definition of insanity, right?"

"Oh, what? That you'll find my picture right next to it in every dictionary?" Denai quipped with a wide grin as she kept typing.

Treena let out a hearty cackle as she agreed with Denai's sentiment. She asked what she was working on and if she needed any help. Denai said she was fine at the moment, but would definitely need Treena to look over her business plan again before she started shopping it around to banks and investors for funds.

"You know I got you!" Treena said with a smile, then turned to leave.

"Hey, T," Denai called to her. "I know I've said it a lot already, but thank you so much for letting me crash here."

"Of course," Treena replied warmly.

"And I promise, as soon as I can, I'll be out of your hair," Denai continued. "I'm already getting calls for more catering gigs next month and..."

"Okay, so we're doing *this*? Cool," Treena interrupted and let out a heavy sigh.

Denai looked at Treena with a confused expression.

"Listen to me," Treena commanded. "*We* are not those people. You are my best friend. Which means there is nothing I would not do for you. There's nothing you cannot ask me for, and to be honest you don't even have to ask. If you needed an organ, I'd be the first one to get tested for a match."

"I know you would," Denai said with a smile.

"So, don't act like you being here is a problem," Treena continued. "If you need it and I have it to give, it is yours. *That* is who we are. If you need a place to stay, you stay with me. If you need money or food or a ride to the damn airport, you tell me."

Suddenly, Denai saw tears forming in Treena's eyes as she continued her speech. Her voice cracked with emotion as she spoke her next words.

"And if you are being abused, you fucking tell me!" Treena demanded as a lone tear streamed down her face. "You do not have me be blindsided by some nurse telling me things about you that I should already know. You do not go through hell without me, and you do not suffer in silence while smiling in *my* face pretending to be fine. Do you hear me? *That is not what we do!* If you go through it, I go through it. *That is what this is!*"

Denai's heart sank as she listened to the pain-filled words of her best friend. Tears began forming in her own eyes as the gravity of everything hit her. It was so natural for her to just keep all of her problems to herself. She learned very early on about the true value of self-soothing and handling things on her own.

Her mother, Claudette, wasn't the most affectionate nor compassionate person in the world – despite being a registered nurse. She would often give Denai the, "You need to figure it out because you're on your own," speech growing up, and now in her adult years, it was the only way she knew how to function.

Denai got up from the bed and went over to Treena, pulling her into a tight hug. She apologized for keeping secrets and promised to share everything with her going forward, even the things she carried shame about. Honestly, that was a large part of the reason why she hadn't told Treena about Ryan's abuse – because she hadn't figured out a way to even explain the experience to herself yet.

Treena assured Denai things will get easier one day at a time, and no matter what, she'd be there every step of the way.

******

Denai could hear things knocking and banging around in Treena's room across the hall, and called out to her to make sure everything was okay. Treena yelled back that she was fine.

"I just keep dropping shit," she said with a giggle.

A few minutes later she came bopping into Denai's room holding a leopard print clutch purse in her hand.

"Girl, what are you doing in there?" Denai asked, referring back to the noises she heard.
"Well, you know how I always purge my closets before the new year, right?" Treena explained.
"Oh, yeah, and I want first dibs on everything before you ship it off to Goodwill," Denai replied in a sneaky tone.
"Oh, good lord!" Treena exclaimed with a giggle. "Okay, fine. Anyway, I was going through all my purses, you know, checking for any money I forgot about."
"Oh, absolutely!"
"As I rifled through this little guy, you'll never guess what I found."

Treena handed Denai a slip of paper that had been tucked in one of the card slots of the clutch she was holding. Denai unfolded the paper and immediately began smiling as memories flooded her mind. It was the note Dell had left for her on the Westin Hotel stationary after they spent the night together.

Re-reading his sweet words warmed her heart, but then a guilty feeling set in. She often regretted not using his number when she had the chance. So many things could've been different, if she had.

"Have you talked to him since?" Treena asked, referring to the jail-break from Ryan's house last week.

"He texts me at least twice a day, once in the morning and once later in the evening, to see how I'm feeling and healing up," Denai said with a shrug.

"That's it? Hot," Treena replied, rolling her eyes. "To be fair though, maybe he's just trying to give you space. You know, after everything with Ryan. Maybe he doesn't want you to feel rushed into some-thing new."

"That makes sense, I guess."

"Nothing says you can't call him, though."

Treena threw her a wink and playfully bounced back out of the room. Denai laughed at her suggestion, but then really considered calling him. Even though Dell had confessed to swiping one of her business cards just to get her number, he had only used it twice. Once to apologize for the whole Destiny fiasco at Treena's birthday event, and the second time was him sending her a text on Thanksgiving.

Considering what she knew of Dell, Denai could only assume that he kept phone activities to a minimum out of respect for her relation-ship with Ryan. At least that had been her excuse for not reaching out to him more often, no matter how much she wanted to.

Denai reached for her phone and dialed the number written on the piece of paper in her hand. Just to play it safe, she never officially saved Dell's number after his first call, because that would have given her too much easy access to someone she was trying to avoid. But, not anymore.

"Hello?" Dell's husky voice floated through the phone with a hint of curiosity in it.

"Hey, you," Denai said sweetly, hesitant to reveal her identity.

"Hey, gorgeous," he replied, his tone saying he already knew who it was.

"How'd you know it was me?" she asked, wondering if had saved her number.

"I'd know that beautiful voice anywhere. How are you?"

Denai felt her skin flush red as she smiled shyly against the phone. She told him she was fine and asked what he was up to. Dell said he was sitting at home enjoying the last few days of his vacation before January came and forced him back into adulthood. They spoke about their nonexistent plans for New Year's Eve, and avoided the topic of Christmas altogether, considering she had ended up in the emergency room two days before and all the drama that ensued afterwards.

She went on to tell him about Treena finding the note he had written and that it inspired her to finally give him a call. He teased her for having him wait by the phone for nine months, but was really happy she called.

"Well, I didn't want to appear too thirsty," Denai teased back.

"Oh, well mission accomplished," Dell said with a laugh.

"So, are you busy right now?" she asked softly.

"Why? You bored with Treena and want some company?" he asked with a chuckle.

"Maybe," she said slyly.

"Send me the address," he said assertively, his voice deep and thick.

Denai quickly texted Dell the address and he said he'd be there in an hour. She gleefully hung up and darted over to Treena's bedroom doorway to let her know Dell was coming over. Treena clapped and cheered, then jokingly said, "This ain't Claudette's house. Over here, when you have male company in your room, leaving the door open is optional." She winked at Denai, who blushed and laughed as she walked back to her room. She decided to hop in the shower as she waited for her guest to arrive.

Nearly an hour later, Dell was ringing Treena's doorbell. When she answered, he handed her a bottle of wine and kissed her cheek before stepping inside. He was also holding a bouquet of roses for Denai, and Treena beamed with joy at the sight of it. *That's what I'm talking about!,* she thought as she pointed him in the direction of Denai's bedroom when he asked about her.

Dell took the stairs two at a time as he anxiously headed towards her open door. He called her name when he stepped inside her room, and followed the sweet sound of her voice to the adjoined bathroom. He peered around the wall and saw her standing at the sink wrapped in a large bath sheet. Her arms, shoulders and legs were exposed with beads of water decorating her skin. He walked up and handed her the roses as he planted a kiss on her forehead.

"Thank you! They're beautiful," Denai beamed as she sniffed the blooms.

"Yeah, but they fade in comparison," Dell said, his voice lowered as he looked her up and down.

"Flattery will get you everywhere," she replied with a smirk as she brushed past him to go out to the bedroom.

Denai came to stand beside her bed, putting the roses in a small vase on the nightstand, and then reached for a jar of skin cream. Dell asked if that was just regular skin cream or specifically for her burns. He noticed the spots where some of the blisters and rashes had been on her legs, arms and back were clearing up quite nicely. Some were barely even noticeable anymore. Denai said that the cream was one of Treena's homemade blends of oatmeal, honey and shea butter.

"She *allowed* me to use the doctor prescribed burn cream for like three days and then said, enough was enough," Denai explained, laughing at her friend's words.

"Smells good," Dell complimented as he sniffed the contents of the jar.

"Yeah, I love it and it's been working wonders for my skin," she said.

"I can see that," he murmured as he stroked her forearm with his fingers.

The feather-light touches set her skin on fire and sent the butter-flies in her stomach on a frenzy. Her breathing became shaky as Dell moved to running his fingers along her thigh, pushing up the hem of the bath sheet as he went. He grabbed the jar and asked if she wanted help putting the skin cream on her body, and all Denai could do was nod as her eyelids fluttered from his touch. Dell whispered in her ear to take off the towel and lie down on the bed as he went to close the bedroom door.

Denai followed his instructions and laid across the bed on her stomach, facing the wall with her feet dangling over the side. She could feel Dell's body heat emanating from behind her as he stood at her feet. He raked his fingers through the creamy, soft shea butter, getting a hefty amount of it and rubbing it in his palms to warm it up. The feel of his strong hands sliding along her calves and the back of her thighs made Denai moan out loud.

She tried to muffle the sound by pressing her face into the mattress, biting down on the comforter, but it didn't help. Dell's lips soon fol-lowed the path of his hands as he kissed the back of her knees, thighs and butt. As he massaged more of the shea butter into her lower back, Dell planted soft kisses along her spine. The sounds Denai made were driving him wild and he was struggling to keep his cool and go slow, like he had so valiantly planned to do.

Denai's back arched at the feel of Dell's weight on top of her. She looked over her shoulder at him and her honey-green eyes were wild with passion. That was all it took to send Dell completely over the edge. He slid his hand under her stomach and rolled her over onto her back.

Dell kissed her with all the passion and hunger that had been building inside of him for months since moving back to Chicago. He held Denai's face in his hand as he continued feasting on her mouth. They moaned and breathed life into each other every second their lips touched.

Denai gripped the hem of Dell's shirt and pulled it over his head. His bare chest and arms were more muscular than the last time she saw them, making his tattoos pop like 3D images right before her eyes. She kissed the trail of them from one shoulder, across his pecks, and over to the other shoulder. The sound of his breath catching in his throat made Denai incredibly wet, or maybe it was the feel of his fingers as they entered her.

Her body tensed up as her thighs clenched around his hand. Dell rubbed circles against her clit with his thumb and inhaled her passionate cries as he kissed her. She gripped his bicep hard and dug her nails into his skin as she felt her body shake from the orgasm wreaking havoc through every part of her. The second she felt the pressure build up in her core, she begged Dell to stop but it was too late. She felt the wetness of her essence shower his hand as he moaned his satisfaction in her ear.

"I'm s-sorry," Denai apologized between gasps of air as she tried to catch her breath.

"What are you sorry for, Baby?" Dell asked with concern in his eyes.

Denai silently looked down at his soaking wet hand resting on her thigh and then back into his eyes. Dell narrowed his gaze, trying to understand why she would be apologetic about that.

"You said sorry the last time too. Why is that?" Dell asked with tenderness in his voice.

"Uh...It's a bit of a mood killer if I told you," Denai said shyly, now avoiding eye contact.

"Try me," he urged gently, stroking her hair with his fingers.

"When you're in a long-term relationship with someone who hates something about you, you just kinda adapt to what they want to make them happy," she explained.

"Meaning what?"

"Sometimes...a lot of times, I squirt and Ryan always hated it. Like, he would get so mad. I think it grossed him out or something."

"Seriously?! Wow, uh ok. So, how did you stop it from happening?"

"Mostly I started faking it."

Dell sat up quickly as if he had just been splashed with cold water. He emphatically asked her to explain what she meant by that. Denai told him that the only way for her to "Shut down the waterworks," as Ryan put it once, was for her to stop completely. So, she started faking her orgasms, and just leaned on masturbating to achieve her *real* happy endings. Denai looked up at Dell's face, trying to read his expression.

He stared into the void, ruminating on Denai's words. Her confession made him understand her so much more, and made his feelings for her intensify in ways he didn't yet know how to explain. So, he decided to show instead of tell. He stood up from the bed, unbuttoned and unzipped his jeans and slid them down his legs until they were a denim pool around his ankles. He stepped out of them, kicking them across the room.

Standing at the edge of the bed, Dell grabbed Denai's ankles, pulling her towards him. He instructed her to take off his boxers, and she happily obliged. She leaned forward and seductively peeled down the waistband of his boxers, kissing each piece of skin she revealed around his pelvis. She pushed the material down further and his already hard penis popped out.

This was the first time she got to truly appreciate the vision of it. It was brown and firm, slightly curved to the left with a large pulsating vein that ran along the top. His helmet glistened in the lamplight with the layer of pre-cum on it, and Denai licked her lips hungrily at the sight of it.

Dell cuffed her chin and tilted her head back, making her look into his eyes. He shook his head "No," as if answering her unexpressed fantasies. When she looked at him questioningly, he just gave a devilish grin as he stepped back and beckoned her to come to him in the middle of the room.

Denai got up from the bed and walked over to Dell. He bent down and scooped his arms between her legs, lifting her up until she was straddling the crooks of his elbows. He gripped her hips and hoisted her up in the air until her pussy was right in his face. He walked over to a nearby wall and rested Denai's back against it as he cradled her hips.

Dell smiled up at her, then slowly grazed his tongue against her pussy lips until they parted, letting him taste her clit. Denai's hands immediately grabbed his head as he wrote his name on every inch of her pussy with his tongue. She clawed at his neck and shoulders as her legs flailed against his arms. Dell's fingers pressed hard into the flesh of her hips as he continued to devour her.

Dell moaned into her core as he tasted her sweet nectar. The sound of her moaning and pleading with him as she ground her pelvis against his face, made his penis get harder and harder. Once again, Denai begged for him to stop because she could feel the tidal wave building behind her walls. The more she pleaded, the faster he flicked his tongue. Her toes curled up tight and her knees locked onto his shoulders as she lost her fight and the dam broke.

He didn't even bother to pull back as she watered his beard with her essence. Denai couldn't muffle her screams anymore. The more she came, the more he licked, and the more he licked, the more she came. Her orgasms crashed through her body one right after the other, firing like a Tommy Gun, as she bucked against him. Dell growled hungrily as he ate and held on tight so she couldn't run. The more he ravaged her, the harder it was for Denai to catch her breath between screams.

The only words she could get out were, "Dell, please," right before another orgasm took over. Leaving her with no energy to apologize for it. Just like he wanted. Dell kissed her delicate lips softly before pulling away and lowering her back down to the floor. Denai's legs felt wobbly as she leaned on the wall for balance and held onto his arms, still trying to catch her breath. He cuffed her chin and asked her to look at him. Denai's eyes fluttered open, trying hard to bring his face into focus.

As his handsomeness came into view, Denai noticed Dell's drenched and glistening beard as remnants of her pleasure dripped from it down his chest. She began to blush from embarrassment, but before she could say anything, he did.

"You can fucking drown me anytime you want to, baby," Dell said seductively. "I want you to cum for me *every...single...time*. Don't stop it. *Please* don't fake it. And don't *ever* apologize for it. *I* love that shit."

Denai bit her lip as she smiled at Dell's declaration. She stood on her tiptoes and kissed his soaked lips – her tongue moving in and out of his mouth, trying to taste herself on his tongue. He pushed her back onto the wall with his body and pressed his hands against it, framing her beautiful face as their kiss continued.

Denai reached down and began stroking his penis, rubbing the pad of her thumb on his helmet. Dell let out a groan as the sensation of her touch made him grow harder. Denai gently nipped at his bottom lip as hers formed a sneaky smile. She kissed him again then quickly dropped to her knees. Dell braced himself, palms still pressed against the wall as he towered over her.

He looked down to see the top of her head moving on a swivel as she dragged her tongue along his shaft from one side to the other. His breathing turned to panting as her tongue licked the underside of his member, dancing along the vein there. When Denai finally took Dell into her mouth, he threw his head back and let out a grunt as his eyes rolled back into his head. He dug his nails into the plaster of the wall and his toes into the carpet as Denai continued to wrap her warm mouth around him, sliding her lips up and down from the base to the tip in slow agony.

She moaned, making her throat vibrate on his penis and it made Dell's knees buckle. He looked down at her in stunned pleasure, and she looked up and winked at him as she continued her vixen play.

"Fuck, baby!" Dell groaned in a breathy whisper. "That feels fucking amazing!"

Denai moaned more as she sucked harder, and Dell didn't know how much more he could take. The second he felt Denai's hand wrap around the base of his penis and start stroking up and down along with her lips, Dell knew that would be the end of him. He moaned louder as he felt himself getting closer and gripped the back of Denai's head.

Dell fell into a pleading of his own as he begged her not to stop. She increased the speed of her mouth and hand as they moved in tantalizing swirls and circles, sending shockwaves through him from literally every angle. He panted heavier and groaned louder until his groans became a guttural growl as he tightened his grip on the back of her head.

Dell buried his face in the crook of his arm, biting into his own flesh as he released every ounce of himself. His body shivered and jerked as he choked back his moans – trying to catch his breath as he came harder than he'd ever had before. He collapsed against the wall, resting his forehead on his fist, as he fought hard not to drop to his knees.

Denai moved from under him and crawled over to the bed. She sat on the floor and leaned her back against the side of the bedframe and mattress. She stretched her legs out in front of her and her arms above her head, smirking in satisfaction as she watched Dell struggle to get his bearings.

"Are you okay?" she asked coyly.
"Peachy!" he replied breathlessly.

Dell stumbled over to the bed and fell across it, no longer having the strength to hold his body up with his own two legs. Denai burst into laughter from her spot on the floor. He let out a lazy laugh of his own that was muffled by the side of his face being pressed into the mattress. A few seconds later, Treena knocked on the door, and Dell yelled out, "We're dead! Come back later!" Her cackling could be heard on the other side of the door as she informed them she was getting ready to order takeout, if they wanted some.

"I think he's full, but I'm down," Denai yelled out jokingly.

"Shiiit! If that's the case, you should be full too," Dell said in her ear as he leaned over the side of the bed.

Denai playfully swatted at him and told Treena they'd be out in a minute. They could still hear her laughing as she went back downstairs. Dell kissed her lightly on the neck and shoulder before rolling off the bed. He shuffled his feet across the carpet as he headed to the adjoined bathroom. Denai licked her lips in appreciation of the muscles flexing in his back as he walked, noticing just how nice his butt really was.

She giggled sheepishly to herself as she stood up and went over to the dresser to finally find some clothes. Denai put on a gray long-sleeved t-shirt with "PINK" in white chenille letters across the front and gray and white checkered pajama shorts. She was raking her fingers through her hair when Dell came out of the bathroom half dressed.

He had grabbed his jeans and underwear off the floor on his way in and put them back on. Denai playfully pouted about him having pants on again, to which he replied, "Oh, don't worry. They're coming right back off later," then kissed her passionately as he palmed her butt like a basketball. Denai giggled with pleasure as she placed her hands on his chest. She kissed his sternum and he kissed the top of her head. Then the two of them went downstairs to meet Treena and decide on dinner.

{ thirteen }

January '23

Dell propped open his office door and opened the blinds, flooding the room with the early morning sunshine. His holiday vacation had come to an end and it was back to business as usual for Dell Hewitt, Attorney-at-Law. In the first week of January, he already had two five-hour court dates and four three-hour acquisition meetings with new clients on his calendar for the week, and it was only Tuesday.

He was just settling in at his desk to start looking over notes for court later, when there was a light knock on his office door. Dell looked up and saw it was one of the partners from his department.

"Hey, Ed," Dell greeted from his seat.
"Hey, good morning, Dell," Ed greeted in return. "You got a second?"
"Yeah, sure. What do you need?" Dell asked.
"Come walk with me," Ed said, sounding slightly cryptic.

Dell furrowed his brow at Ed's invitation as he rose from his chair and followed his boss out of the office. They walked down the hall and ended up at one of the conference rooms. Ed threw open the door and asked Dell to step inside. Dell continued to watch him suspiciously as he stepped through the door, and what he saw on the other side made his face fall flat.

Seated on one side of the long meeting table were the Chief Human Resources Officer, the Human Resources Business Partner for the Mergers and Acquisitions team, and another one of the Managing Partners over Mergers and Acquisitions. However, out of everyone in the room, it was the sight of Ryan Lattimore sitting next to the HR team that made Dell's jaw clench with annoyance. He could only imagine what game Ryan was playing at this early in the morning.

Dell was instructed to grab a seat at the table, which he immediately declined until someone explained why he was there and what this was all about.

"We just want to talk for a moment, Dell," Ed explained after taking his seat at the head of the table.

"About?" Dell pressed, still standing with his hands in his pockets.

"Dell, please," the Chief HR Officer pleaded, gesturing to the empty chairs.

Dell let out an exasperated sigh as he unbuttoned his suit jacket and sat down on the unoccupied side of the table. He put his arms on the armrests and looked at the eyes of every person watching him. Once Dell was seated, Ed explained why they were all gathered there.

"Dell, it's been brought to our attention that a physical altercation has occurred between you and Ryan," Ed explained. "Now, though it happened outside of work, it did involve two colleagues not only from this office, but from the same department. And we'd just like to get to the bottom of it."

Dell scoffed quietly while straightening his tie as he listened to Ed's deposition. He looked across the table at Ryan, whose face still bore signs of their second run-in with each other regarding Denai. Ryan had severe bruising around his nose, two black eyes and a split top lip, as well as multiple superficial scratches and scrapes on his face and hands. Dell admired his literal handiwork as it sat on display for the whole firm to see.

Ryan had made the arrogant mistake of coming to Treena's house the same night Dell had come over. Dell and Denai were lying in bed, cuddled together after having ordered takeout with Treena and exhausting themselves with another round of love-making when they heard raised voices coming from downstairs. Dell quickly dressed and headed down to check on the commotion and saw Ryan trying to force his way into Treena's house.

Dell wedged himself between them and shoved Ryan away from the doorstep. He reminded him of the last time they saw each other and asked if he hadn't learned his lesson from then? Ryan said he was over this whole charade of Denai's temper tantrum and she needed to come back home. By this time, Denai had made it downstairs to witness his tirade. Dell continuously shoved Ryan backwards every time he tried to maneuver his way around to get inside Treena's house.

Denai and Treena both shouted for him to go home, that she was not coming back, and their relationship was over. All facts Ryan refused to accept. So, in true fashion he hurled insults, curses and threats like an Olympic Champion in the Shot Put. The louder he got, the louder the women got, and the fact that it was well past midnight on a quiet neighborhood street were all the necessary ingredients to finally make Dell's rage boil over.

He issued one last warning to leave immediately, and Ryan responded by throwing his first and last punch. That was all the ammo Dell needed to launch an attack of his own. He beat Ryan senseless, tossing him like a rag doll across every inch of Treena's front yard, before dragging him to his car parked on the street.

That is where Dell had left him and the last time he had seen him. Now here Ryan sat, crying "victim" for a beat down he absolutely earned.

"So, we're really doing this?" Dell asked Ryan, not looking at him.

"Excuse me?" the partner seated next to Ryan asked.

"Huh, Ryan? You really want to do this? Today?" Dell repeated as his eyes finally met Ryan's.

"We just want to get to the bottom of this, Dell. That's all," Ed offered.

"Alright. Let's do it," Dell quipped confidently.

He rubbed the palms of his hands together and cracked his knuckles, then leaned forward and clasped his hands together on top of the table.

"Ryan made the unfortunate mistake of showing up where he wasn't wanted while I was there," Dell said plainly.

"And what does that mean?" the HR Business Partner asked as their eyes widened.

"It means that Ryan Lattimore has a propensity for violence towards women," Dell said. "An act I have witnessed with my own eyes, not once but twice, and both times against his ex-fiancée, whom I believe you all are familiar with."

Audible gasps and murmurs filled the room as all eyes were set on Ryan, who began to shrink under the scrutiny.

"I'll admit to a physical altercation occurring between Ryan and myself," Dell continued. "But, it was done in the defense and protection of two women he threatened. As you said, it happened outside of work and any amount of billable hours. I do not deny nor regret my actions, and if I am to face disciplinary action, then I ask what next steps will be taken for my fellow combatant with a fondness for domestic violence? Especially that which has been documented by way of hospital records."

More shocked chatter erupted around the table and Dell sat calmly, swiveling his chair back and forth as he watched Ryan's house of cards come tumbling down. Ryan tried frivolously to contest what Dell had said, but his account of everything was far too detailed to be considered false. Not to mention the air of confidence surrounding Dell that signified he had nothing to hide and no reason to lie.

Ed and the HR reps thanked Dell for his candor and told him he was free to go. He pushed away from the table, holding Ryan's gaze steady. Dell stood up, buttoned his jacket, and tugged at the cuffs and lapels to straighten them. He gave a two-finger salute to the room and bid them all a good day as he traipsed out unscathed and unbothered. As he passed by the glass window of the conference room, he could see Ryan coming under fire from the same cannons he had tried to put Dell in front of.

Shaking his head and trying to stifle his laughter, Dell headed back down the hall to his office to continue on with his day. "There goes ten minutes of my life I'll never get back," he mumbled to himself as he entered his office.

******

Denai arrived at *Plein Air Cafe* near the University of Chicago's campus at one o'clock on the dot. She stepped inside and was overcome by the scent of brewing coffee, flavored syrups, sugar and baking pastries. Quaint cafes were one of her favorite places to go, just because of the ambiance and energy inside. She was glad Iris Lattimore had chosen this place to meet.

Iris had called Denai to wish her a Happy New Year and invited her out to lunch to catch up. It had been a few weeks since Denai had seen or spoken to the woman she loved like a second mother, and even though she and Ryan had broken up, she wasn't ready to completely cut ties with Iris. Especially, since Denai hadn't told her about the split yet.

Denai spotted Iris seated on the enclosed patio with another woman at the table. As she got closer she realized the other woman was her own mother, Claudette. Her presence was very unexpected if for no other reason than she had said on more than one occasion how much she couldn't stand Iris.

Claudette always complained that the woman came across as up-pity, bougie and acting as if she were better than everyone else. Denai gave up on trying to change her mother's mind about Iris a long time ago. Once Claudette formed a thought or opinion about something, it was cemented as fact from that point on.

Denai took a deep breath and forced a smile on her face as she approached the waiting duo. She greeted Iris first with a warm hug and a kiss on the cheek. The smile Denai gave Iris was genuine and full of excitement because she had missed her very much. Whereas, the exchange between her and Claudette was a bit awkward and strained, which really wasn't that uncommon as of late.

The three ladies sat down and placed their coffee orders as they perused the menu. Denai asked her mother how things were going at the hospital and was she still working a lot of overtime? Claudette said she was and would continue to do so for as long as it was offered.

"That's what us single women have to do when we don't have a man to take care of us," Claudette snarled slightly as she flipped through the menu.

Denai rolled her eyes and instantly regretted having asked her mother anything.

"And how about you, Ms. Iris? How have you been?" Denai asked in a sweet tone, trying to mask her annoyance.

"Well, let's just say that Christmas break was certainly not long enough," Iris said jokingly. "Speaking of, we missed you guys at the party this year."

Iris was referring to the Lattimore's annual Christmas party that was always a big to-do. The house would be completely decked out in festive fanfare provided by professional decorators, and a full feast prepared by professional caterers. The house would be filled from top to bottom with revelers and eggnog drinkers singing carols offkey and way too loud.

With Denai being from such a small family, it was always a welcomed treat to attend the Christmas party at Isaiah and Iris's house. This was the first time she had missed it in three years.

"Yeah, I missed you guys too," Denai replied shyly. "Ryan didn't come either?"

"No, he said he was feeling a little under the weather," Iris replied. "He said with all the traveling he had been doing lately, he didn't know if it was just a regular bug or something else and he didn't wanna risk it. So, he stayed home."

"How you don't know what's going on with your man, lil' girl?" Claudette mused from across the table.

Denai looked up wide-eyed at her mother because the question caught her off guard. Since she left Ryan's house two days before Christmas following his last blowup and was staying with Treena temporarily, Denai hadn't spoken to anyone else about what happened between them. Anytime her mom asked about Ryan, she'd always give straightforward, vague answers that didn't require too much detail and then she'd quickly change the subject.

Denai considered doing that very thing again today, but decided it was time for people to know the truth, no matter how ugly or uncomfortable it may be.

"Well, uh...Ryan and I broke up," Denai finally said after taking a generous sip of water.

"Oh no! Why?" Iris asked with sadness in her voice and eyes.

"Because I left him," Denai answered plainly.

"You what?!" Claudette exclaimed angrily from her side of the table, nearly dropping her coffee cup.

"Why, Denai? What happened?" Iris asked sincerely, reaching across the table for Denai's hand.

Denai took several deep breaths that she disguised as just blowing on her hot coffee. For a split second she felt a twinge of fear and guilt, because she knew the truth of what had really gone on in her relationship with Ryan would crush Iris. He was her only son and she doted on him constantly, even in the moments he disappointed her. The longer Denai sat with that knowledge, the more uncertain she became of just how Iris would react. There was only one way to find out.

"Ms. Iris, Ryan was abusive," Denai confessed slowly. "In every way possible. Verbally, physically, financially, all of it. I was being abused often, and it got worse and worse until I ended up in the hospital. That was the last straw. And that's why I wasn't there for Christmas."

Denai watched the realization of her words set in as Iris visibly collapsed under the weight of such a truth. She clasped her chest with one hand and covered her mouth with the other as tears welled up in her eyes. The gravity of knowing that the son she had raised and poured all her love and values into had grown up to be just like the men she fought against every day in Family Court was too much to bear. Iris asked Denai to tell her everything that happened, which Denai adamantly begged her not to ask for, but she wanted to know.

Begrudgingly, Denai gave her account of the first time Ryan physically hurt her when he pushed her down the stairs during their argument about her unpaid tuition last year. She told Iris that was why they had broken up the first time, but he apologized and proposed soon after, so no one knew about it. Denai spoke about Ryan forbidding her to work and exercise any amount of independence in her own life; and how him putting his hands on her increased month after month since becoming engaged.

Denai's words delivered one crushing blow after another to Iris's heart. It pained her to watch it happen, but Iris urged her to get it all out. After Denai finished revealing everything to Iris, including that she had fully moved out and returned the engagement ring to Ryan just to show how serious she was, the sweet woman thanked her for sharing her truth.

Iris apologized for her son's behavior and poor treatment because that is not who she raised him to be. She expressed her love and adoration for Denai with the utmost sincerity. Claudette, however, had a different energy.

"What did *you* do?" Claudette asked dryly, with her arms folded across her chest.

"Excuse me?" Denai asked, her eyes narrowed in confusion.

"Ryan is a good man," Claudette replied. "He did everything for you. Gave you whatever you wanted. Took care of you for over three years, and just outta nowhere starts *abusing* you? He wouldn't do that. So, what did *you* do?"

"Claudette!" Iris scolded with a shocked look on her face.

"You don't know my daughter like I do," Claudette retorted. "Her attitude. That mouth. Nah, it's more to it than just what she's saying. I know it."

Denai fell back in her chair in complete disbelief and stunned silence. She looked at her mother's face, trying to determine if she was being serious with her line of questioning. When reality hit that Claudette was not only very serious, but was fully expecting an answer she deemed acceptable, Denai lost it.

"So, let me get this straight," Denai started as she leaned forward and put her arms on the table. "Your only child...*your daughter* tells you the man she's been dating and living with has been abusing her in every way. She tells you she's been hospitalized by said abuse and you want to know what she did to *deserve* it?!"

"You know how you get!" Claudette angrily replied.

"Wow, Ma. Wow!" Denai exclaimed softly as she tossed her linen napkin on the table.

Denai grabbed her purse off the chair next to her and stood up. Iris tried to stop her, but there was no way Denai was going to stay at that table. She hugged Iris and thanked her for all of her kindness and love over the years and especially for today. She apologized again for having potentially tainted Iris's image of her only son in any way, and encouraged her not to blame herself for the actions of a forty-year-old man.

The two women hugged tightly, as Denai tossed one last scowl in her mother's direction before leaving the patio and disappearing back inside the cafe. Iris wiped the tears from her face as she watched Denai leave her sight. Taking a few quick breaths to get her nerves together, Iris turned around to see Claudette sitting there looking unfazed while sipping her caramel latte. The sight of it sent Iris's blood boiling, but she kept her composure.

"Well," Iris exhaled as she started putting on her coat.

"Don't let Denai and her lies ruin lunch for you. We can still eat," Claudette said, her face frowning up.

"Oh, no ma'am," Iris said, snatching up her purse. "There's not enough hunger in the world that would ever make me share another meal with you."

"Excuse me?" Claudette said through gritted teeth.

"I believe Denai, because, sadly, I know my son, and if you knew my son as well as you claimed, then you'd believe her too. And the fact that you don't and *she's your daughter*, is a damn shame."

Iris stormed away from the table following the same path Denai had taken, leaving a stunned Claudette alone just as the waiter was dropping off the check.

******

Denai was sitting at Treena's kitchen table typing away on her laptop. Several times, Treena had to wave a hand in front of Denai's face just to get her attention. Each time she'd laugh and apologize for her extreme tunnel vision, but Treena said she completely understood, and was actually headed into her office to do the same thing.

"I'm about to work on some marketing materials and client follow-ups for these buyers," Treena explained as she grabbed two bottles of water from the refrigerator.

"Working hard as always," Denai praised as she blew on her cup of mint tea.

"You're one to talk," Treena teased. "What you got going on over here anyway?"

"Menus and grocery lists for your two open houses coming up, plus some other events I booked," Denai said.

"Let's go!" Treena exclaimed as she high-fived Denai excitedly.

After Denai returned home from the lunchtime fiasco with her mother, she went straight to work on her catering business. Claudette's comments about Ryan doing everything for her, literally made Denai's skin crawl. Partially because she knew it was true, but also because she realized it was all done as a way to control her life.

Denai had quit her job because Ryan claimed he wanted to take care of her, but it was really just to make her more financially dependent on him. She didn't have money unless he gave it to her. She moved out of her mother's house into his. Even the car she was currently driving came from him. Luckily, she had enough presence of mind to make him put it in her name only when they picked it out.

Once her May graduation date came and went without her getting the degree she had worked so hard for, all because Ryan held the power to deny her such an achievement, Denai set out to start her catering business anyway with dogged defiance. She never wanted to be in that position of dependency ever again. So, she had spent all of last summer researching and compiling information and ideas to put her business plan together.

After meeting with Treena in September to get her blessing on the business plan and portfolio, Denai hit the ground running. Quietly promoting her culinary skills any way she could. Utilizing her network of friends, and even some of Treena's own business partners, Denai built up a small clientele and worked diligently until that list grew. All the while, keeping it hidden from Ryan and her naysayer of a mother, because she knew neither of them would be happy about it. Her perseverance would not be praised, but punished.

Now with Claudette's seething words still burning holes in her memory bank, Denai wanted to push herself even harder to be successful at something others said wouldn't work. The next four weeks of Denai's calendar were booked solid with orders, events and consultations for services, and she couldn't be happier. Treena high-fived her again and said she was so proud of her, making Denai beam with joy as she went back to work.

Denai was editing photos of some dishes she had made and readying them for posting on her social media pages when her phone rang with a FaceTime call. A wide smile quickly spread across her face when she saw Dell's name flashing on the screen.

"Hey, you," Denai greeted cheerfully when his face showed up on screen.

"Hey, gorgeous," Dell's deep baritone caressed her eardrums through her earbuds.

"How are you?" she asked, still smiling at the phone resting on the stand next to her laptop.

"Now? Fantastic," he said flirtatiously. "How 'bout you? How goes it?"

"Eh, had a pretty shitty day, but life goes on," she said with a shrug.

"Hmm, did you really have a *whole* shitty day? Or was it just something shitty that happened today?"

"Okay, Mr. Perspective!"

Dell laughed and insisted that Denai not let one bad moment ruin her entire day. He said it was definitely a skill he had to learn himself, but he was willing to try if she was, too. She agreed, but made him go first.

"Lead by example, Mr. Hewitt," Denai urged with a smirk.

"Ugh, fine!" Dell huffed jokingly. "Well, mine is just boring work stuff."

"So?" she pressed.

"You right!" he agreed.

Dell had considered telling her about his early morning run-in with Ryan and the partners, but decided against it. As far as he was concerned, Ryan wasn't worth the time or energy either of them would expend just by mentioning his name. He and Denai were moving on in their very own bubble of bliss, and there was no place for Ryan Lattimore in it.

So, instead Dell talked about being frustrated with work because he had spent all morning preparing for court later that afternoon, only for his time to be pushed and moved to another day. It wouldn't have been so bad, except that he now had two cases scheduled on the same day, less than an hour apart. It wasn't an uncommon occurrence, but it certainly was one of his least favorite things.

"I just hate having my schedule disrupted like that," Dell said with a heavy sigh.

"I completely understand," Denai empathized. "I'm sorry that happened. I used to clerk for some of the guys there when I was an admin. So, I definitely know how annoying that can be."

"Yeah, I know it comes with the territory, but that shit is still wack as hell," he said with a chuckle.

"It really is," she agreed with a laugh of her own.

"Okay, your turn."

"Ugh, I was hoping we could skip me."

"Nope!"

With an exasperated sigh, Denai told Dell about how what was supposed to be a simple lunch with Iris and Claudette had completely gone up in flames before they could even order appetizers. She talked about revealing the truth of Ryan's abuse and mistreatment to the mothers, and how heartbreaking it felt to look Iris in her eyes while doing so. Denai then told him about Claudette's response, and that sent Dell fuming.

"You know, the more you tell me about this woman, the less enthused I am to ever meet her, Babe," Dell said with a gruffness in his voice.

"I get that," Denai said softly, sounding pained as she recalled her mother's words.

"Denai," he called her name gently.

"Yeah?" she replied, her eyes low with sadness.

"Look at me," he prompted. "There is nothing you did or could ever do to deserve what Ryan did to you. He's a weak ass coward, and that is his shame to carry. Not yours. Okay?"

Denai nodded and sniffled softly, trying to shake off the negative thoughts attempting to stir back up in her mind. She was grateful for Dell's kind words, and she knew he was right. It would just take some time for that truth to set in and take root.

"I never thanked you for what you did that night either," Denai said, referring to the night he helped her escape Ryan's house.

"Oh, I beg to differ," Dell replied with a sinister smirk.

"You are so nasty! You know what I mean," Denai fussed, trying to hide her laugh.

"I know what you meant, and I meant what I said. Your gratitude was felt and well-received. Both times," he teased with a wink.

"You make me sick!" she said, covering her face shyly.

Dell reassured Denai that he understood what she was saying and there was no need to thank him. He would do it all over again if he had to, without hesitation. Hearing his words warmed Denai's heart and sparked her curiosity.

"Why did you do it?" Denai asked, her head tilted in anticipation.

"What do you mean?" Dell asked in return, his eyes narrowed in confusion.

"I mean you didn't have to come to the hospital or the house," she explained. "You didn't owe me that, and the last time we saw each other you were so mad at me. So, why did you come?"

"Because it was you," he said without hesitation.

Dell told her the second Treena said her name while on the phone, his heart started racing with the hope that she was coming to their game night, but when the fear flashed in Treena's eyes his heart dropped. Once he heard she was in the hospital there was no question or doubt about whether or not he'd be by her side.

"Checking on you, protecting you, it was all instinct," Dell continued. "It just came natural. There was no other choice. No other option. My heart wouldn't have it."

"Aw, Dell," Denai swooned, covering her smile with her hand.

"It's one thing to hear about it, but to actually see you laying in that bed...the bruises and burns...I couldn't leave you. I *wouldn't* leave you."

The next thing Dell said took Denai completely by surprise.

"And as for what I said, I was wrong for accusing you of using me," Dell confessed. "I was just trying to hide the fact that I was hurt and a little pissed that you were with someone else and I didn't want to accept my loss for what it was."

"From your perspective, all signs pointed to the situation being something other than what you originally thought," Denai said, trying to soothe him. "You were mad, I get it. You had a right to be."

"Nah, I didn't," he replied quietly, shaking his head. "Then the look in your eyes...I saw you flinch...I scared you. Knowing everything you've been through, I'll never forgive myself for doing that to you."

"You didn't mean to. I forgive you," she said sweetly.

"I appreciate that, Love, but I don't deserve your forgiveness just yet. But, I'll do everything in my power to earn it, if you'll let me."

Denai smiled and blew a kiss at the phone screen to seal their agreement. The tenderness in his voice and sincerity in his eyes told her Dell meant every word he said, and if given the chance, he'd prove it to her as often he needed to.

******

Denai skipped up the walkway to E-Man's front door, hoping to catch Dell before he got started with his day. The bright Saturday morning sun threaded through the trees and made the snow-covered ground sparkle. It added a welcomed warmth to the city that had been missing for weeks.

"Oooh, look at you all sweaty!" Denai squealed as she stepped across the threshold into E-Man's house.

"Moving furniture will do that to you," Dell replied, sounding out of breath.

Dell had finally closed on his new house in Oak Park and was in the process of moving everything in this weekend. His Saturday morning consisted of emptying out the storage unit he had been renting since his return to Chicago. It was filled with all of his belongings from his condo in Detroit, plus some new things he had acquired since being back in the city. Dell was in the middle of breaking down his bed and television stand when Denai stopped by.

"Just moving furniture does that to you?" Denai asked suggestively with a smirk.

"And this face," Dell flirted as he leaned in for a kiss.

"Mmm, good answer," she said, cupping his face in her hands.

Dell pressed Denai's body against the front door with his hand resting right above her head. The moment their lips met, they both let out a blissful sigh and throaty moan. He slid his hand inside her coat and gripped her waist as he feasted on her mouth hungrily. Their tongues tussled passionately as Denai's arms encircled Dell's neck and she massaged the back of his head. The feel of her fingers on the nape of his neck made Dell melt into her.

"You busy right now?" Dell asked in a breathy whisper in between kisses.

"I got time," Denai panted as she ran her hands across his damp, bare chest.

"Yeah, but he don't!" E-Man shouted from behind them, carrying a box down the stairs.

Dell pressed his forehead to Denai's and groaned with irritation as she giggled. He looked over his shoulder to find his cousin glaring at him and fussing about, "Not having all damn day to help him move his shit," before dropping the box in the middle of the living room and heading back upstairs.

"*Shut up*, nigga!" Dell yelled up the stairs behind him.
"*Hurry up*, nigga!" E-Man yelled back.
"I think he's losing patience," Denai giggled.
"His fault," Dell said smugly as he went back to kissing her.

Denai laughed against Dell's lips as she pushed on his chest. He huffed in disappointment as he pulled away. She grabbed his hand, lacing her fingers through his, and looked into his eyes. Dell pulled her to him and released a low growl as he cupped her face with his free hand and started kissing her again. He was just about to lay her down on the couch when E-Man angrily called his name from upstairs.

"This motherfucka!" Dell grumbled through gritted teeth as he pulled away from Denai for the third time.

He accepted the fact that now wasn't a good time to pounce on her because he was, in fact, busy and had someone waiting on him. Didn't make him any less pissed off about it, though.

"Let me get back to work before I kill this nigga," Dell groaned as he put it on a red t-shirt that had been tossed on the couch.
"Yeah, that's probably the best idea. I've seen him angry and it's not pretty," Denai grimaced.
"You've also seen me angry," he replied, cutting his eyes at her.
"That I have," she confirmed with a nod.
"And now I'm angry *and* horny. Terrible combination," he said with a huff.

"Well, just let this be an incentive to get all moved in so we can christen the new place without interruption," she said with a sneaky smile as she drew circles on his chest with her finger.

Dell bit his bottom lip and nodded in agreement as he fought the urge to throw her down on the couch anyway. He offered her a drink as they headed into the kitchen.

"What you got going on today?" Dell asked, handing her a bottle of water from the refrigerator.

"Guess I'm kinda moving too," Denai replied before taking a sip.

"You leaving Treena's already? Damn! That was faster than I expected," he joked.

"Hush!" she said, swatting her hand at him. "No, I, uh...I'm moving my catering equipment out of my mom's garage today."

Denai told Dell about how she was stashing all of her catering supplies in her mother's garage because Ryan would pop a blood vessel if he saw them. She said it was also much safer keeping it in the garage because her mom was always skittish about going out there and hardly ever did.

"This way I keep everything out of sight of them both," Denai explained.

"Reeeeally starting to hate these people," Dell grumbled, referring to Ryan and Claudette. "Why you ain't tell me? I could've helped you move it out."

"Actually, you moving into your house this weekend kinda inspired me to make this move for myself," she admitted. "And it's really not that much stuff to grab."

"That's not what I asked you," he said firmly, his eyes fixed on hers. "Why didn't you tell me?"

"I knew you would be busy," she replied with a shrug.

Dell stepped forward, closing the gap between them. He cuffed her chin, tilting her head back so their eyes could meet.

"I am never too busy for you. Just tell me what you need, okay?" Dell said, his voice firm but gentle.

"Okay," Denai said with a shy smile.

******

Denai pulled up to her mother's garage door in the alley in a rented U-Haul van. She hopped out and pulled the back doors open, then flipped the latch on the side gate and went into the backyard. She opened the side door to the garage and hit the light switch as she stepped inside. The fluorescent bulbs flickered eerily before flooding the garage with dim light. Denai pushed the button next to the light switch to raise the garage door.

She was loading a stack of serving trays and burners into the back of the van when her mother came charging into the garage wearing a ratty purple bathrobe, while wielding a cast iron skillet and yelling like a crazy person.

"Denai?! Girl, I thought you were a burglar!" Claudette exclaimed.

"Nope," Denai replied dryly.

"What are you doin' in here? What is all this stuff?" Claudette asked with a furrowed brow.

"This is my catering equipment," Denai said matter-of-factly.

"Catering equipment?! Why the hell do you have catering equipment?" Claudette shrieked with her hands on her hips.

"I don't know, Ma. Maybe because I'm a caterer!"

Denai lifted a large box off the ground that held her KitchenAid mixer and slid it into the back of the van. She was snatching up boxes and stacks of supplies one after the other and angrily shoving them into the van while her mother stood there watching in aggravated silence. She hadn't said a word since hearing that her daughter was working as a caterer. Claudette didn't know which was worse – the fact that Denai was doing it or that she knew nothing about it.

"Well, why are you keeping *your* catering equipment in *my* garage?" Claudette asked sarcastically.

"Because, Ma, it was literally not safe for me to keep it anywhere else," Denai answered in a huff.

"Meaning what?"

"Meaning I've gotten my ass beat for less in Ryan's house. God forbid he found out I was working for myself."

"Girl, don't you start that again!"

Denai slammed the doors of the van shut after loading the last box inside. She turned and marched towards her mother with pure rage in her eyes. Claudette squared her shoulders and gripped the handle of the skillet tight.

"I am your daughter!" Denai exclaimed. "*I* am your child! And the fact that you give more credit to the nigga who remodeled your kitchen as a Mother's Day gift than the daughter you actually gave birth to, just fucking baffles me!"

"You watch your fucking mouth!" Claudette barked.

"You know, when I came home after Ryan and I broke up the first time," Denai continued. "You never even bothered to ask what happened or even if I was okay. Just wanted to know how soon I'd be moving back out. I tell you Ryan's been abusing me and you looked me in the face and asked what did I do to deserve it?"

"Denai, that is not..."

"And now I tell you that I'm finally pursuing my dream of being a chef and caterer, but that I've had to do it in secret because it was literally not safe to do out loud, and you still refuse to believe me. And frankly, I'm done trying to convince you to be on my side for once."

Denai ripped the keys to Claudette's house from her key ring and slammed them into the palm of her mother's hand. A lone tear rolled down Denai's cheek as she backed away, shaking her head in disappointment at Claudette. She climbed into the van and started the engine. Taking two deep breaths and feeling an immediate sense of calm, Denai threw the van into gear and drove off down the alley, sending the tires sloshing loudly through the snow. She felt the weight fall off her shoulders as she turned out onto the street, barreling down the road towards her new future.

{ fourteen }

February '23

"Okay, braids!" Denai exclaimed when Treena walked in the house.

She had gotten her signature bright pink mohawk put into knotless box braids of the same color that draped across her shoulders and down to the middle of her back. Treena giggled at Denai's compliment as she dramatically ran her fingers through the braids. Denai was fluffing her own short curls in the mirror on the closet door in the living room while waiting for Treena to get back from her early morning hair appointment.

"These things were necessary if I'm gonna be sweating in a hot kitchen with you all day," Treena joked as she tossed her coat over the arm of the couch.

"You got a point," Denai chuckled as she touched up her lip gloss in the mirror.

"I thought this was a catering job? Not a date," Treena teased as she elbowed her friend in the side.

"Don't mean I can't be cute," Denai replied, smiling with her tongue between her teeth.

"You right!" Treena said before darting upstairs to change.

Dell had finally finished moving into his new house and commissioned Denai to cater his semi-housewarming and Bears Game watch party today. She was so flattered that he even asked and he told her there was no one else he'd trust. So, today Denai was on cloud nine. While she had prepared and delivered food for numerous clients' events before, today was her first official run at catering and serving for an all-day event.

She was feeling a bit nervous, but was truly grateful for the opportunity to stretch herself into a new skill. Any chance to shine in her newfound independence, Denai welcomed with open arms. However, to avoid being overwhelmed with the day's task, she asked Treena to assist again, and she happily obliged.

Treena bopped down the stairs wearing one of Denai's custom made navy blue polo shirts with her new logo on it, a pair of fitted dark denim jeans that hugged her hips tightly and black wedge booties. She had pulled her braids up into a bun on top of her head and donned russet brown lipstick. Denai rolled her eyes at the sight of her.

"What?!" Treena asked in a high-pitched voice, feigning innocence. "You can't be the only cute one!"
"And there it is," Denai replied with a laugh as she shook her head.

Denai flipped up the collar of her own polo that was paired with fitted khakis that showed off her petite curves and navy blue knee-high Polo riding boots. She popped pearl studs into her ears, batted her eyelashes in the mirror one last time and grabbed her North Face fleece jacket from the closet.

A few minutes later, Denai and Treena loaded all the pre-made food and serving supplies into Treena's chrome Jaguar F-PACE SUV and headed for Dell's house to get set up. The thirty-five minute car ride was full of laughter and bad karaoke as they sang along with the R&B mix playing on WGCI that morning.

When they pulled in front of Dell's house, Denai was impressed just from seeing the outside. This was her first time coming over, because Dell was adamant that he wanted to get unpacked and all moved in before she did.

"I don't need you thinking I'm a slob," he had told her every time she asked about coming over.

Denai and Treena grabbed two tote bags each full of serving utensils and table decor from the backseat to take in first. They jogged up the concrete front steps and rang the doorbell. A few seconds later, E-Man opened the door.

"Hey, Ms. Denai," he greeted warmly with a smile.
"Hey, E-Man!" she greeted in return and gave him a quick peck on the cheek as she stepped inside.
"Ms. Treena," he said, his smile now gone and tone flat.
"Hey, E-Man," she replied with a smirk, sounding flirty.
"*E-Man*? Hmm, interesting," he commented with his eyes narrowed and jaw tight.

He welcomed the ladies inside and told them Dell was in the basement setting up the gaming area but would be up shortly. E-Man then showed them to the kitchen where they could get themselves situated.

"D said he wants everything set up in the dining room kinda buffet style just to make it easier. Other than that, this is your show," he explained, while giving them a tour of the kitchen so they'd know where everything was located.

E-Man then offered to grab the rest of the supplies and equipment out of the car for them. Treena decided to go too – so she could corner him for a moment – while Denai started unpacking the tote bags. She was sitting a tray of deviled eggs in the refrigerator when she heard Dell trotting up the basement steps. Denai pretended not to hear him just to see if he'd notice her first. She quickly got her answer.

"I have never loved khaki pants more in my life," Dell said when he reached the top of the stairs and spotted her standing at the sink.

Denai dropped her head and exhaled a laugh at his comment. He came up behind her, wrapped his arms around her waist and trailed the tip of his tongue along the side of her neck, making her moan softly. Dell slowly dragged his tongue up to her ear and traced its edges, giving her goosebumps. Denai bit her bottom lip as his breath tickled her skin.

"Sir, you had me come here to work," Denai said, her words wrapped in soft giggles and moans.

"Party doesn't start for two more hours," Dell said in her ear, his voice deep and thick.

"I have to prep, though," she said, slowly losing the battle against her hormones.

"You just gotta prep for me," he whispered as he popped open the button on her pants.

Denai squealed and pushed away from the sink, sliding out of Dell's embrace. Each time he tried to reach for her again, she swatted his hand away, dancing around the kitchen as he chased after her. Dell caught the hem of her shirt before she could make it through the archway leading to the dining room and turned her around, pressing her body against the doorjamb. Denai looked up at him with a laugh so childlike and a smile so joy-filled.

"Jesus! These eyes," Dell exhaled as he looked deep into her honeygreen orbs decorated with black glittery eyeliner.

He gently grabbed her face and pulled it close to his, connecting their lips in a tender kiss. Dell whispered against her lips how much he missed her, then kissed her again. Denai gripped his waist and pulled him closer, deepening their kiss. She had no idea how she was going to get through the rest of the day focused on working his event, when all she really wanted to do right now was work his body. *This is gonna be a looong day,* Denai thought to herself as she traced Dell's lips with her tongue.

******

E-Man worked in total silence as he moved in and out of Treena's SUV loading up the two wagons with Denai's burner racks, serving pans, jugs of water and other supplies. Each time Treena tried to step in to help, he'd just take whatever from her hands while looking at her with the coldest, blank stare. After the third time, she decided to address the proverbial elephant on the sidewalk.

"Is there something bothering you?" Treena asked, folding her arms across her chest.

"You called me 'E-Man,'" he replied through pursed lips.

"Okay?! That's your name," she said with a confused shrug.

E-Man sent the SUV's backdoor slamming shut as he spun on his heels to face Treena. He didn't know what frustrated him more about her. Her avid avoidance of anything emotional or sentimental when it came to him or how hard it was for him to actually stay mad at her while looking in her eyes. Deep hazel pools that drowned him every time as they drew him in to touch her smooth butter pecan skin. Despite how much Treena rattled his nerves, E-Man was determined to stay strong in his conviction.

"When we first met I told you everybody calls me 'E-Man,'" he said, taking a step towards her. "And you, with all your attitude, said 'Well, I'm not everybody else. So, what do *I* call you?' You remember that?"

"Yeah, I remember," Treena said, her arms still folded defiantly.

"I told you to call me 'Emmanuel.' Nobody's called me that since my granny died, because I don't let other people use my real name." he said with heaviness in his voice. "But, I let *you* call me 'Emmanuel,' because I didn't want you to be like everybody else. You were special. I *wanted* you to be special, and then today you looked me in the face and called me 'E-Man' just like everybody else does."

E-Man shook his head in disbelief as he held Treena's gaze. She stammered trying to find the right words to soothe the pain swimming in his eyes, but there was nothing she could say. He exhaled a, "Tsk," before grabbing the handles of the wagons and pulling them towards the porch steps. E-Man hoisted each wagon up to his chest and carried them up the stairs and into the house one-by-one, leaving a bewildered Treena standing by the car.

"I thought y'all got lost," Denai called out from the dining room when she heard the front door open.

"Aye man, you could open a food truck with all this shit you lugging around," E-Man grunted as he dragged the weighed-down wagons through the living and dining rooms and into the kitchen.

"Ha! I'll keep that in mind. Thank you, E-Man!" she sang as she finished unpacking the table decorations.

"You're welcome, sweetie," he said dryly.

"You okay?" she asked.

"I'm just waiting on twelve o'clock."

"Why twelve o'clock?"

"Because then it'll be acceptable for me to start drinking."

E-Man gave Denai a gentle squeeze on the shoulder before heading for the basement. She watched his retreating back curiously because she had never seen him like that before. Denai turned her attention back towards the living room when she heard Treena come in, who also looked visibly bothered by something. *What the hell happened out at that car?* Denai silently wondered.

******

"Aye, bro, can I get in ya business real quick?" E-Man asked as he chalked the end of his pool cue, waiting to take his shot on the pool table.

"When are you *not* in my business?" Dell asked sarcastically as he sank the fifteen ball into the left corner pocket.

"Dude," E-Man said with an exasperated sigh and rolling his eyes.

"What's up, bruh?" Dell asked with a chuckle, looking up from the pool table at his cousin.

"What's the deal with you and Denai? Like where are y'all at?"

"Oh, well...uh...we tryna see some shit."

E-Man palmed his face as he and Dell fell out laughing. Dell told him that since Denai's breakup with Ryan was still pretty fresh, he was being careful and intentional about not rushing her into anything she wasn't ready for just yet. He couldn't even imagine what that healing process would look like for her, but he fully intended to be there for her every step of the way, in whatever way she needed him to be.

"Okay, but like how does that actually work?" E-Man asked, a confused frown marring his features.

"Simple," Dell replied as he sank another ball into the corner pocket of the poll table. "I respect any limited ability or total inability she currently has to reciprocate the energy I give to her. But, I don't let any of that affect the way I choose to continue to treat her or how I feel about her. Make sense?"

"Kinda," E-Man said as he took his turn on the pool table.

"Look at it like this, the better she's treated during her healing period, the safer she feels to allow herself the right to be happy and to be loved correctly," Dell explained.

"Damn, that's kinda deep," E-Man replied, nodding his head in agreement.

"You know who gave me that gem? Good, old Pastor Randall Denton," Dell said with a smile, referring to his step-father.

He explained that when his step-father came asking for his blessing to marry his mother, Annette – as a show of respect for him being the "man" in her life even though he was only fourteen – Dell asked Randall if he was sure she was the right woman for him? Annette Denton (née Hewitt) was a bit of a hellion and a man-eater back in the day, with a venomous tongue fueled by a pack-a-day Newport habit.

To Dell, she was the Queen of the World and the sweetest woman he'd ever known, but he also knew about her temper and ability to rip folks a new one when circumstances called for it. She and Randall were polar opposites. Randall Denton was an ordained Deacon, at the time, and training to become a Pastor. He was gentle, calm and soft spoken outside of the pulpit.

He didn't drink, smoke or use profanity. He barely even raised his voice when he was arguing with someone. Randall's easy-going nature could warm the coldest hearts, but Dell still felt he was no match for Annette. Thankfully, Randall had proved him wrong, and there were sixteen years of wedded bliss to show for it.

"Randall honored Mama's history with love and relationships and made it a point to understand the woman she had to become in order to survive in this world," Dell continued. "So, the woman we know and love today was born out of the safety and freedom Pops provided with the way he loved her. And that's what it's all about, bruh."

"Man, you make that shit sound so easy," E-Man replied with a huff.

"Treena putting you through it, huh?" Dell asked with a chuckle.

"Bruh! It's like every time I think we're making progress, she flips on me. Feel like I'm banging my head on a brick wall."

"Well, I don't know her that well, but, I will say this, I don't think all of your efforts have been in vain. Don't give up just yet. You may find out just how much she's worth the headache."

Dell gave E-Man a pat on the shoulder before jogging up the basement steps. E-Man exhaled a heavy sigh as he marinated on his cousin's advice. It was true that Treena Thompson was frustrating the hell out of him, working his last nerve and depleting his patience. For him, it had been nearly a year of trying to reconnect and get close to her since the night of his birthday last March, and every time he thought they were making headway, she'd throw him for a loop.

Part of him really believed his feelings for her might not be mutual, but now after listening to Dell, E-Man wondered if there was more beyond the surface with Treena that he hadn't seen yet. He followed Dell's path up the steps and his heart skipped a beat when he heard Treena's laugh coming from the kitchen.

Couldn't leave her ass alone if I wanted to, he thought to himself as he followed the sweet sound that tickled his ears.

******

Dell's housewarming kick-back was in full swing. He had invited some family and childhood friends and it became an endless loop of reminiscing and embarrassment. There was a lot of "I remember that time when Dell..." going on, and Denai was eavesdropping trying to get more intel on the man who sent her heart fluttering every time he was near. Every so often she would quietly giggle to herself at something said about him or the way he tried to protest and say how something wasn't his fault.

Denai and Treena were putting the food out on the bar in the dining room, setting up everything buffet style for the guests, when they heard the chime of the doorbell. Dell had run upstairs to change his shirt because his first one had gotten stained by some salsa, leaving E-Man to manage crowd control. He opened the door without looking through the peephole, and immediately regretted it.

"What the hell are you doing here?!" E-Man barked when he saw who was on the other side of the door.

"Well, hello to you too, Emmanuel," Destiny replied sarcastically.

"I told you about that shit," he said gruffly with a raised eyebrow. "Now answer my question.

"I'm here for the party," she said flippantly.

"Bullshit! He would never invite you."

"He didn't. Trish told me about it."

"So, you decided to show up to someone's house uninvited by the *owner* of said house? You a bold motherfucka."

Destiny pushed past E-Man and stepped inside the house. A few of the other guests cheered and greeted her warmly, while others eyed her skeptically. E-Man frowned at the sight of Destiny mixing and mingling with people inside Dell's house, and then a sudden sense of dread washed over him.

From the foyer, he snuck a glance at Denai in the dining room and saw the way her face frowned then fell at the sight of Destiny. Shaking his head, E-Man darted up the stairs to retrieve Dell and let him know his home had been infiltrated.

Denai squinted her eyes tighter and tighter the longer she looked at Destiny, who was shimmying out of a leather coat to reveal a black nylon catsuit. *Does this bitch not own anything else?!* Denai mused to herself as her blood ran hot. Out the corner of her eye she could see Treena watching her as the reality of Destiny's arrival set in.

Denai looked over at her best friend, who was now looking at her with wide eyes that silently said, "Oh, shit!" and "What the fuck?!" simultaneously. Denai angrily rolled a sheet of foil over the top of a pan of chicken wings, then stormed off through the kitchen to the bathroom on the other side.

Meanwhile upstairs, E-Man rounded the corner into Dell's bedroom, bursting in without knocking.

"Uh, my nigga, we got a problem!" E-Man exclaimed when he entered the bedroom.

"Uh, we do?" Dell asked, confusion evident on his face.

"Yes! Nigga, Destiny is here!" E-Man said gruffly through clenched teeth.

"What?! Why?!" Dell asked, his voice higher than normal.

"She said Trish told her about the party, and she decided to pull up."

"What the fuck?!...Did Denai see her?"

E-Man just pursed his lips, closed his eyes and nodded slowly. He heard Dell release a string of curse words under his breath as he hurriedly brushed by and headed downstairs.

Once Dell got to the bottom of the stairs, he snuck a peak around the wall and sure enough, there was Destiny sitting just as cozy as she pleased on the corner of his sectional. He mumbled a few more curse words before rounding the corner to his right that took him down a short hallway to the kitchen.

Dell saw Treena at the sink rinsing dishes and slid up next to her.

"Where is she?" Dell asked quietly, referring to Denai.
"Bathroom," Treena said softly.
"Is she pissed?" he asked nervously.
"Wouldn't you be?" she retorted.
"Fuck!" he expelled in a whisper, then turned to go back down the hallway towards the guest bathroom.

Dell had just raised his hand to knock when the door suddenly opened, revealing the object of both his concern and desire. Denai was startled at first, but then her face quickly frowned up at the sight of him standing there. She shook her head in annoyance and attempted to push past him to leave the bathroom.

Dell gently, but firmly, pressed his palm to her stomach and moved her backwards into the bathroom as he followed her inside. He closed and locked the door before pressing his back against it.

"Dell, what the hell..." Denai stammered in frustration as he moved her into the bathroom. "What are you doing?"
"I get that you're pissed, but you don't get to storm away from me again. Not in my house, anyway," Dell said firmly, with his hand still on her waist.
"I'm not pissed. I'm working," she said dryly with a stoic expression.

Denai tried again to get by and leave, but Dell was a statue at his post against the door. She angrily asked him to move and each time she did, he'd just shake his head and remain still.

"Dell, can you please..." Denai began, but was interrupted.

"Baby," Dell said softly as he pulled her close to him and pressed his temple to hers, with his lips by her ear. "Please don't be mad at me."

"I-I'm...n-not mad," she replied, feeling her resolve weaken from him being so close to her.

"Yes, you are, and I get it," he continued. "But, I need you to know I did not invite her or ask her to be here. Besides just wanting to be messy as hell, I don't even know why she's here, but she is *not* here for me. I promise."

Dell placed soft kisses to her temple, cheek and neck as he pleaded for forgiveness. He knew Destiny's presence was not only a problem for him, but it was definitely one for Denai, especially now. Though they were still somewhat unofficially together, the last thing Dell wanted to do was give Denai any reason to feel disrespected or like she couldn't trust him.

He'd be damned if Destiny, of all people, would be the cause of any contention between him and the woman in his arms.

"I'm sorry, baby," Dell whispered against her ear as he stroked her lower back. "Please don't be mad at me. Okay?"

"Okay," Denai whispered in return as her eyes fluttered close.

"I will make her leave," he promised as he cupped her face in his hands.

"No, it's okay. Today's about celebrating you. There's no need for drama," she said, shaking her head.

"Are you sure?"

"Yeah, I'm sure. It's okay...I mean it's *not*, but whatever."

Dell leaned forward and kissed Denai's lips, softly at first and then it intensified as their tongues met and danced together. He gripped her hips and moved her backwards; cupped her butt in his hands and lifted her up onto the edge of the sink. Denai wrapped her arms around his neck, palming the back of his head in her small hand and massaging the short curls of his mohawk. A move that always made him putty in her hands.

Dell moaned into her mouth at the feel of her touching him and at how good she tasted. He trailed kisses from her mouth to her cheek and down to the right side of her neck. He traced her pulse with his tongue, making Denai twitch with desire as her grip tightened around his neck. She moaned softly into his ear as her breathing turned to aroused panting.

Between the way his tongue flicked along her neck and his fingers going under her shirt to caress the skin of her lower back, Denai could feel her panties getting wetter and wetter. She clung tightly to Dell's shoulders when he began nibbling on her shoulder beneath the collar of her polo shirt. She pressed her thighs against his hips, pulling him closer to her, and he welcomed the feeling.

Dell brought his right hand around and popped open the button of her khaki pants with two fingers. Denai flinched at the act and tried desperately to gather her senses.

"No, no, no. Dell wait," Denai panted as she grabbed his forearm.

"What's wrong?" Dell asked, breathing heavily against the side of her face.

"Baby, I'm working. We can't do this right now," she said, trying to stifle a giggle.

"You're entitled to a thirty minute break," he said slyly as he went back to kissing her neck.

"Dell," she groaned with a smile as she pushed on his shoulder.

Dell released a groan of his own as he dropped his head onto her shoulder. Denai rubbed his pack comfortingly and laughed when he fake cried into her shirt. Begrudgingly, he stood up and placed a kiss on her forehead before pulling away from her. Denai slid off the edge of the sink and buttoned her pants back up, taking several deep breaths to try to calm her own horny nerves.

"That's twice today," Dell said, sounding out of breath. "I don't know how much self-control and strength you think I have, but the answer is *none!*"

"Stop it! You have plenty of self-control," Denai replied with a laugh as she swatted at him.

"Yeah, when you're *not* around," he emphasized. "But, you've been here all day. You have no idea what that's doing to me."

Denai looked up at Dell through her eyelashes to see him dragging his eyes over every inch of her body as he bit his bottom lip lustfully. She could see his prominent erection through the front of his dark gray sweatpants, and licked her lips to keep from drooling. Just then, Denai got a devilish thought as a sneaky grin spread across her face.

She stepped towards Dell and pushed against his chest with her small hand until his back hit the wall behind him. He eyed her curiously, trying to figure out what was going on, but he soon got his answer. Denai slipped her dainty fingers inside the waistband of his sweatpants and boxers and pulled them down to his knees in one fluid motion. Dell blinked rapidly as he watched her every move.

Denai stood on her tiptoes and kissed him lightly on the lips before dropping down to her knees, nearly disappearing out of sight. Dell's sharp intake of breath was music to Denai's ears as she held his manhood in her left hand while craning her neck to the right, licking at the seam of his balls. She swirled her tongue around them before drawing them into her mouth, lightly rolling them around like marbles between her lips.

As she continued teasing him with her tongue, Denai stroked his penis up and down with the firm grip of her hand. The dual sensations made him cough out one moan after another. Dell bit down on his bottom lip, trying to muzzle himself, but it was a losing battle. The second he felt Denai's warm mouth wrap around the head of his penis and her tongue swirling around it, his knees buckled and he said, "Fuck!" as he released a heavy sigh.

Dell covered his face with both hands as he felt Denai's wet mouth slip and slide along every inch of him. She would periodically pull him from her mouth and run the tip of her tongue along the underside of his penis, which made him groan from deep within his chest every time. He desperately gripped the towel rack on the wall next to him as he held on for dear life. He could feel the knot forming in his stomach, letting him know his release was on its way.

Denai moaned onto Dell's penis, making her throat vibrate against his flesh – a move she knew drove him crazy. That was the move that made the dam break. Dell latched on to the sides of Denai's head as he moaned and whimpered at the feel of an orgasm crashing through him. His entire body twitched and jerked as he released every ounce of desire that had been building up in him all day long.

Denai slurped and lapped up every drop, moaning at the taste of his essence. Dell panted and begged her to stop because he was so sensitive, but that just excited her more. He slowly slid down the wall listlessly as Denai made one final swipe of her tongue along the tip of his penis. He dropped down to the floor, completely spent and out of breath.

Denai let out another sinister giggle as she stood up and turned towards the sink. She quickly washed her hands, rinsed her mouth, leaned over to kiss Dell atop his head and giddily bounced out of the bathroom.

Dell let out a euphoric sigh as he stumbled back to his feet, pulling up his boxers and sweatpants practically in slow motion. He went over to the sink and threw some cold water on his face, trying to get his bearings. As he surveyed his reflection in the mirror, Dell smiled to himself.

There was nothing or no one that could do anything to ruin his mood today. Not even Destiny's party-crashing ass. He realized in that moment just how lucky he truly was and it was all thanks to the amazing woman who had just skipped out the bathroom after devouring his soul.

"I fucking love her," Dell said aloud and then jumped in shock at his words.

He looked around the bathroom as if trying to be sure no one else heard him, then looked back at his reflection wide-eyed. Had he really just confessed to being in love with Denai Powell? Was it just the post-orgasm euphoria talking, or did he really feel that way about her? Based on the butterflies in his stomach, Dell believed he knew the real answer.

He shook his head in disbelief and splashed more water on his face before leaving the bathroom.

******

"You did all of this?" a woman named Marie asked Denai as she sat down another mixed fruit tray on the coffee table.

"I sure did," Denai said excitedly, smiling at the woman.

"Giiiirrrlll! You got a card or something? Imma need you," Marie replied with her own excitement.

"I sure do!" Denai said, pulling a stack of business cards from her back pocket and handing one over.

Marie said she had two bridal showers coming up soon and was going to need catering for them. Denai let her know she would be more than happy to help if her calendar permitted it.

"I provide two different services," Denai explained. "I can either prepare and drop off, where I make the food and do setup for the event and then you're on your own. Or, I can do full service, like today, where I'm there for the duration of the event to help with anything you might need related to the food."

"Okay, okay! I like!" Marie exclaimed as she fanned the business card in her hand.

"Just give me a call or text so we can set up a consultation. It's complimentary, but it is required."

"Understood. I'll definitely be calling you, sis."

Denai thanked Marie for her consideration and began making her way back to the kitchen. As she was walking, a man came up and tapped her on the shoulder. She turned around to find a tall, dark and handsome man standing there who bore a striking resemblance to Dell. She wondered if he was one of the many cousins she'd heard about earlier.

"Hey, how you doing? My name is Evan," he said.

"Hi, Evan. I'm Denai," she greeted with a sweet smile and firm handshake.

"Sorry to bother you," he started. "But, I saw you earlier and I just had to come over and..."

Evan's words trailed off when he caught a glimpse of Dell, who was in the dining room grabbing a drink from the bar. He was mid-pour when he spotted Evan doing what he does best, and immediately became incensed with jealousy. Dell silently locked eyes with Evan across the room and gave a short shake of his head. When Evan acted like he didn't understand what was going on, Dell narrowed his glare and swiped his hand across his throat signaling for him to "Cut it out!"

Evan quickly glanced at Denai then back at Dell and the realization finally clicked. He subtly nodded his understanding and redirected his conversation with Denai.

"Uh, I just had to come over to say great job with what you've done here," Evan continued, shifting gears and leading with a professional compliment almost flawlessly.

"Oh, thank you," Denai said graciously, still smiling with her hands clasped in front of her body.

"Quick question for you. Do you only do catering work?" he asked, tilting his head to the side.

"Uh, I guess that depends," she replied with curiosity in her voice.

"I'm a personal trainer and some of my clients are looking for a personal chef to help with their meal prep. Is that in your wheelhouse?"

"Anything with food is in my wheelhouse."

Evan lifted his eyebrows and smirked, pleased by Denai's confidence. He asked for one of her business cards and said he planned to call very soon to discuss a potential partnership opportunity. She gleefully handed him the card and thanked him for considering her. Evan nodded respectfully before turning around and heading back towards the crowd in the living room. He could feel the heat of Dell's eyes on the back of his head, and didn't even risk looking back at him.

Dell made a beeline for the kitchen, following Denai's path, and made quick work of finding out what his womanizing, manwhore cousin had said to her. When she revealed their conversation to him, he just quietly nodded with his eyes still narrowed and jaw hitched tight.

"Why do you ask?" Denai asked, eyeing him quizzically.
"Because Evan is sneaky," Dell said plainly, still frowning.
"What does that mean?" she wondered.
"It means he'll try any way he can to get with a woman he's attracted to," he explained. "I just hope his offer to you is genuine and not some bogus plot to get next to you."
"Are you jealous?"
"Yes."

Dell's tone was flat, but direct. However, it wasn't just him being jealous. He was also annoyed, because this wasn't the first time Evan had tried to make a move on a woman Dell was with. It's like there was no line he wouldn't cross.

Now, Dell suddenly regretted inviting him in the first place. Between Evan and Destiny still lingering around, he had half a mind to end the party early and put everyone out, but he knew that would be wrong.

The feel of Denai's lips pressed sweetly to his cheek made Dell snap back to reality and release the tension in his shoulders. It was funny how quickly he melted like ice on a hot day at her slightest touch. He turned to face her and brought his lips down to hers. Just as their fleshiness touched, they heard a gasp come from the kitchen doorway. It was Destiny.

Dell looked over the top of Denai's head and snorted a laugh at Destiny's shocked expression. Denai looked her up and down, still trying to ascertain why she was even there in the first place. Dell hooked his index finger under Denai's chin, turning her face back towards him. He cupped the side of her face in his palm and leaned in, kissing her passionately.

He licked and nipped at Denai's lips as he continued to devour every inch of her mouth. They moaned in unison as the kiss became more intense, and it wasn't until they heard the front door slam shut that they broke off their kiss and started laughing hysterically.

E-Man came around the corner into the kitchen to see what had finally expelled the demon known as Destiny and erupted into his own fit of laughter when he saw Dell and Denai doubled over at the sink. He walked over and slapped hands with Dell as they clinked their drinks together in celebration. It wasn't clear who was the happiest to see her go, but the trio definitely shared in the excitement, nonetheless.

<h1 style="text-align:center">{ fifteen }</h1>

Denai was tying the handles of a trash bag together when Dell walked into the kitchen. He had just let the last of his guests out the front door and came to see if she and Treena needed any help with clean-up. When he spotted Denai trying to hoist the bag out of the trash can, he sternly went, "Aht! Aht!" and she cracked up laughing and threw her hands up in surrender.

"You know the clean-up is a part of the service provided at Plated by Powell Catering?" Denai informed him with a smirk.

"Plated by Powell Catering?" Dell asked with a raised eyebrow.

"Yeah, I think that's what I wanna go with. Coming up with a business name is hard!" she replied, stomping her foot and pouting.

"I like it," he complimented with a soft shrug and quick peck on her cheek.

Denai beamed with pride as a wide smile spread across her face. Dell was only the second person she had told about her naming idea – Treena, of course, being the first – and she was so grateful for the positive feedback. With so few people in her corner these days, she truly appreciated the ones who stayed and took their role in her life seriously.

"Oh, and as far as your providing of a service, I don't give a damn," Dell chimed as he headed for the backdoor. "You ain't handling trash in front of me. Thus, why I stepped in and dealt with Ryan for you."

Denai scoffed a laugh as she threatened to throw a box of matches at Dell, who stuck his tongue out and winked before slipping out the door. She shook her head and giggled at how true his statement was.

"Well, he was kinda trash," she said to herself, as she headed out into the dining room to finish packing up.

"Who was trash?" Treena asked as she pulled the plastic covering off the buffet bar.

"Ryan," Denai said plainly.

"Ooh, a whole landfill in an Armani suit," Treena scoffed and shook her head.

"Damn, Treena!" Denai said, screaming with laughter.

The ladies gathered the last of the supplies and loaded them back into the vinyl wagons. As they were putting on their coats, E-Man perked up from the sectional in the living room.

"Y'all ready to load up and head out?" he asked, not tearing his eyes away from the television.

"Yeah, I think we got everything," Denai replied, as she tugged on the zipper of her jacket.

"Aight, let me grab my hoodie out the basement and I'll help you get everything out to the truck," he said with a grunt as he pushed himself up to stand.

"Thank you, Emmanuel," Treena replied softly.

The sound of his name on her lips made him stop in his tracks. E-Man turned his head slowly until his gray eyes met her hazel ones. They were locked in an intense stare that made all the air on the first level of the house thick with combustible sensual tension. Denai watched the silent, heated exchange between the two of them and bit the inside corner of her bottom lip to keep from smiling. She heard

Dell come back in from taking out the trash and decided to slip into the kitchen to give Treena and E-Man a moment alone.

"Wh-What did you call me?" E-Man stammered finally, his throat dry and husky.

"What I always call you," Treena said with a light shrug, trying to hide her own smile.

"S-say it again," he pressed as he began walking towards her.

"Thank you, *E-mman-uel,*" she repeated slowly in a sultry voice.

E-Man bit his lip and moaned quietly in the back of his throat as he finally came to stand in front of her. He gripped the lapel of her coat and pulled her body to him. He lowered his mouth over hers, tasting the spearmint freshness of her breath as she began panting in wicked anticipation.

It was something about the hunger in his eyes and the forcefulness in which he handled her that made Treena's soul quake. It took every ounce of her strength not to beg E-Man to take her right here and now. The fire in his eyes said he'd want nothing more, as well.

"You're very welcome, Treena," E-Man said against her lips, his voice deep and commanding. "And thank you."

"F-For what?" Treena stammered in a whisper before running the tip her tongue over her lips and slightly grazing his.

"Mmm," he groaned when he felt the wetness of her mouth against his. "For always being you."

E-Man released his hold on her and pulled his face away. He searched her eyes, trying to figure out at what point did he lose part of himself in them. He slowly licked his lips again as he dragged his eyes from her face and roamed them all over her body. The feel of E-Man's eyes on her was more intense than his hands had been, and Treena had to pinch her knees together to calm the throbbing between her legs.

He stepped around Treena without uttering another word and headed for the basement to retrieve his hoodie, leaving her standing there speechless and wanting. E-Man gave a quick head nod to Dell and Denai as he passed through the kitchen, and they watched until his back disappeared down the stairs before they started snickering.

Denai told Dell what she had seen between E-Man and Treena in the other room and that she didn't understand what they were waiting on to just pull the trigger?

"I mean, it's not like they haven't done it before," Denai said casually with a shrug.
"Yeah, but I don't think it's that simple," Dell said.
"What do you mean?" she asked.

Before he could answer, E-Man emerged from the basement shoving his head through the neckhole of his sweatshirt. He told Denai he'd get everything loaded into Treena's truck while she finished saying her goodbyes to his cousin. Just then, Dell decided he didn't want it to be "goodbye," not even just for the night.

"Come back," Dell insisted, pressing his lips to her ear.
"Are you asking me or are you telling me?" Denai pondered as she tilted her head to give him more access.
"I'm pleading," he groaned as he moved down to her neck and kissed her pulse.
"Oh, is that what that was?" she asked snickering.
"Please, Baby, Baby! Please!" he begged in an exaggerated tone as he tightly wrapped his arms around her waist.

Denai burst into a fit of giggles as she tried to wriggle herself loose, but not really wanting to leave his arms. She told him she had to go home and help Treena unload her truck and put all the catering stuff away.

"It'll probably be a couple hours before I'm able to get back over here," Denai informed him when she finally freed herself from his embrace.

"That's fine. I'll be here, waiting patiently," Dell said sweetly as he kissed her knuckles.

"Patiently?" she asked skeptically.

"Okay, I'll do my best," he said, rolling his eyes.

"Uh huh," she replied. "Well, I'll try not to keep you waiting too long."

Dell pulled Denai to him and captured her face in his hands, looking deep into her eyes. Seeing his reflection in those beautiful golden-green pools made his heart skip a beat and confirmed his greatest suspicions. Denai had invaded his every waking thought, and sometimes even as he slept. There were times he'd pass by someone wearing the same perfume she had worn the night they met and his mind would become flooded with vivid memories.

He had only known her for a handful of hours, but he spent months missing everything about her. Now, here she was, literally in the palms of his hands, and he never wanted to let her go. Dell tracked featherlight kisses across Denai's forehead, on one cheek, across the tip of her nose and then the other cheek. Her eyelids fluttered closed, making her lashes brush against his face as he kissed her.

They both smiled peacefully each time his lips touched her skin — skin that felt so soft and warm and adored by this man. Dell finally planted a kiss on her lips, inhaling her breath into his lungs like the life-force it was. Denai gripped his ribs with her small hands, sending shockwaves coursing through his chest and stomach.

He ached for her. He longed for her. He wanted to spend every minute of every day with her, if he could. He needed her in the most dire way — in his arms, in his bed, in his home, in his life. This moment right here, right now in his kitchen, let Dell know, without any shadow of any doubt, that Denai Renee Powell was the one. There was no point in fighting it anymore.

They pulled away from their intimate embrace and Denai palmed the left side of Dell's face, silently letting him know she'd be back. He turned and kissed her palm, and then she glided out of the kitchen, through the dining and living rooms and towards the front door. Just as Denai's hand reached for the doorknob, Dell called out to her from the dining room.

"Hey!" his heavy voice booming through the empty rooms.
"Yeah?" Denai replied in a stunned tone as she turned to face him.

For a brief moment, Dell paused just to silence his nerves. He gingerly slipped his hands into his pockets, squared his shoulders, angled his head and licked his lips. Denai lifted her eyebrows curiously, still waiting for a response. With the chandelier glowing behind his head like a heavenly halo, Dell slowly mouthed the words, "I...Love...You."

After deciphering what he said, Denai exhaled a small laugh, first in shock and then in pure palpable joy. Without any further hesitation, she placed her hand on her heart and mouthed, "I...Love...You...Too," right back to him.

Dell dropped his head and smiled as the warmth of their shared declaration washed over him. He looked at her through his eyelashes, still smiling and shaking his head almost in disbelief — or maybe it was more so relief. Denai blew him a kiss and then slipped out of the front door, almost bumping into E-Man, who was on his way back inside.

As she giddily plopped into the front seat, Treena looked at her and asked what had her so chipper?

"Dell just told me he loves me," Denai revealed, her eyes sparkling and smile wide.

"What?! Oh, my God!" Treena exclaimed with excitement. "Well, girl, what the hell are you doing in here?! You should be in there pouncing on ya man!"

"Ha! I'm coming back. Gonna unload this stuff and get my car," Denai informed her.

"Aight, I guess that's an acceptable answer," Treena said sarcastically as she rolled her eyes.

Treena pulled her SUV away from the curb and began firing one question after another at Denai as they drove down the street. She asked out of genuine curiosity because not only was she really excited for her best friend, but she also really wanted to know how she did it? Denai had been to hell and back again with her most recent relationship, and most of her wounds were still fresh — the ones you could see and the ones you couldn't.

Yet, here she was freely allowing herself to fall again; to be open again, without any second thoughts. Treena was truly amazed, and maybe even a little inspired. She listened intently, hanging on to Denai's every word as they drove back to the South Side of the city.

******

Denai nervously pulled on the belt of her dark navy blue vinyl trench coat, making sure it was tied securely around her waist. She fussed with the buttons, fastening and unfastening them, trying to decide which look she wanted to do. As she let out a frustrated sigh – immediately regretting her decision to do any of this – she absent-mindedly rang the doorbell.

"Shit!" Denai chastised herself as she tugged at the belt one more time before hearing Dell's gruff voice through the door asking, "Who is it?" She jumped at the sound and released another heavy sigh before saying, "Well, we're here now," to herself.

Denai announced herself on the other side of the door and he quickly opened it. The sight of his warm eyes and bright smile put her a little at ease. She dropped her eyes to the ground, then slowly, seductively pulled them back up until they met his. A sneaky grin formed on her lips and it made Dell inhale sharply.

He grabbed one end of the belt and swiftly pulled her into the house. Denai giggled as she trotted past him. She strutted further inside with slow, measured steps and began loosening the knotted belt around her waist. Dell stood in the middle of the living room watching her every move.

He drank in the sight of her draped in a fitted trench coat with tall black leather high-heel boots latched to her calves and thighs. Suddenly, he was conflicted on whether he wanted her to keep them on or not. Denai did a small pirouette, turning to face Dell, who's mouth fell open in pleasant surprise.

She had untied the belt and put her hands on hips, pushing the coat open to reveal a lacey lilac-colored bra with matching thong. The delicate material clung to her breasts as some of their fleshiness spilled over the top; the straps of the thong held on to her hips like a familiar lover. The pastel hue against her brown skin looked like a pure work of art to Dell's eyes.

He ravenously licked his lips, trying to keep from drooling, as his eyes roamed over every inch of Denai's visible skin. Dell made mental notes of what and where he'd kiss first – he planned to make it one long, deliciously agonizing process. Denai slid the coat off her shoulders and down her arms, dropping it to the floor in one smooth motion. She rubbed her hands across her midsection and over her breasts, pushing them together and making them spill over the top of the bra even more.

Dell couldn't stand the tortuous teasing anymore and took four quick steps forward, closing the gap between them. He ran his knuckle across her bosom, drawing small circles on her skin, tracing the outline of her heart-shaped birthmark. Then he slid his finger between her breasts and hooked it on the center of her bra, pulling her closer. Dell bent forward and Denai met him halfway.

Their lips touched and it felt just like the first time. The heat, the passion, the desire, even the nervousness that formed knots in the center of their stomachs.

Denai slipped her hands beneath the hem of Dell's gray tank top, pushing the material up his torso as her hands blazed a trail of fire along his skin. She could feel his abs clench and twitch at her touch and it turned her on just knowing the effect she had on him. Dell ran his hands down the sides of Denai's body, circling around her hips and coming to firmly grip her butt with his strong fingers. He lifted her up and she happily wrapped her legs around his waist as he carried her over to the sectional.

Dell sat down with her straddling his lap. He ran his hands up her back, unclasped her bra, hooked the straps on his index fingers and pulled them down her arms. He cupped her breasts in his warm hands and rubbed the pads of his thumbs over her taut nipples. Denai exhaled a moan and began grinding her hips against his lap, bringing his erection to life through his basketball shorts. He leaned forward and started circling her nipples with his tongue, one right after the other. Denai arched her back in ecstasy as the feel of his wet tongue matched the wetness pooling between her thighs.

She gripped his shoulders tightly when she felt herself about to explode. Denai had never experienced a nipple-stimulated orgasm before and it rushed through her body, settling in her core. She cried with pleasure when Dell flicked his tongue faster and faster, and she swore she could feel the exact same sensation between her legs. Just as Denai screamed Dell's name, she collapsed onto his shoulder, spent by the first of what she knew would be many more releases.

Dell could feel the wetness of Denai's orgasm soaking through the thin material of her thong and his shorts, and it drove him wild. He lifted her up just enough so he could pull his shorts down to free his throbbing penis. Denai looked down at his thick, rock-hard flesh and instantly began salivating. She pulled her leg across Dell's lap, bringing her knees together to kneel on the cushion beside him. Denai leaned over and lowered her head into his lap, taking the full length of him into her mouth.

Dell sucked in air through clenched teeth as he stretched his arms out across the back of the couch. He dug his nails into the tops of the cushions when he felt Denai's tongue lapping at the head of his penis. The sensation was enough to nearly drive him over the edge, but he wasn't ready to fall yet. Dell palmed Denai's face with one hand and her shoulder with the other, halting her taunting tongue action.

He moved to stand up and told her to stay just as she was – face down, ass up.

Dell stood behind her, perching one foot on the couch and the other on the floor. He pulled her thong to the side and entered her slowly, inch by delicious inch, until he was fully engulfed by her feminine essence. He exhaled a throaty groan, followed by a string of profanity as he moved in and out of her, one powerful thrust at a time.

The heels of Denai's boots clicked together while her butt slapped against the skin of his pelvis and lower stomach. All of it mixed with their moans and echoed beautifully throughout the entire lower level of the house.

Denai could feel herself getting close to losing it and didn't want to ruin Dell's brand new sectional. She reached back to grab his wrist as she turned to look over her shoulder. Her eyes darkened by the desire that filled them and full lips parted as she panted and gasped with pleasure.

"Baby!" Denai moaned loudly out of pleasure but was also trying to get his attention.

"Mmm, yeah, Baby. That's it," Dell groaned, feeling her sex tighten around his.

"Oooh, Ba-Baby, I don't wanna fuck up your couch," she cried, her grip on his wrists getting tighter in anticipation of the build-up.

"Fuck this couch!" Dell exclaimed as he sped up his thrusts.

Denai gave up the fight to hold on and screamed in ecstasy as she showered Dell with her wondrous waters. Drenched and harder than he'd ever been in his life, Dell lost his own battle of wills. He gripped her hip tightly with one hand and the back of her neck with the other as he thrusts harder and faster. Denai deepened the arch in her lower back when she felt herself about to cum again, and that only increased Dell's direct access to the entirety of her core and her G-Spot.

"Fuck!...Fuck!...Fuck!...Fuck...me!" Denai screamed as he pounded into her.

"Gladly!" Dell replied in a devilish tone as he reached around and began fingering her clit.

Denai bucked against him as the dual sensations set every nerve in her body ablaze. She could feel her toes curl inside her boots as she clung to the couch cushion for dear life. She dropped her head to the plush surface, biting and screaming into the fabric as Dell shredded every fabric of her being right there in this living room.

His grunts got deeper – letting her know he was reaching his peak just as she was nearing hers once again. In perfect unison, they both spilled forth every ounce of themselves. They gasped and coughed, trying to catch their breaths and stop spinning in the euphoric haze that followed their shattering orgasms.

Denai fully collapsed onto the couch and Dell fell right on top of her. They laughed drunkenly, still fighting to come back down from their sex cloud . Then he started kissing the back of her neck and shoulder, before moving up to her hairline just by her ear.

"I want you to actually *hear* me say it," Dell said groggily. "I love you."

"I love you, too," Denai replied, her voice cracking as a tear formed in the corner of her eye and ran across the bridge of her nose.

"Happy tears, I hope?" he asked with concern in his voice when he heard her sniffle.

"Very happy," she answered with a smile in her voice.

"Mine are too," he said, quickly swiping a lone tear from his face with his knuckle.

Dell moved off Denai to lay on his side and pull her body to him so they could spoon on the couch. She raised her legs in the air to pull off her boots and get comfortable. Dell grabbed a blanket that was draped over the arm of the couch and threw it over them. Before long they were drifting off to sleep, while he lightly stroked her hip with his thumb.

Denai hummed softly to herself as she gave in to the exhaustion. She had spent mostly all day at Dell's house catering his party – playing hostess and chef at the same damn time. Not to mention all the time she spent in the morning, beforehand, doing her pre-preparations. Denai couldn't remember the last time she'd felt this tired from working all day, and then Dell worked her over all night until she nearly screamed herself hoarse. Totally worth it, though.

Just before she fully gave in to the slumber, Denai remembered something.

"Dell?" Denai called out softly.
"Hmm, yes, baby?" Dell replied, sounding half asleep.
"I love you," she said sweetly.
"I love you, too," he said back.
"But, you still gotta finish paying me for that party earlier."

Dell sat up on his elbow and looked down at Denai in disbelief. He shook his head and mumbled, "Cutthroat," under his breath as he laid back down. The last thing he heard was Denai's child-like giggles as his favorite lullaby before finally drifting off to sleep.

{ EPILOGUE }

March '23

"So, what you and Bae getting into this weekend?" Treena asked as she plopped down on the couch.

"Girl, he leaving me!" Denai said with a pout as she popped another taffy grape in her mouth.

"What?!" Treena exclaimed, lurching forward and looking at Denai through squinted eyes.

"No, no. Not like that," Denai said, laughing and waving her hands. "He's going out of town with E-Man for his birthday."

"So, why you not going?"

"Because I guess it's kinda like a guys trip sorta thing."

"When are they leaving?"

"I'm not sure of the exact time, but I know it's at some point tonight after Dell get's off work."

Treena's squinted eyes darted back and forth as she ruminated on Denai's words. Dell and E-Man were going out of town for the latter's birthday, and neither she nor Denai had been invited. The theory of it being a "guy's trip," seemed plausible, but it was also unacceptable to her – not that she was owed anything.

Treena often found herself pondering on the conversation she'd had with Dell awhile back about E-Man. He had advised her that his cousin was genuine in his efforts of pursuing her and that his feelings were much deeper than those tied to a mere one-night stand. She constantly straddled the fence on what to believe and what to ignore, but one thing she couldn't dismiss was his consistency.

E-Man always handled Treena with care and shows of affection. He never downplayed or tried to hide any of what he felt for her, but she was so skittish about love and relationships for a multitude of reasons. So, anytime it felt like E-Man was getting too close, she'd pull back and create this awkward distance between them.

Usually, he had some patience for her anxiety-laced antics, but for about the last month or so, something had changed. Now, it was E-Man putting distance between them, and the idea of that actually scared Treena. *I've fucked this up, haven't I?* She had been wondering that for weeks now.

Treena popped up off the couch as if the cushion beneath was suddenly too hot. She made a mad dash for the stairs leading up to her bedroom. Denai called after her to ask what was going on, but never got an answer. After a few minutes, Denai made her way up the stairs and headed for Treena's room.

Denai stopped short in the doorway when she saw Treena filling up a travel bag propped open on her bed. She was grabbing handfuls of clothes and just tossing them into it. Denai wondered if anything Treena pitched in that bag even matched. She started to ask, but watching her best friend whiz by, darting from one side of the bedroom to the other, was beginning to make her dizzy.

Denai stepped inside and jumped in front of Treena to halt her steps. Treena stared at her through wide eyes as she loosely cradled a pile of clothes.

"What?!" Treena asked loudly with raised eyebrows.

"What are you doing?" Denai asked with her arms stretched out in front of her, blocking the path to the bed.

"I'm packing," Treena said matter-of-factly.

"For?" Denai pressed.

"For Emmanuel's birthday trip."

"T, we weren't invited, and I'm sure that was for a valid reason."

Treena scoffed and tried to push past Denai, but to no avail. Though Denai was small, she was surprisingly strong. She wrestled the pile of clothes out of Treena's arms and dumped them on the bed with a sigh, then grabbed Treena's hands and held them tightly.

"T, listen to me," Denai began. "If he wanted you to go, he would've invited you."

"What if he did want to invite me and I fucked it all up?!" Treena posed, her face tight and voice high with emotion.

"What are you talking about?" Denai asked, dropping Treena's hands.

"I'm talking about wasting a year's worth of opportunity to see if there's any real potential with me and him, all because I was too scared to risk it."

Denai tilted her head to the side and narrowed her eyes, trying to understand Treena's point. She explained how hard E-Man had been trying since they first met to really get close to her – dating her like a proper lady and showing her that it is more than possible for her to find a really good man in this lifetime.

When Treena really sat and thought about it, instead of fleeing from it, she realized that Emmanuel Tipton may very well be the per-fect man for her. The perfect man who was now opting not to invite her out for his birthday!

"What if Dell didn't invite *you* because Emmanuel asked him not to? Because he knows that you and I are a packaged deal?" Treena said. "So, if you go on the trip, I'll more than likely show up to go too, and he doesn't want that."

"T, I don't think that's the case," Denai said gently, rubbing her friend's arm comfortingly.

"Well, I won't know for sure until I ask him," Treena replied as she pushed by and finished packing.

"And that requires an overnight bag?"

"It does."

******

Denai and Treena pulled up outside of E-Man's house just as he and Dell were in the driveway loading luggage and coolers into the trunk of a Black Ford Expedition. Dell smiled with narrowed eyes when he saw who it was, because while he was always happy to see Denai, he was surprised to see her right now. They had spoken earlier while he was at work, and she hadn't mentioned anything about stopping by, and she knew that he was headed out of town tonight. Nonetheless, he headed over to the car just as she hopped out of the passenger seat.

"Hey, Babe," Dell greeted as he pulled her into a hug.

"Hi!" Denai replied cheerfully, laying her head on his chest.

"Hey, Treena," he called out to her.

"Hey," Treena replied dismissively without looking at him.

"Did I do something?" he asked with his face twisted up.

"No, not you. Him," Denai said, gesturing towards E-Man who was still by the truck.

Treena's boots crunched loudly in the snow as she marched towards E-Man, still unsure of what she'd actually say once she got over to him. He was shifting the bags around in the trunk to make room for a large cooler, and when he bent down to pick it up, Treena put her foot on top of it. E-Man slowly moved his eyes up from her boots to her face, staring blankly and blinking at a turtle's pace.

"Going somewhere?" Treena asked with a smugness she didn't mean.
"Nope," E-Man replied dryly.
"So, you lying to me now?" she asked, putting her hands on her hips.
"Treena, I really don't have time…" he began, but stopped and just shook his head as he yanked the cooler from under her feet.

E-Man loaded it inside and stepped back to pull the trunk door down. When he turned to head back in the house for a last minute check, Treena was standing so closely behind him that he slightly bumped into her. She put her hands up to brace for impact and ended up resting her palms against his hard chest.

Even through the thick material of his hoodie, E-Man could feel the heat of her touch searing his skin and he instantly became undone. All gruffness and impatience started slipping from his grasp, no matter how hard he tried to hold on.

"I'm sorry," Treena said the loaded words softly as she looked up at him with big doe eyes.
"Nah, that's my bad. I didn't see you," E-Man apologized as he tried to back up and put space between them.
"Where are you going?" she asked, her hands still resting on his chest.
"Cabin in Wisconsin," he answered.
"Without me?"
"Huh?"
"You're going for your birthday, right?"
"Yeah."
"Celebrating birthdays together is kind of our thing, no? At least, I thought it was, but you're going out of town and didn't even tell me…or invite me."

E-Man watched Treena's face closely, trying to determine if she was being earnest or not, and what he saw took his breath away. She was serious. There was a twinge of pain in her eyes that matched her voice. She was actually looking forward to celebrating his birthday with him.

Considering it was this very time last year when their paths first crossed and they literally spent the entire night together. Then fast forward a few months to E-Man surprising Treena at her own birthday celebration and how excited she was to see him. It had practically become their new unspoken tradition.

"I didn't think..." E-Man started, but stopped himself.

"What?" Treena asked, finally dropping her hands to her side.

"Ms. Treena, would you like to go to cold ass Wisconsin to celebrate my birthday with me?" E-Man asked tenderly, tucking a wisp of hair behind her ear with his finger.

"I...Yes," she exhaled the words and shuddered at his touch.

"How much time do you need to get packed?" he asked as he grabbed her hand and stroked her knuckles with his thumb.

"My bag is already in the car," she confessed with a giggle.

"Stay ready, right?"

"Always!"

E-Man chuckled as he pulled Treena into his arms. He called out to Dell, who was still standing with Denai by Treena's truck. He told him that Treena was crashing their cabin trip and Dell was more than welcomed to bring Denai with him now.

"I appreciate you standing in solidarity with me at first, though," E-Man said and gave Dell a thumbs up.

Dell smacked his lips and shook his head, scolding himself for not making a bet with E-Man that he'd cave before they even left the state.

"You need to go home and get stuff?" Dell asked.

"My bag is packed in the backseat," Denai said with a grin.

"Just in case, huh?" he asked with a grin of his own.

"Just in case," she replied with a sly shrug.

Dell and Denai shared a laugh as he grabbed hers and Treena's bags out of the car. As Denai followed him over to the truck, she quietly reflected on how differently her life looked now compared to just one year ago. Going on a couples' road trip and cabin stay with the man she loves and her best friend with a man she's equally as crazy about, even if she couldn't admit it yet. Four lives had been changed for the better and it all started with one night...

Until next time...

ShaRhonda is originally from Maywood, IL, and currently resides in Metro Atlanta, GA. She is a self-proclaimed "Unhinged Creative," as well as owner and operator of **S.L.S. Publishing, LLC.** She has been published multiple times across various indie publications, including three self-published collections of poetry and a host of other projects. ShaRhonda holds a Master's Degree from National Louis University in Chicago, and currently works a "cushy 9-5" as a means to fund the dream of being a best-selling author some day. In between her many passion projects, she moonlights as a freelancer, content creator, copy writer and editor, and avid reader of fiction and poetry.

Follow along on her writing journey & check out her merch brand **The S-L-S Collection**